# THE RAIDERS

**THE RAIDERS 1**

# ROB JONES

This is a work of fiction. Names, characters, organizations, places, events, and incidents are either products of the author's imagination or are used fictiously. Any resemblance to actual persons, living or dead, or actual events is purely coincidental.

Text copyright © 2017, 2018 by Rob Jones

No part of this book may be reproduced, or stored in a retrieval system, or transmitted in any form or by any means, electronic, mechanical, photocopying, recording, or otherwise, without the express written permission of the publisher.

www.robjonesnovels.com

ISBN-13: 9781979603133
ISBN-10: 1979603138

Printed in the United States of America

*For My Family*

# THE RAIDERS

# CHAPTER ONE

The hunt was electric. Kiya felt the man's fear as he stumbled down the steps and strained his eyes in search of an exit. The Ravens watched him too, each circling around the vaulted chamber to cut off any possible escape route.

But their prey was fast and knew the building better than any of them. Fumbling a door handle in the dark, Monsignor Bruno Scala, the head of the Vatican's Archivum Secretum pulled on the heavy oak door until a crack of light appeared in the darkness. It lit up the old man but he moved into the shadows before they could get to him and then he was gone, slipping away through a stone archway beyond the door.

Kiya whistled in the low light and ordered Tekin and Dariush to follow her into the corridor after Scala. The Ravens mustered, and once again she felt the adrenalin coursing through her veins like fire as she moved after the fleeing man; the lethal Bride flanked by her two Ravens…

Through the archway now, and Scala was clambering up a short series of stone steps at the end of a twisting corridor. Lit only by a couple of bare electric bulbs, the desperate man's shadow bobbed up and down along the ancient stone wall as he once again slid from view.

Kiya resumed her pursuit, pushing out into the subdued darkness of the tunnel and making her way toward the archway. She heard Tekin and Dariush moving swiftly a few paces behind her.

The chase exhilarated her because she knew she would win. She knew in her heart that the old man could never escape from the thing which hunted him – the thing of which she was just a tiny part.

And when she caught her prey tonight, the Lion would be pleased and he would reward her lavishly with his promise to elevate her to a Soldier. She had dreamed of it since the day she had joined them. To think it was only hours away gave her a bigger adrenalin rush than a needle full of ephedrine.

To be lifted out of the mass of humanity as they had done to her, to give her the answers most sought but never learned, was enough of a gift, but to move from Bride to Soldier in less than a year... Her heart quivered as thoughts of secret rituals flashed through her mind. They said the pathway to Soldier was one of the hardest... but she was certain the Lion would guide her.

"There!" Tekin said. "He went to the left."

Her carob brown eyes flicked up and saw the Raven pointing to another door at the end of the tunnel.

Dariush rushed up behind them. "Did you see him, Kiya?"

"Yes – come on!"

They sprinted along the corridor and burst through the door, finding themselves outside in the moonlight. They were on the roof, and ahead of them Monsignor Scala was slipping and sliding on the tiles as he made his way along the apex. He was struggling to reach another door a few hundred meters to the north at the base of a clock tower.

"He's getting tired," Kiya said, her own chest rising and falling with the effort of the hunt. She smiled. "Very tired."

Scala clutched at something hanging around his neck and called over to them as he swung open the door. "Do not move settled things, you demons! Do not drag this out of the ancient past!"

He turned to slip inside the door but Kiya had tired of the chase. She pulled a shuriken throwing star from her pocket and threw it across the rooftop. The sharpened steel blades spun into a blur and flashed silver in the moonlight as it zoomed through the night and buried itself in the throat of Monsignor Bruno Scala.

The old man's eyes almost burst from their sockets as he realized what had happened. Reaching up for the star he pulled it from his neck. The blood pumped from his jugular as if he were a slaughtered pig. He fell to his knees as his blood pressure rapidly dropped.

"I have taken him," she whispered. She heard the reedy voice of the pipes as they floated through her mind. She closed her eyes and saw the sun setting over the Nile Valley. The priests were dancing around the temple and chanting to the sun god.

She opened her eyes.

Vatican City.

She walked across the apex of the roof with the Ravens behind her. To the rest of the world they were nothing more than three silhouettes in the light of the crescent moon, but to Scala they were judge, jury and executioner.

Kiya held out her hand. "Give me the ankh."

The old man was breathing hard, and blood bubbled out of his mouth when he spoke. "Quieta non movere!!" His fearful, hoarse voice made the Latin sound even more ghostly as it echoed across the rooftops. "Do not move settled things!"

"Goodnight, Monsignor," Kiya said, and gently closed his eyes as the old man slumped back against the clock tower. As his last breath left his dying body, she snatched the ankh from his dead hands and held it up to the moonlight. The symbolic value of the shape was as ancient as time itself, and she couldn't resist staring at it:

Her eyes danced over its ancient beauty. It was made of gold, as the legend had said it would be, and it was encrusted in precious gems – diamonds, rubies and sapphires. She followed the moonlight reflecting off the gold and saw what she had been hoping for – a carefully carved lined of symbols stretching all the way up one side and down the other. This would change the world forever.

"This is our treasure?" Tekin asked.

Her smile was the only reply.

"Then we must leave," said Dariush. "The sun will rise soon."

Slipping the ankh around her neck and scanning the streets of the Vatican City for any sign of trouble, Kiya the Bride was satisfied she had completed her mission and it was time to return to the Lion's den.

# CHAPTER TWO

The two sports cars were neck and neck as they raced along the road below him. From up here on the ridge, out in the Arizona desert, the man in the sunglasses was able to track them easily with the naked eye but now he wanted to get closer to the action. He pushed his glasses up on his forehead and lifted an old pair of army binoculars to his eyes.

He watched the cars with approval as they fought for supremacy along the desert highway. The Bugatti Veyron was in the lead, but the Lamborghini Aventador was closing fast and as they approached, the hot wind carried the sound of their powerful engines to his ears.

Behind them was a Honda, a family hatchback.

He grinned and shook his head.

*Crazy kid…*

A shallow bend raced up to meet the speeding cars and the Aventador made a break for it. Up on the ridge, the man smiled; it was a textbook move: the Lambo took the inside line in a hurry, drew level with the Veyron in the braking zone and then floored the throttle, overtaking into the lead and beating the more powerful Bugatti to the apex.

The Bugatti fought back, taking advantage of another long straight, but then the inevitable happened, and the little Honda ripped past both the Veyron and the Aventador and streaked toward the horizon until it merged with the shimmering mirage.

The man on the ridge laughed. He imagined neither Caleb Jackson nor Virgil Lehman were too happy about the kid getting the better of them on the bend, but the race wasn't over yet and now they were on another straight, heading back in his direction. He tossed the binoculars into his hired Ford, fired up the engine and drove down the winding track that would lead to the finishing line – the old ranch Caleb called home.

The drive was short. He could see the ranch after the first bend and two minutes later he was parked up in the front yard and leaning on the hood. He heard the two sports cars revving wildly as they approached the property, and wondered if Caleb or Virgil had managed to snatch victory from the jaws of defeat and humiliation.

When the Bugatti appeared first, he saw that the older man had won after all, and that meant the kid would have to try again another day.

The Veyron's eight litre, quad-turbocharged engine growled like an angry monster as it pulled up outside the garage and then a moment later the Aventador swerved in behind it. Both drivers killed their engines at the same time and then climbed out of their cars into the silence of the desert.

Caleb Jackson shook his head as he walked over to the man in the shades and raised a beefy, tattooed arm to remove his own pair of Wiley's sunglasses.

"Fuck me, if it isn't Jed Mason…"

Mason pulled off his shades and returned the smile. "In that case I'm glad to say it *is* Jed Mason."

Caleb laughed, but the smile quickly faded. "Been too long, Jed."

Mason nodded.

Virgil and Mason shook hands. "I was glad when you called, Jed."

"How's Amy?" Mason asked.

"Like any six week-old girl," Virgil said, beaming with pride. "She keeps me and Jen up nights but she's cute as a button. But hey – what's this all about?"

Mason said, "Wait till Mr Risk and his Honda arrive and I'll let you know."

The highly-tuned Honda turned into the property at last, steam pouring from its radiator grille. Milo Risk climbed out, ran a hand over his hair and joined them.

"How's it going, all?" Milo said.

Caleb raised a hand. "Howdy, Milo. What the hell are you doing here? I couldn't believe it when I saw you in the mirror."

"He asked me to meet him here," the young IT specialist said, jutting a smooth, untanned chin at Mason. "All cool, V?"

"Just dandy," Virgil said. "Saw your little problem back there on the road. Too bad."

Milo managed a stoic shrug. "I saw you two are still measuring each other's dicks with these cars of yours. You deserved the humiliation."

"He has a point," Mason said. "The car thing is bordering on an obsession, Cal."

The kid had a wide grin on his young face. "Oh, man… your faces when I hit the gas on the Honda."

"Sleeper car," Caleb rumbled. "The last refuge of the scoundrel."

"The techno-geek, more like," Virgil said.

Milo laughed. "You know what they say, Virgil – better a techno-geek than a library nerd."

Virgil looked confused. "I'm a polymath, anyway – *do* they say that?"

Caleb broke things up. "Why are you here, Jed?"

"You know why."

Caleb looked up at the sky before locking his eyes back on Mason. "I thought we agreed no more jobs?"

"We did."

Milo looked at Mason. "Big?"

"Bigger than anything we ever did before."

Caleb sighed. "I've heard it all before, besides – I have another job on the horizon."

Mason cocked his head. "Another job?"

"Sure – is it so hard to believe that someone other than the great Jed Mason might want to employ me?"

"Not at all. Who's the idiot?"

"Old friend of mine who used to work for the NSA."

"Used to?"

Caleb kicked a stone across the yard, put his hands in his jeans pockets and scratched a line in the dirt with his boot heel. "You might say he's trying to set up on his own."

"And when is this job?"

"I'm expecting a call any minute now."

Mason sighed. "Come on, Cal. Just for old times' sake? If we pull this off we're all set for life – and our kids too. That's presuming you can find a woman stupid enough to hook up with you."

"That big, huh?"

Mason nodded. "What about you, Milo?"

"I never turn down a pay check."

"Virgil?"

"I don't know… I have Jen and Amy to think about now."

"Nice Lamborghini," Mason said. "You buy it with money you made with my team, or money you made pissing about with poker?"

Virgil looked down at his dusty boots.

Caleb crossed his arms and tried to look casual. "What's the job?"

"Asset extraction."

"The best damned asset recovery crew in the world," Virgil said, briefly looking up from the ground before returning his eyes to his boots again. "So I kinda worked that out already, Jed," he said. "That's sort of what RAIDERS is: Rapid and Incognito Deployment, Extraction and Rescue Service. I need some detail. What are we talking about here – stolen jewels, kidnapped royalty?"

"One of the most famous objects in the world has been stolen, but no more details until you're on board. You know the way I roll."

"Come to think of it," Caleb said, a broad white smile spreading on his tanned face. "I *am* kinda bored racing cars."

"I knew you wouldn't let me down," Mason said. "Virgil?"

Virgil looked up from his boots. "If you're putting the team back together, does that mean *she* will also be joining us?"

Mason nodded. "Sure."

Caleb laughed.

Milo sighed.

Virgil pretended to cry.

\*

She leaped over the temple's ridge tile, twisting in mid-air as she somersaulted down to the gable roof. Landing like a panther, the setting sun flashed in her eyes as she regained her balance and scanned for the enemy. High above the temple, the Japanese mountains rose up into a salmon-pink sky.

# THE RAIDERS

From up here on the roof of the Hall of Buddha she could see nearly the entire monastery, from the sōmon gate in the west to the sōbō where the monks lived. She scanned the entire site and then she saw one, scuttling along the roofed portico passage which connected the Zen rock garden with the Dharma hall. It looked like it could be Shen, or maybe Shintaro. It didn't matter: whoever it was had let his guard slip and now she had found him.

She climbed down the pagoda roof, one tier at a time until she was close enough to lower herself onto a lower sloping roof belonging to the belfry, and then shimmied down a drain pipe until she was on the ground. She could see it was definitely Shintaro now, and he was weaving in and out of some pine trees, diligently cloud-pruned by her very own hands.

She ran with the grace and speed of a leopard in pursuit of the fleeing monk. With the thrill of the hunt electrifying her blood, she pounded after the man, determined to bring him down and improve her personal best. He was heading toward the karakado, a gate in the west of the temple compound with an arched roof.

She paused for breath. Darker now, and the sun was sinking into the cypress forest to the west of the temple. She sprinted again, feeling the warm air rushing into her lungs as she hunted down her prey. She was almost on him when the head priest, or Jushoku, swung the wooden bell hammer in his right hand and struck the enormous suspended gong. The sound rippled out over the compound and everyone froze where they stood.

The hunt was over.

Zara Dietrich walked over to the Jushoku and bowed. "Why have you stopped the games?" she said in perfect Japanese.

The Jushoku returned the bow but said nothing. Instead, he pointed his chin over her shoulder. She turned around to see nothing less than three ghosts.

With her guard dropped, one of the monks lunged toward her, but the Jushoku clapped his hands together. "Stop!" he said in stern Japanese. The man froze on the spot, gave a shallow bow and took a step back. The other monks followed his lead and backed away from the American woman dressed in black robes.

Now, Zara walked over to the ghosts, shaking her head gently in disbelief.

One of the ghosts spoke. "Zara Dietrich," he said. He was still leaning against the wall with his hands in his pockets. "Fancy meeting you here…"

Zara wiped the sweat from her forehead and walked closer to him.

He pushed off the wall to meet her. Caleb and Milo stayed back.

Zara slapped his face so hard the sound of the smack sent a number of Pacific swallows flying into the air for safety. "You have some nerve, Jedediah Mason."

Mason didn't flinch, but he felt the pain vibrating away from his cheek and over his ear. The slap was meant to hurt, and it did, but it hadn't meant to harm. "I deserved that."

"Sure did," Caleb called over.

"If I was her, I'd have slapped both sides of your face at the same time," Milo said.

Zara gave him a sharp look. "You're not me, Milo, so keep it zipped."

Milo gave a sloppy two-fingered salute and said, "Sir, yes sir!"

Zara rolled her eyes and then looked back at Mason. "Seriously, Jed – how could you walk back into my life after what happened?"

"We can talk about that later," Mason said. "Right now I have a job, a big job, and I need to know if you're in or out."

"Where's Virgil?"

"New York. Saying goodbye to Jen and Amy. He's meeting us at the job. Are you in?"

She shook her head and gave a smile that said: I just cannot believe you're asking me this. "No."

"At least think about it," he said. "This is the gig to end all gigs."

The Jushoku spoke in Japanese. "Should we stay?"

"No, Jushoku," Zara said, knowing none of the ghosts would understand a word. "I can deal with this."

The monks faded away into the darkness, leaving Zara alone with the three men and a cool, rising wind ushered in by the night. "Don't talk to me about gigs, Jed. My father died chasing the gig to end all gigs."

"And what *would* Jimmy do?" Caleb said. His low voice was heavy in the silent yard.

Zara lowered her voice. "Do *not* bring him into it."

"You brought him into it," Milo said.

She let Milo's words hang in the air for a long time as she studied the way the last rays of the sun were striking the pagoda roof above her head. "The gig to end all gigs, huh?"

\*

The film crew following Ella Makepeace along the London sidewalk was small – Gus, the director was doubling as the soundman and then there was Sandy with the HD broadcast camera on his right shoulder.

Mason, Caleb and Milo leaned up against a wall and crossed their arms as they watched Ella do her thing and astonish the crowd. Zara walked over from a café with some green tea and joined them. "Has she wowed them all yet?"

"Not yet, you're just in time," Milo said. "Check out the bird she's with now."

"You mean woman, right?"

Milo glanced at Zara and smiled. "Sure, that's what I said – check out the woman she's with now."

Zara watched Ella carefully as she misdirected the young woman with a series of deft movements and gentle commands. "There goes the watch," she said.

"And now she's got her mobile phone out of her bag too," said Milo.

"And next up," Caleb said, "is her pashmina."

"Woah," Zara said. "That's crazy."

"It's just common or garden variety sleight of hand and misdirection," Mason said.

"I meant Caleb knows that thing's called a pashmina," she said with a wink. "I'd have thought you'd call it a massive handkerchief."

"Hey," Caleb growled. "I have my feminine side like anyone else."

"Caleb?" Zara said.

"What?"

"You're about as feminine as a GMC Sierra with spike lug nuts and bull bars."

"That's two miracles today," Milo said. "Not only does the legendary Caleb Jackson know that enormous scarf is called a pashmina, but the even more legendary Zara Dietrich knows of the existence of spike lug nuts."

"I'll spike your lug nuts in a minute," Zara said. "I grew up on the road, Gomer."

"Nice," Caleb said, and he and Zara shared a high five. "Wait a minute – why is Zara even more legendary than me?"

"Her dad was Jimmy Dietrich, Cal. He toured with Aerosmith, Guns and Roses and about a million other bands. When you throw in the fact she's a Silat guru, well... this shit adds up, you know?"

"Heads up," Mason interrupted. "Looks like she's finished filming this segment."

Mason approached Ella and when she saw him, her eyes lit up and the world-famous smile appeared on her face. She recognized him at once, but she wasn't letting on for the camera. "What about you, sir?" she said casually. "Will you take part in our TV show?"

Mason took off his shades and cleared his throat. "Why not?" He cast an uncertain eye at the camera on Sandy's shoulder.

"Try not to look at the camera," Gus said. "We'll just have to cut it out in edit."

"You might be able to fool these guys," Mason said, locking his eyes on Ella. "But you're not going to get one over on me."

"No?"

"No."

"In that case, why do I already have your Rolex and wallet?"

She waved them at the camera and the crowd applauded.

Mason laughed. "Dammit, Makepeace. How do you *do* that?"

"Tricks of the trade, Jed. Tricks of the trade." She and Gus decided to call it a day and Sandy pulled the camera off his shoulder with weary sigh.

"So why are you here?" she said.

"Job."

She gave him a knowing smile. "What sort of job?"

"He wants you to put on a production of Purcell's Dioclesian," Milo called out. "We're retrieving a mystery item – stolen apparently. What do you think?"

"Jesus, Milo," Zara said. "Why don't you just put an ad in the New York Times?"

"Sorry."

Mason took his shades off and looked into Ella's bright green eyes. "Well? Just for old times' sake?"

"I want a fair cut, Jed. None of this you get fifty and we split the rest bullshit."

"When did I ever do that?"

"Two years ago in Moscow."

"Ah."

"V?"

"With his family. Meeting us in Istanbul."

"Istanbul, eh?"

A nod.

"I don't know, I have Ben now."

"He'll understand."

"Maybe. And what about the seventh member of our team?" she said, peering over his shoulder.

"She's on site already, getting some transport sorted."

"And we're splitting the money evenly?"

"We are."

She smiled. "So we have a deal, then?"

"As long as you don't do some crazy hypnotist shit on me and make me give you my split of the cash, then yes."

"Great," she said. "And thanks for giving me that idea, by the way."

# CHAPTER THREE

"Get this right, and we'll never work again."

He could still hear the Englishman's words as he walked into the sprawling campus of Harvard University. Looking at all these spoiled brats sliding from privilege to good fortune and back to privilege again, he hoped to hell the Brit was right. For these students, life was just a matter of surfing Daddy's money all the way to the beach house but for him it was about street fights and pain and rage.

The visceral hate he felt for them rose like acid inside him until it was high enough in his throat that he almost choked, and that went for the assholes who called themselves professors too. If anyone in this world deserved a good pounding it was these guys, but today only one of them was going to get what she deserved.

He crossed Oxford Street and disappeared into the shadows of the Hoffman Laboratory. The narrow path ran along the south side of yet another opulent park of oak trees and smooth lawns. The smell of freshly cut grass drifted on the warm evening air. Up ahead loomed the Harvard Museum of Natural History but the building that formed its southern wing was his target tonight.

He turned and looked over his shoulder before entering the large building. It was the habit of a life spent getting up to no good in the toughest parts of town, and he never fought the urge away. He'd never trusted a single soul in this crap hole of a world and he wasn't about to start now. If he did, he knew he'd be dead before you could say *betrayed*.

Had coming here tonight meant trusting Linus? Never. Brick? Never. Jansons or Cruise? Never. These people were his crew. Led by that Limey Linus, what he felt for them was no more than professional respect. He watched their backs and they watched his and if any of them turned on him he'd cut them up like a snake. That's what happened to anyone who crossed Kyle Cage.

Had been like that since he was a kid and wouldn't stop till he was in his grave, Amen.

He raised his right hand to make sure the Browning Hi Power 9mm was still in his inside pocket and skipped up the last few steps of the Natural History Museum. Yes sir, old habits die hard. A lot of people also die hard, he mused, and a second later the large red brick building had completely swallowed him up and left only the peaceful students outside.

"Get in, get down and get out," Linus had said. He spoke to the Spiders like they were his goddam soldiers, but then like he'd just thought – old habits die hard. Before being court martialled for assaulting a senior officer, Linus Finn was a Colonel in the British Army – some kind of Guards regiment, maybe. He forgot. He respected Linus, but he wouldn't trust him any further than he could throw him. Nothing personal. He just gave off that vibe.

Inside now and Cage turned to the right and started to walk to his target. Linus had made him remember the route by heart the night before and go through it all day. No asking for directions. No looking at maps. "You have to look like you're supposed to be there, Kyle," he had said in his clipped English accent. "Not some itinerant barrow boy looking for an upmarket shag."

Cage didn't know what most of that meant, but he caught the drift all the same. Linus never talked about himself, but it was obvious the guy had a background of old money. But not Kyle Cage, no sir. He was born on the back seat of a stolen Cadillac and never even knew his father. He had no interest in knowing him, even though his mom had the shortlist down to six. He'd fought his way to adulthood on the roughest streets of Chicago and he didn't mind who knew it. One thing he did mind people knowing was that to this day he couldn't read or write. That was why he learned to memorize the map like Linus had told him to – he knew he wouldn't be able to read the signs inside the museum.

It had nothing to do with barrows and shags and whatever the hell Linus was talking about.

He continued down the long corridor. His alligator boots clicked on the polished tiles as he moved closer to the target. On either side, the doors of various offices and rooms punctuated the walls of the corridor, but the words on them were meaningless to him. It didn't matter – there was nothing wrong with his memory and that told him to keep on going.

Up ahead now he saw a large sign with a series of letters on it. He knew from memory that he was now in the Peabody Museum of Archaeology and Ethnology, and that meant it was time to go to work and earn his money. Reaching the door he needed, he caught a glimpse of his face in the polished window. It looked back at him like a ghost, and there on the spectre's neck was the tattoo that had changed his life forever: a black spider.

They all wore the black spider tattoo with pride – Molly, Iveta, Bjorn and him – and they did it because Linus told them that was the rules. When Cage asked Linus who told *him* to have the tattoo, he broke eye contact and changed the subject. It was the only time Kyle Cage had ever seen the old Colonel look fearful.

And that was their crew. Not a family. A family loved one another. Love was not the bond that held the Spiders together. It was something else altogether – a grotesque cocktail of greed, fear, hate, revenge. He didn't know what else, but whatever it was, it kept them together like the Mafia.

Pushing the door open, he was stopped immediately by two large men in black suits. They were wearing shades and earpieces. He knew at once they were her protection. Maybe government men, or former government.

"Not so fast, son," one of them said in low, measured tones.

The other one raised a wide shovel-hand. "ID?"

He let them push him back out into the corridor. It would be easier this way.

"It's right in my p-p-pocket, sir," he said, deliberately stuttering and trying to look as nervous as possible.

He reached into his pocket with his left hand, but at the same time he reached around his back with his right hand and grabbed the Browning. The two men drew their weapons but it was too late. Cage fired the silenced rounds into their chests – two in each in as many seconds and they tumbled down to the floor in streaks of dark blood.

Cage smiled, replaced the weapon, stepped over the bodies and made his way inside, finding himself in a large research library. This is where she was supposed to be – somewhere in here among these stacks of books and journals and a handful of nerds who felt it was necessary to work on this crap so late into the day.

A man sitting behind what he guessed was some kind of checkout desk looked down at him over the top of his glasses. He wore a tweed jacket with those leather patches on the elbows, and Kyle Cage guessed he'd worked in here long enough to sniff out street trash like him.

And he was right.

The old man raised his head. "Are you looking for someone?"

Cage kept his cool. "I need to speak with Dr Evangeline Starling."

"I see. Are you a student of hers?"

Cage lowered his head and his mind raced. He might not be able to read words but he could read human nature better than anyone. He knew this old asshole was a second and a half away from lifting that Big Ole Phone on the desk and calling the Harvard University Police Department.

"Actually, *sir*," he said. The word 'sir' stuck in his throat like razorwire, "Yes, I am."

The old man looked down at him, and Cage looked back, fixing his eyes on him and never letting go.

A few seconds passed as the man processed the situation, and then he moved to pick up the phone.

"Who's asking for me?"

Kyle Cage and the man at the desk both looked over to the stacks. A beautiful young woman was walking toward them. She placed a journal down on the desk and gave both men an honest, inquisitive smile.

"I am." Cage said.

"Are you one of my students?" Dr Starling said, her Texan accent ringing out in the hushed silence.

"Not exactly."

The man sighed and lifted the receiver to his ear. "Right, that's it."

"You bet your fuckin' ass it is, Peabody," Cage said, and pulled the Browning out of his pocket. He fired three times into the man's chest and blasted him back off his chair. He crashed into the wall behind the desk and slid down dead to the floor.

The students and academics in the library hardly knew what hit them. They all panicked and made for the exits. Evangeline Starling was still looking at the long line of blood and tissue that the man had left behind on the wall as he slid down.

Cage turned around and fired on the fleeing people, mowing them down with extreme prejudice and nothing in his eyes but a cold determination to survive at any cost. The bullets exploded in the silent learning space with a fierce savageness, but Dr Starling surprised and impressed Cage by what she did next.

She kept calm and didn't scream.

"What do you want?" she said.

An old academic tried to make a run for the door from the stacks but Cage saw him and fired. The rounds tore through him and cut him down in a heartbeat. He thudded to the floor, briefly clinging to a book-laden trolley before finally collapsing into the blood-splattered carpet.

"I asked what you want?" she said again, defiant.

"You're coming with me," he said.

She looked down at one of the students. He was half-dead and lying on his face a few meters from them. She was horrified to see that the bullets had blown his lungs partly out of his back and they were now inflating and deflating like balloons. She thought she was going to be sick. This was the kind of thing her grandfather had refused to talk about whenever anyone asked him about the time he got back from France after World War Two.

"I don't understand."

"You will do," Cage said. "Don't make me hurt you, Dr Starling."

# CHAPTER FOUR

Death was only seven seconds away. One false move was all it would take to fall the fifty-two floors down the outside of the Istanbul Sapphire and hit the concrete below. That wasn't seven seconds he wanted to experience.

Jed Mason marked the glass pane with a black cross and carefully placed a suction cup over the center of it. He set the wheel-holder to seventy centimetres and gently traced a circle in the window to make sure he'd gotten everything right. He pulled a small bottle of cutting fluid from his bag and squeezed it thickly into the score-line, but as he wiped the sweat from his forehead, he dropped the bottle. He cursed as he watched it fall hundreds of meters to the ground, disappearing long before it hit the street far below.

Once he had seen someone leap from a skyscraper back in his home town of London. What had surprised him most was the noise. When the jumper hit the ground it sounded like someone firing a cannon. He could never forget that noise but thankfully the plastic bottle went down without a fight.

He pushed around ten kilos of pressure against the wheel-holder and gently moved the cutter around in a clockwise direction until he had made a full circle. Then he retrieved a glass tapper from his bag and set the intensity to minimum before placing it on the score-line and pressing it against the window. He released the bolt and opened a section of the glass. A clean cut would require him to do the same from the other side but that was impossible, and besides, he didn't need a clean cut.

He heard his earpiece crackle. "How are we doing?"

"I'd be doing better if you'd stop interrupting me, Milo," Mason said.

When he'd gone full-circle he pushed gently on the window with the suction cups and it popped out in a perfect circle. He placed it inside the room before pulling himself through and landing quietly on the carpet inside. He checked the way was clear and then walked across the plush office to the door on the far wall.

"I'm in," he said.

"Received, Jedediah," said Milo.

"Just make sure the chopper's ready, Milo, or I'm a dead man walking. And don't call me that."

"We're all good to go, Jed," Milo said. "Kat called in a second ago."

"Good, because we all know what happened to the last man who tried this."

The radio silence that followed told him everyone knew. Another crew had attempted this mission just a few days earlier and one of them had ended up in a high rise trash compactor on the penthouse's mechanical floor.

"You're the best, Jed," Milo said. "Just remember that."

Maybe.

Mason opened the door and looked into the corridor. He moved silently along the corridor and passed various expensive works of art hanging on the walls before reaching the door he needed. It was locked, but they always were, and better than that, this was just a common pin-tumbler.

From his bag he got his tensioner spanner and a rake and placed the spanner in the bottom of the lock plug. He pulled back on the spanner until he got the pressure right and then slid the rake in the top of the keyhole, sliding it back and forth until he got the small gap between the driver pin and the key pin to line up with the shear line. Five seconds later the pins aligned and he was able to pull the spanner around and open the lock. The door was opened.

He stepped inside the room and it almost took his breath away. He was looking at the definition of opulence crafted in Persian rugs, floating staircases and a wall-window giving a view of the entire Istanbul skyscape. An ocean of thick, plush pile carpet in pale cream stretched in every direction and grand mahogany furniture was carefully placed all over the apartment.

He shook his head. Luxury penthouse apartments at the top of exclusive skyscrapers were a world away from where Jed Mason grew up. Those mean streets were a distant memory now, blurred by the years and darkened by more recent pain. But their legacy lived on, and under the surface was a tough, stubborn man who had learned to look after himself the hard way.

The intel they had from one of the apartment cleaners was that the safe was behind the large reproduction of the Mona Lisa hanging behind the desk. It was expensive intel and now was the time to see if it was money well spent. Mason stepped down into the sunken part of the room and walked across the thick, cream carpet until he reached the wall. He removed the fake Mona Lisa from the hook and breathed a sigh of relief when he saw the safe. It was a substantial gun safe, but he knew at once he could crack it.

Milo's voice in his earpiece. "You got some company, Jed."

"Who?"

"Two men in the living area directly below the study. They're heading toward the stairs right now. I'm tracking them with the Sunagors."

"How long?"

"Up the stairs, across the mezzanine and then they're with you. Maybe ninety seconds unless they stop to give each other a massage or something."

Mason sighed. "And how likely is that, Milo?"

"I'd go with ninety seconds," Milo said. "If they go to the other side of the apartment I'm going to lose them, but if they head over to you then we're good."

"All right, I'm on it."

He needed at least thirty seconds to get out of the room and head to the exit if he was going to make the escape plan work, so that meant less than sixty seconds to open the safe and get the asset.

There were three basic ways to open a safe. The first was with the key, or code, the second was to blow it with explosives, and third was Mason's way.

He focused on the safe's dial so closely that the rest of the world vanished from his mind. Concentrating hard on the sensation of the dial as it turned in his fingers, he was able to detect the slightest drop in resistance. Just through touch, he got the first number in less than twenty seconds. This was the result of thousands of hours of spin-testing every type of safe on the market and learning how all the various tumblers fell inside the lock mechanisms.

"How we going, Jed?"

"Just lining up the lock gates under the fence, Milo."

Mason turned the final wheel until the fence dropped down into the lock and retracted the bolt.

"Ten seconds, Jed."

"I'm in."

The safe was open with ten seconds to spare and Mason hurriedly opened the door to reveal a long steel tube which was resting on top of a pile of large denomination Turkish and American bank notes. He checked quickly to make sure the asset was inside and then he slid the steel tube inside his bag.

Job done.

He turned to leave, but he was out of time.

Someone was opening the door.

# CHAPTER FIVE

Moments earlier, and looking to her right, Ella Makepeace saw the broad grin on Caleb Jackson's face and was glad he was in the van with them today. Urban climbing up the side of the Istanbul Sapphire might be Jed Mason's idea of a good time but he could keep it. Ella's idea of a good time usually involved a sun lounger, a large tumbler full of gin and tonic and enough ice to sink an aircraft carrier.

"You think he's nuts, don't you?" Caleb said.

Virgil chuckled. "I think he's crazier than a soup sandwich."

"Me too," Milo said, passing the Sunagor binoculars to Virgil. "Mad as a box of frogs."

Ella shrugged her shoulders and leaned forward in the front seat. The cheap vinyl squeaked as she peered up through the windshield and took in the sight of a very tiny Jed Mason in the luxury penthouse. He had made his way up the western side of the eight hundred-foot skyscraper posing as maintenance on a suspended scaffold. It had looked fragile enough when it was on the ground, but now it was dangling off the top of the skyscraper it looked like a toy. She watched it swaying in the hot Turkish breeze and hoped he knew what he was doing.

"Yes," she said almost in a whisper. "I think he's totally nuts."

Zara looked at her. "Why is he nuts?"

Ella and Caleb both turned to Zara at the same time but Ella answered. "Because he risked his life on that stupid contraption, for one thing."

"How long was he planning this?" Zara said, and then before anyone in the van could answer she said, "Weeks! That's how long. This job is a big fuckin' deal to him, Ella – to us all. If that means Jed goes up the Sapphire then he goes up the Sapphire, for fuck's sake. Besides – he likes playing spiderman."

"He knows what he's doing," Virgil said. "He's never screwed up a job yet and he's not going to start today so everyone just chill out."

"Virgil's right," said Caleb.

"As always," Virgil said. "And not just about Jed either. I'm also right about the Lambo."

The smile dropped from Caleb's face. "Like hell, you are!"

Zara looked confused. "Huh?"

"Oh, the V-Man here is advancing an argument that the Aventador has more cajones under the hood than the Veyron."

Now Ella looked confused. "What?"

"They're talking about cars," Milo said.

Zara turned up the aircon. "And Virgil couldn't be more wrong."

Virgil put his binoculars on his lap and spun around in his seat. "Hey!"

Caleb raised two palms in a peacemaking gesture but his smile said it all. "It's just the way it is. My car is faster than Virgil's..."

"But not my tuned Honda," Milo said with a smug smile. "As you were."

Caleb sighed. "As I was saying, my car is faster than Virgil's and he doesn't like it because it makes him feel inadequate in the pants department." He leaned forward and placed his two heavy hands on the young man's shoulders. "Virgil? Would you *like* a ride in my Veyron?"

"Fuck off, Caleb."

Ella Makepeace was enjoying the banter. She was the black sheep of the Raiders, only joining them on occasional jobs when the circumstances demanded it. She had studied psychology and law at Cambridge and was headed for a career in counselling, but all that ended sharply one night when she went to a late night show in the Comedy Store and saw Zack Marvin.

Marvin was a stage hypnotist and conjuror who dabbled in mesmerism, and after a few short minutes, Ella was hooked for life. She spoke with Marvin backstage and a year later she was on the stage, amazing audiences with her own act. Not long after that Zack Marvin's agent arranged a meeting for her with a television production company called Magikal Productions. Her first TV show was a national success, and the second series went international. Ella Makepeace was a household name.

When she was filming the third series, her old friend Milo Risk got in touch.

He had a favor to ask, and when he told her about it she couldn't wait to help.

An American-Greek millionaire had fled the United States with his son after losing a custody battle with his wife. The job was simple: get the son back to New York and make a quarter of a million dollars each. Her skills proved invaluable, and she became an unofficial Raider.

Her memory was broken by Zara. "It's not even that big a deal," she said. "I could get in that penthouse with my head up my ass."

Caleb laughed. "But I thought Buddhist monks were suppose to be good?"

"I'm *not* a Buddhist monk, gunslinger," she said.

"No?"

"No. And the term is *bikkhuni*. I am a woman, if you hadn't noticed."

"Oh... I'd noticed."

This time she turned to face him. "Do you need your ass kicking again?"

At five-foot nothing, a threat like Zara would have made Caleb Jackson roar with laughter, he was, after all, a six-foot-two former US Army Ranger, but Zara Dietrich was a Silat guru. Silat was Malaysia's martial art and considered one of the most lethal in the world. Like most people who met Zara, Caleb had found out about Silat the hard way.

Virgil turned in his seat. "I'd pay to see you kicking Cal's ass."

"Get those binoculars back on the building, nimrod," Zara said.

Virgil turned back and trained the binoculars on the penthouse. "Shit, they're approaching the door!" he said.

"You think he can make it?" Ella said.

Caleb, Milo and Zara all answered at the same time: "Yes."

Virgil continued to train the powerful binoculars up at the penthouse. "Shit, they're opening the damn door!"

# CHAPTER SIX

The door burst open and two men walked into the room. They looked shocked, and clearly weren't expecting to find an intruder in the property. Without asking any questions, they each made their way toward Jed Mason.

Mason slung the bag containing the asset over his shoulder, took a step back and made a quick study of his opponents. They were built more substantially than the gun safe behind him, and now they were moving toward him with dark expressions on their unshaven faces.

They wore expensive suits – not tailored, but good stuff. One of the men had an undercut hairstyle with shaved sides and the rest pulled back into a jet-black pony tail. The older man's was a buzzcut – silver stubble all over.

"Sen de kimsin?" said Undercut.

Mason didn't speak a word of Turkish. "I'm here to collect something."

"You are English?" the man said.

Mason smiled. "Guilty as charged."

Buzzcut spoke next, his accent thick and heavy. "What are you doing in here?"

"This is private property," said Undercut. "Mr Omar said nothing about you."

They both noticed his gloves and bag at the same time and Undercut said, "Hırsız!"

"I'm presuming that's not an offer of tea and biscuits then?" Mason said.

The two men looked at each other for a second as they exchanged a few words in Turkish, and then they padded toward him. The man with the shaved head rolled his jacket sleeves up as he got closer. "I'm going to enjoy this."

"Just hang on a minute," Mason said. He took a step toward Buzzcut and examined his suit, rubbing his lapel gently in between in his finger and thumb. "No – sorry. Thought it might be Fielding and Nicholson, but on closer inspection it's just a pile of shit."

The man grinned to reveal at least two broken teeth and then swung a violent punch at the Englishman. It was a punch heavy and angry enough to kill, but Mason knew it was coming. He dodged the blow with a millimeter to spare and then brought his elbow up, sharply jabbing the man in the throat and collapsing his windpipe.

Undercut barged into the fray, swinging his fists like a palooka, as Mason's old boxing instructor would have said.

Mason distracted him with a bolo punch – an undercut-hook combination favored by Sugar Ray Leonard. It struck him hard and knocked him on his heels.

"Army Boxing Champion," Mason said with a wink. "Did I mention that?"

The man grunted as he regained his balance and searched for a weapon. He snatched up one of the fire irons from the marble hearth and weighed it in his hands. "Istanbul's dirtiest street fighter," he said in a thick accent. "Did I mention that?"

"Didn't have to, mate," Mason said. "I can smell it from here."

The man growled with rage and ran toward the intruder. Raising the poker above his head, he swung the poker down hard in a bid to smash it across Mason's head but the Englishman was faster and slipped to the side.

The poker crashed down on an antique table and smashed a lamp to pieces.

Before he could turn and take a second swing, Mason was on him, pummelling his back with jabs and then swinging another savage uppercut up into his ribcage.

The man turned and fought back, landing a good punch right on Mason's jaw and nearly knocking him out. He staggered backwards, knocking over a number of Mr Omar's finest antique ornaments as he went but it still wasn't enough to arrest his fall.

He went down on his back and crashed into the carpet. Lucky. His skull struck the step leading down to the sunken lounge and for a second he thought he was going to lose consciousness.

A mind-numbing pain coursed through his head. If he went out now he would wake up upside down in a basement with duct tape over his mouth. Milo wasn't kidding when he'd talked about the last man caught in this apartment. In the Turkish underworld, Omar Dogan was as serious as you got. Waltzing into his private apartment and stealing from his personal safe wasn't going to end well if you got caught.

Confused by the blow to his skull and the eye-watering punch that put him down in the first place, he now struggled to focus on the men as they padded over to him, one still nursing his bruised throat. They were grinning. They thought they had won.

"I told you this was private property," said Undercut.

"You should have listened to him," Buzzcut chimed in casually. He even slipped his hands into his pockets for a few seconds and slouched against one of the interior pillars. "Now we have to kill you and dump your body in a landfill. I've got better things to do with my time, believe me."

Mason shook his head back into focus and got to his feet. He bobbed and weaved as the man stormed toward him, swinging punches left, right and center. One of the men fought back hard, but the Londoner returned fire again, striking the Turkish bodyguard under the chin. The impact forced him back on his heels once again and he threw his hands out for balance.

Seizing the initiative, Mason grabbed one of his hands and forced it back against the top of his forearm until he heard a loud snapping noise. The man howled in agony and collapsed to his knees to nurse the wound and Mason ended the brawl with a hard left, smashing the man in the side of his head and putting him out for the count.

"No flash knockdown for you, lad," he said.

Buzzcut rejoined the fight but was still struggling to breathe properly from his windpipe punch. He flicked open a switchblade and padded over to where Mason and Undercut had brawled a few moments ago in the center of the plush apartment.

Mason saw the knife. Things were getting out of control. Army boxing champion was one thing, but that didn't usually involve fighting armed men. He grabbed Buzzcut's knife hand with his left hand as he piled his right hand up into the guard's jaw. Holding him tight he was able to put his body between Buzzcut and the knife, and then he brought his hand down hard on his wrist and belted the knife from his grip. He kicked it away with his boot and then brought his elbow up into the man's throat for the second time.

Buzzcut gasped for air like a freshly landed fish on a jetty.

Mason moved in for the kill. "Is it that you can't learn, or won't learn?"

The gasping man was on his knees now, unable to breathe and eyes full of genuine fear.

Mason delivered a catastrophic overhand punch and knocked the man down into the sunken lounge beside his associate. Stepping over the fatally wounded man, Mason moved to the window and talked calmly into the mic. "Milo – I've been rumbled and I'm going to need to get out of here ASAP."

"All right," Milo said. "We saw. I'm looking at the schematics of the apartment right now. Where are you? I can't see you anymore."

"To the east of the study in some kind of recreation room."

"Okay, I see it. You need to go to your right and you'll see a corridor. Go to the end and then take the first left. This gets you to the stairs that lead up to the roof."

Mason followed Milo's instructions until he reached Omar's private staircase and ran up the steps to the door. He slammed the panic bar on the inside of the heavy security door and was blinded by the bright Turkish sunshine.

"I'm out!" he said.

"Good stuff, Jed," Milo said.

Mason raised his hand to block the sun and scanned the sky. "But where the hell is Kat?"

"She's on her way!" Milo said.

He heard shouting and the sound of men clambering up the steps behind him. "I hope she gets here in about two seconds, Milo, because it looks like I've got some more trouble on the way."

He slung the bag over his shoulder and ran as far from the door as he could, but then more of Omar's men were on the roof. This time they had knuckle-dusters and scimitars.

# CHAPTER SEVEN

Making contact with the Persian was always unpredictable and dangerous, because the Persian was unpredictable and dangerous, and Schelto Kranz knew it better than most. As he waited for the man to answer the Skype call, he realized he was wringing his hands in fear and fought hard to make them still. He controlled himself but the sensation had left him bereft of his confidence, and in awe of the sort of power held in the Persian's hands.

"Kranz," the Persian purred menacingly. "How good of you to call me."

"Thank you, sir."

The Persian studied his face for a moment. "You look nervous. I hope you're not going to disappoint me today."

"Not at all, Amadeus. I bring good news." He swallowed with anxiety as his eyes crawled all over the silhouette image of the man on the iPad screen. Why did he always hide his face like this? Kranz was Dutch aristocracy, with enormous wealth and power, and yet the Persian put him on edge more than anyone else in this world. He supposed that was the way of things in the Order. The Hidden Hand moved around the world in the shadows, flitting in between the gaps of reality like phantoms. The making of their deeds was never seen, but always felt, and usually by millions of people.

"Then share this good news with me. I like good news."

"Kiya and the others had a successful hunt."

The Persian leaned back in his chair and the light behind him shone through into the camera, burning itself on Kranz's eyes. He blinked and looked away, but then his superior resumed his normal position and blocked the light once more.

"We have the ankh?"

"Yes, sir – and there is more good news."

The Persian breathed out slowly. "You have the woman?"

"Finn and the Spiders took her into their custody a few hours ago. She is already on her way to one of our temples."

The Persian gave a low chuckle. "So, easier than we had anticipated. I am most impressed with your work, Kranz."

"Thank you, sir. I hope you will find the time to mention my work to the Sun-runner…"

The Persian cut him off. "That is not the way of Occulta Manu, Kranz. The fact that you would even propose such a thing makes me question your suitability for promotion to higher offices."

"I beg your apology, sir."

Kranz cursed himself for mentioning such a stupid thing. He didn't even know the identity of the Persian and here he was trying to use his superior as a messenger to curry favor with the Sun-runner, of all people. Was he insane? The Order had a strict hierarchy: Raven, Bride, Soldier, Lion, Persian, Sun-runner and then the Pater. He had to show he knew his place within it.

"You are to update me when we have the information from the ankh."

"Yes, sir."

After the Persian cut the call, Kranz sat for a long time and stared at the dead screen in silence. It felt good delivering such important news to him, but had he made a terrible mistake asking for his success to be taken to the Sun-runner? Lions never spoke with Sun-runners, and as for asking a Persian to do his bidding for him… he prayed he would not be a dead Lion for giving into his vanity and greed like this. They all knew what had happened to Morton Wade after his expulsion from the Order, and none of them wanted to be on the outside like that, in the cold… unprotected. Pushed away from the warm embrace of the Pater.

On his desk, a black plastic telephone rang. He licked his lips, took a deep breath and answered it.

"Mr Kranz?"

It was Matthias, his personal assistant.

"Yes?"

"The German Minister for Foreign Affairs is on the line, sir. He wants to discuss the up-coming trade summit."

"He'll have to wait," Kranz said.

"But it's the Minister himself, sir."

"And I am the Minister of Foreign Affairs of the Netherlands and I am dealing with a more important matter at the moment."

He cut the call. Matthias would deal with it. He was very good at that and he could trust him to keep Dieter happy. Kranz had more important things to consider than an international trade deal. That was child's play compared with what the Persian was demanding of him.

He rose from his studded leather swivel-chair and stepped across the plush carpet of his office. Studying the skyline of The Hague beyond his tinted window, his mind began to dance around the joys – and fears – that a conversation with the Persian could bring. Insignificant men like Dieter Müller, the German foreign affairs minister, could not hope to understand the level on which men like the Persian moved around the world.

Kranz moved to his lavish drinks cabinet and poured himself a chunky Courvoisier. Downing the first in one, he breathed out hard as he poured number two. This second one he sipped more slowly as the brandy unleashed his mind from the fears that usually kept him in place. He glanced over his shoulder to make sure no one was in the office – it was a ridiculous act of paranoia. He lowered his voice to a mumbled whisper in case someone in OM had bugged his office – not so paranoid this time – and started to mutter: "Raven, Bride, Soldier, Lion, Persian, Sun-runner…"

He reduced his voice now to almost nothing. "Pater… who are you, Father?"

He stopped.

This was dangerous territory.

He finished the brandy and opened the window of his office, allowing the warm summer air to blow over his face. He was being reckless. Talking to the Persian in that way, and now speculating about the identity of the Father… If he was not very careful indeed, he would surely be a dead Lion soon enough, and yet would that bring the peace he craved, or did the Father control the afterlife as well as the world around him?

He shook the thought from his mind. It was too dark to contemplate. It was time to bring his mind back to the hunt once again. Kiya had done well. She was solid, efficient and ruthless. She was a good Bride and would make a fine Soldier. That, at least, was one decision that as a Lion he was able to make for himself.

They had the ankh, and they had Starling, the one woman who could translate its ancient poetry. Now all he had to do was to persuade her to read the symbols and the ancient Egyptian ankh would lead them all the way to one of the greatest treasures imaginable. Surely then his efforts would be recognized by Amadeus and he would be nominated for elevation to Persian himself.

And anyone who got in the way of that would not be long for this world.

# CHAPTER EIGHT

Mason searched the sky above the roof of the Sapphire but Katherine Addington was nowhere to be seen. He scanned the Istanbul skyline for any sign of her but drew a blank. "Where are you Kat?" he said into the mic.

"She's on her way, Jed," Milo said.

"Yeah, you just said that, and now I have three guys with knuckle dusters and swords heading my way."

"She's almost there!"

Mason sighed, and continued to step away from the men. "What the hell does that mean, Milo?"

And then he heard her voice. "It means I'm four minutes out."

"Kat!"

It was good to hear the sound of her voice. He and Kat Addington were as close as couples got, and no one ever dared come between them. But it was turbulent. The good times were great, and in the bad times they fought like cat and dog, but they had come through so much together.

Mason glanced over his shoulder at the door. "How long now, Kat?"

"Three minutes. I'm just passing over Maslak."

One of the men stayed at the door, while the other two came closer. He studied them for any signs of weakness as they moved toward him. He didn't much like that they were tooled up with swords, but they still had to be faced down. He guessed they'd seen their buddies downstairs in the penthouse and didn't want to make the same mistake. Two of them were holding antique Ottoman scimitars in their hands and one was pushing a brass knuckle duster on his right hand. With Kat still three minutes out he'd be lucky to get away with his life this time.

Jed Mason had nowhere to run.

The roof of the Istanbul Sapphire had become his prison now, and there were only three ways out – through the door now guarded by one of the sword-wielding men, over the side and a two hundred and sixty-one meter drop or on the rope ladder of Kat's Robinson R22 chopper… but where the hell was she?

The two men moved toward him fast now. They were going to attack at the same time. As Mason confronted the man with the scimitar, Knuckle Duster ran around behind him and swung his armed fist at him.

He ducked and the fist sailed over his head, but at the same time Scimitar slashed his blade through the air and almost sliced an inch-deep gouge in his neck.

"I'm in deep shit, Kat!"

"Two minutes."

Knuckles laughed and brought the brass rings down on Mason's jaw, blasting him over on his back and nearly knocking him out. Mason's world began to spin as he tried to recover from the impact of the knuckle duster. The skyline of Istanbul zipped around a few times but gradually the stars started to fade as he came around.

Both men approached him.

"I'm going to enjoy killing you, English man," Scimitar said.

"Tell me if I'm overstepping my bounds, but have you ever considered seeing a psychiatrist?"

The man was stony-faced and slashed the sword through the air. Its curved blade reflected the sunlight and dazzled Mason's eyes. Whoever this guy was, he knew how to handle a blade. To underline the point he threw it in the air and caught it in the other hand, and now he lunged forward, aiming the tip of the steel at Mason's heart.

The canny Londoner knew the moves thanks to his army boxing, and quickly sidestepped the attack and allowed the man to fall past him. Seizing the moment he brought his fist around into his flank and hammered him hard. Scimitar staggered back but Knuckles charged into the fight.

"One minute, Jed. I hope the asset's nice and safe."

"Safe and sound, Kat – just… *hurry up!*"

Mason spun around and powered a fist into Knuckle Duster's face. He fell on his knees and grunted in pain, but Mason wasn't done with him yet. He brought his right leg up and powered a solid kick into his ribs. Never kick a man when he's down, his instructor used to tell him.

*Except when they're trying to kill you, old son.*

And then anything goes.

Mason judged the kick's aim and power as if he was trying to launch a rugby ball over the crossbar from the halfway line. Ribs cracked and the man cried out as he rolled over on his back and clutched at his broken bones.

Mason padded forward and fired a no-nonsense right cross into his face. He belted him hard enough to knock him out. He turned on the other man who was swinging the scimitar in his face once again.

The blade slashed past his head with millimeters to spare, and his only play was to use the bag as a defense. He pulled it from his shoulder and held it up like a shield. The man slashed the blade a second time, slicing through one of the straps like a hot knife through butter. The bag fell out of his hands and tumbled over onto the floor.

His opponent lunged forward, but this time Mason was ready and side-stepped to the left before powering a punch into his face. His head cracked back and Mason smacked the sword out of his hand before unleashing a brutal volley of punches into the man's stomach. He finished things off with a head butt and then the chopper finally arrived.

As it descended down toward the roof, he sprinted over to it, snatching up the canvas bag on his way. Back at the door, another man had joined the man with the sword and they were sprinting toward him.

"Throw the bag up!" Kat yelled.

Mason scrambled for the bag and tossed it through the chopper's door. Kat grabbed it and put it in the co-pilot's seat.

"You need to come lower!" Mason yelled, but his voice was drowned out by the roar of the engine and the tremendous downdraft of the rotor wash. He knew it was dangerous for her to come any lower because of the risk of the rotors hitting the many aerials. "Lower the rope!"

Now the men were pounding across the roof toward Mason.

Kat leaned out of the open window and called down to him. "Goodbye, Jed. It's been nice knowing you, but it's time we went our separate ways."

Mason stared up at the chopper almost unable to believe what he had just heard. "What are you talking about? They're going to kill me!"

"Say goodbye to the other Raiders for me, won't you, darling?"

He felt the chopper power up and move away from the skyscraper's roof. The rotors speeded up and increased the downdraft. It knocked him off his feet and blasted him back onto the roof. He watched helplessly as Kat Addington, the love of his life, lifted the Robinson high above the Sapphire and made a sharp turn to starboard, peeling away into the bright Turkish sunlight with the asset in his bag right next to her.

"What the hell's going on?"

Milo's voice.

"She's gone," Mason said, his voice weak and confused.

"Speak up, Jed."

"I said *she's gone!*"

"What are you talking about?"

"Kat... she just took my bag and flew away."

"Jesus..."

"I'm in trouble, Milo. I need back-up."

"On it."

And he would be on it. They were asset extraction specialists after all, and now he needed extraction, but still, he could hardly believe what Kat had just done.

Had he imagined it?

He felt gutted. He felt hollowed out.

He felt two heavy hands grab him by the shoulders and heave him up to his feet, and then a savage punch in his stomach. He collapsed forward with all the air knocked out of him and began to cough wildly.

The other man tore the mic and earpiece from him and ground it to dust under his boot heel. "You won't need this."

"And now you come with us," the other said. "Your girlfriend might not love you anymore, but now you have a date with a trash compactor."

# CHAPTER NINE

This time, the strike knocked him clean out of his chair. He fell back onto the floor and his skull smashed into the concrete. The blow had almost dislocated his jaw and made him lose focus for a few seconds. For a moment, it looked like he was seeing the world from the bottom of a swimming pool.

Jed Mason shook it off and took a deep breath. An hour ago he had told the others that it would be a dangerous mission but the pay off would be worth it – but now he was starting think again. There are some things that are not worth five million dollars, and as the heavy-set man punched him in the face and hauled his chair upright again he was starting to think this was one of those things.

The smell and taste of his own blood washed over him as he scanned his new surroundings. As expected, the men had dragged him into the mechanical floor directly below the penthouse. These were the places that housed the building's electrical generators and HVAC systems. Through a beaten, swollen eye he saw a series of metal tubes leading from a water-cooled chiller plant in the corner and vanishing in the ceiling above his head.

And the trash compactor.

Mason had been in tougher scrapes, but this situation could easily get out of control.

"Who are you working for?"

Mason fixed his good eye on the man. "I'm a self-employed man."

The men looked at each and started to laugh. "You're a dead man."

Without warning, the man rushed him and powered a mighty punch into the side of his head. His felt the blood froth up in his mouth and spill over his swollen lip. It felt like he was drowning in hot copper, and as he spat the blood out it ran down his chin and almost made him throw up.

"Mr Omar is a nice man, but it was a mistake coming here and stealing from him. If you tell us where the item is, we will feed you into the trash compactor face first. If you don't tell us where Mr Omar can retrieve what belongs to him, you go in feet first, Trust me, that's not nice."

"Well, I can see I'm spoilt for choice."

The man smashed him with a left jab. Mason couldn't duck, bob or weave anymore. He was too badly beaten. He barely knew what day it was, but one thing was still very clear in his mind – the sight of Kat Addington smiling at him as she turned the R22 into the sun and flew away, stranding him on the roof.

Leaving him for dead.

Letting these men feed him into an industrial trash compactor.

How could she do such a thing? The betrayal was so raw it hurt more than the beating he was getting at the hands of these men.

Another blow to the face, this time delivered by the smaller man. The impact cut his upper lip and knocked his head back hard. Stars flicked in front of his eyes like pieces of shredded aluminum sparkling in the sunlight. He felt sick again.

The nausea climbed higher inside him every time he saw her face... the face he had loved, the lips he had kissed. She was the woman he wanted to marry, and yet she had stolen the ultimate prize from him – from them all, torn it away from him the way she had ripped his heart out.

"So... where is the item?"

"I don't know..."

It was the truth.

"Feed us lies, and we feed you into the compactor – feet first."

"She robbed me – you saw it. I threw the bag into the chopper and she just flew away and left me for dead."

"She left you for dead all right, but I don't believe it when you say you don't know where she is. Where did the chopper come from? Where is it going?"

"Are you deaf?" Mason said, raising as much energy as he could muster after such a savage beating.

Another blow, and another. Brutal fists rained down on his face. He felt the men's knuckles smashing into his swollen cheek bones, and now he was seconds from passing out. "I... don't know... where she...."

The bigger, older man turned to his protégé. "Turn on the compactor."

"No... wait."

"Put it on slow, Mehmet."

"Yes, boss."

Mehmet trudged across the mechanical floor and turned the machine on. Its motor began to whine and Mason felt the vibration through his chair.

Kerem, the bigger man, picked up a chair and walked over to the machine. It was a solid chair with metal legs and a wooden seat, but when he dropped it into the compactor the machine crushed it as if was made of papier mâché. The older man turned and gave Mason an innocent shrug. "You see why it's better if your head goes in first, no?"

Mason's reply was to spit out more blood.

"That way, it's over in a second, but if your legs go in first it's very painful. Trust me, I've used both methods on men who have incurred the displeasure of Mr Omar."

*Goodbye, Jed. It's been nice knowing you, but it's time we went our separate ways....*

The hopeless sense of treachery and betrayal was slowly giving way to anger and rage. Kat Addington was a highly skilled extraction specialist. She knew all the tricks. She had contacts all over the world. But he was better, and so were the other Raiders. Together, they would track her down and...

Suddenly he was aware of the old man right up in his face. He was gripping him by the chin and forcing him to look into his eyes. Sweat was beading on his forehead and running down his nose. When he spoke, it dripped off and landed on the floor in a tiny splash.

"Last time I ask you. Where is Mr Omar's property that you stole?"

Mason's head was swimming now. He was no longer sure what was happening. He could still hear the whine of the trash compactor and something about Kerem told him he wasn't the type to bluff.

*Say goodbye to the other Raiders for me, won't you, darling?*

He heard her say it over and over again, but the upper class English accent that once chimed his heart strings now made him feel nothing but hatred and revenge.

Milo.

Milo and the others would get him out of this.

But how?

Then he heard a scream. At first he thought his fevered imagination had cooked it up, but then he heard it again. A man's scream. It sounded like Mehmet. Something was happening in here. Kerem had released his chin and was fighting with someone using a metal bar as a weapon.

Mason turned his face and strained to see through his battered, swollen eyes.

His heart started to pound with hope – was that Zara?

It was hard to see through eyes almost sealed up with dried blood, but if it was Zara then these two men would end up begging for the trash compactor before too long. He almost felt sorry for them.

For the next thirty seconds he was reminded strongly of a program he'd once watched about how lionesses hunt and kill to feed their young. Watching the two heavy-set Turkish men desperately trying to keep up with a Silat guru was in many ways more painful to watch than seeing a baby gazelle getting brought down on the African savannah.

At least the TV show blurred out the really graphic parts.

When she had finished pummelling them, she strolled over to Mason and cut his hands free with her knife.

"Aaand you're welcome," she said.

"How did you get here?"

"Same way you did, but I took the scaffold to the roof."

"Thank God. She betrayed me, Zara," Mason took a deep breath. "After all the times we shared together she double-crossed me and left me for dead, not to mention the fact she stole the damned asset as well."

"No, she didn't," Zara said.

"What do you mean?"

"What do you think I was beating those two assholes with?" She held up the steel bar, and now in the peace and quiet Mason saw for the first time it wasn't a steel bar at all, but the steel tube he had recovered from Omar's safe.

He was astonished. "You have the asset! How?"

"Some freaking idiot left it lying around on the roof."

"It must have come out when I dropped the bag up there!"

"You think?"

Mason changed the subject. "We're going to need to get out of here in a hurry, and when I say here I don't just mean this building, but Turkey."

"No problem," Zara said. "Cal just got another call from his old buddy. Turns out he was in Germany on a job and when he found out we were in Istanbul he made the trip down."

"Sounds like this guy's pretty serious about getting Cal on board. I wonder what the job is?"

She shrugged. "We're not going to find out in here," she said.

"Where is he?"

"At the airport."

"So let's get going."

"Can you walk?"

He nodded and held up the asset. "Whatever this mysterious job is, we have to get this back to its rightful owner before the world finds out what happened."

# CHAPTER TEN

"Ezra Goddam Haven."

The man in the black suit returned Caleb Jackson's smile and the two men clasped hands in a solid shake. "It's been a long time, Caleb."

They were standing in a hangar over in the general aviation apron of Istanbul Atatürk Airport. "You can say that again." The former Ranger and CIA man looked at Ezra shrewdly. "Maybe not long enough?"

"I see you haven't changed."

"What the hell are you doing in Turkey, Ezra?"

Ezra Haven studied the confused faces of the Raiders, dwelling for several seconds on the badly beaten face of Jed Mason, and then glanced at his watch. "Like I said, I have a job for you, and since we spoke last it's gotten way more serious."

"What is it?"

"On the plane first."

Mason took a step forward, still battered and bruised but now thinking clearly again. "Just wait a minute. I trust Cal with my life, but until someone tells me just who or what the hell you are, me and my team aren't going anywhere."

Ezra's mouth curved into a respectful grin. "I can understand that, but I think just this once it might be smart to get on the plane. Your little stunt at the Istanbul Sapphire has not gone unnoticed. It's being reported as a bungled robbery and murder by a foreign thief and just about every alphabet agency in the country is hunting you down. Unless you want to spend the rest of your life in Silivri Prison I'd trust your friend and get on the Citation. Plus, there's a medic on board who can take a look at you."

Mason fixed his eyes on the man in the black suit, determined not to waver or show any weakness. What he'd said about the Turkish authorities was true and the last thing he wanted was for his crew to get arrested and broken up and scattered around the country in different prisons. On the other hand, this guy could be anyone. Even if Caleb had known him once, there was no way to know who he was working for now.

He turned to look at his old friend. "Who is he, Cal?"

"He left the CIA at the same time as me, and the last government job he had was with the DIA."

Ella frowned. "What's that?"

"Defense Intelligence Agency," Caleb said, still smiling at his old friend. "But you're freelance now, right Ezra?"

Ezra's smile faded. "We need to make tracks, Cal."

Mason sighed impatiently. "Can we trust him?"

"For sure," Caleb replied, returning his attention to his old friend. "But I still want to know why you're here. Seems like one hell of a coincidence that you show up at the same airport, and at the exact same time."

"I need you, Cal. You and your team. You're the best."

"It's not my team, Ez. I told you that already. It's Jed's crew."

Mason stepped forward. "And what the hell do you know about my crew anyway?"

Ezra replied without hesitation. "Caleb Jackson: former US Ranger, bomb disposal expert. Give him a screwdriver and he can build anything. Zara Dietrich: former LAPD with a rocky past. Silat guru, not to mention just about every other martial art under the sun. Sharp, inquisitive, takes shit from no one. Milo Risk: one of the world's greatest computer programmers and hackers. On the watch lists of more governments than I can count. Virgil Lehman: Brilliant classicist and polymath scholar. Like a walking Smithsonian. Ella Makepeace: a stunningly talented hypnotist also specialising in mentalism, mind control and mesmerism."

Mason held back the grin. "And what does your research say about me?"

A pause. "Jedediah Mason: a broken soldier who came back from the brink of terrible personal tragedy. Weighed down by a crushing guilt. A brilliant strategist and leader."

"I don't know…" Everyone recognized Mason's doubtful tone. He still wasn't convinced.

The man in the black suit turned on his heel and started to walk across the tarmac toward the jet. "Take it or leave it, Mr Mason. I hear Turkish prisons are some of the worst in the world."

Mason looked at his crew. Zara shrugged, Milo gave an uncertain smile and Caleb raised his arms into the air in a 'What the Hell?' gesture. Virgil pulled an uncertain face and put his hands in his pockets. Mason had hoped someone might help him out, and then she did.

"He's telling the truth," Ella said.

Mason's face got serious. "You sure?"

She raised an eyebrow and gave him a condescending look. "Yes, I'm sure. I do this for a living, Jed."

As Ezra started to climb the air stairs, he called across to Mason and the others. "Is that sirens I can hear?"

Mason knew he had no choice, and started to walk toward the plane with his friends right behind him. Whatever was inside the private jet had to be better than a Turkish prison. They climbed on board, greeted the medic and then the plane taxied to the runway and prepared to take off.

The Citation was the same kind the CIA used for covert flights, especially extraordinary renditions. It was fast and small and could land just about anywhere, but now it was climbing out of Istanbul Atatürk Airport at four thousand feet per minute with the Raiders crew on board.

At cruise, they unbuckled their belts and Ezra Haven started to talk.

"First off, as Caleb says, I'm no longer with the DIA. I was, but no more. I transferred to the NSA. That's where I really wanted to be after the CIA and I finally got there, but now I'm freelance. I work for a private consortium."

Ella sighed. "Christ, it's like being in a bowl of alphabet soup in here."

Ezra laughed. "Sorry, sometimes those of us on the inside can forget what it sounds like. The NSA is the National Security Agency. They're one of the highest intelligence agencies in the US and responsible for monitoring foreign intel and counterintelligence. They're also responsible for cryptology and breaking any codes that need to be broken and they're in charge of US Cyber Command which deals with cyber warfare issues. I have many contacts there."

"Wow," Ella said, visibly impressed.

Mason sighed. He looked much less impressed. "That's all fantastic, but why are you talking to us? I presume all of this is not just your quirky little way of catching up with your old pal Caleb here."

Ezra Haven dipped his head for a moment and nodded in recognition of Mason's justified frustration. After a few moments he began to explain. "A few hours ago one of my key researchers was kidnapped in a violent assault on her workplace. Her name is Dr Evangeline Starling and she was taken by a professional snatch squad who attacked Harvard University to get at her."

"Who was the squad?" Caleb asked.

Ezra looked at his old friend with an apologetic smile. "I can't tell you that at this stage. It's classified."

"But you know?" Mason said.

"Yes, we know. We have a positive ID. We ran some stills from the university CCTV system through our extensive computer records of known felons."

"Why was she taken?" Zara said.

"I can't tell you that either, sorry. It's highly classified."

"So what the hell can you tell us?" Mason said.

Ezra looked like he understood his frustration. "I can tell you that the kidnapping of Dr Starling represents the gravest national security threat since the Cuban Missile Crisis and we have to get her back no matter what the cost."

Mason frowned as he listened to Ezra calmly talk about national security threats and missile crises and kidnapped researchers. "Why am I here, Mr Haven?"

"I've known Caleb for over twenty years," Ezra said firmly. "We lost a great agent when he left the agency, but he's one of the best asset extraction specialists there is. You all are. I originally contacted him a few days ago to help protect her, but now I want him to get her back. I want you *all* to get her back."

Mason laughed. "You want *us* to get your missing researcher back?"

Ezra was stony faced. "I don't see what's so amusing about it."

"You don't? Try the fact that you were in the NSA and could rustle up just about any team of specialists in the US to get any job done no matter how dirty – and yet you're asking me and my crew instead."

"I understand."

Caleb started to look uncomfortable for the first time since the airport. "So what's the deal, Ezra? Why did you bring this to me the other day, and again now? Why us and not someone still in the government?"

"I'm glad someone asked me that," he said, flashing Mason a withering glance. "Many reasons. Let's start with the fact that any extraction team sent into a foreign country is going to take a lot of paperwork and land on a lot of desks. Putting it bluntly, there are hostile factions within the US intelligence community who represent a threat to our national security. If any of these factions learns of our attempt to rescue Dr Starling it's no exaggeration to say that we could see the collapse of government in America. Plus, I'm freelance now and just don't have the kind of influence needed to get government forces deployed."

A long, heavy silence filled the cabin of the Citation. Like the rest of his crew, Jed Mason hardly knew how to respond to what he had just heard. When he spoke, his voice split the silence like an axe through dry wood.

"I'm not risking the lives of my team without knowing who we're up against. I don't care if it's highly classified or not. Either you tell us who took your researcher or the deal's off right now. Final word."

Ezra sighed and looked to Caleb for support, but he didn't get any.

"Sorry Ezra, but Jed's the leader of this crew and he's right. I'm with him on this one."

Ezra rubbed his nose and stared into the middle distance for a few tense seconds. In the background, the medic fussed with a first aid box but Mason pushed him away. The Londoner guessed Ezra was wrestling with his conscience about just how much to tell them all. He was in the army once and he understood classifications, but he wasn't going to budge on this one. Not one inch.

Then Ezra Haven relented. "All right, but what I'm about to tell you has a code word classification, ranking it above Top

Secret. It's what we call SCI, or Sensitive Compartmented Information."

"Spit it out, Ezzie," Zara said. "I want my afternoon nap."

Ezra was clearly wrestling with something in his mind, but then he rubbed his face, let out a deep sigh and started to speak.

# CHAPTER ELEVEN

"The group who took Dr Starling call themselves SPIDER," Ezra began. "This stands for Special Infiltration, Deception and Emergency Retrieval."

"Sounds like us," Zara said.

"It sounds like you," Ezra agreed. "And they have similar skills, but there the similarity ends. Unlike you, these men and women dedicate their lives to evil. They're all thieves and ex-cons."

"Not like us, then."

"No. The Spiders were in prison for serious crimes – murder, blackmail, intimidation and violent armed robberies, not to mention art and jewel theft, kidnap and smuggling – especially drugs."

"Who's their leader?" Mason asked.

"In the field they're led by a man named Linus Finn."

"Is he the top dog?" Caleb asked.

"No. The boss was a man named Horst Vogel, but he died in mysterious circumstances on the Berlin underground. Now Finn's controlled by a woman known as the Black Widow. We have strong suspicions she's working for someone else. We've been watching bank accounts and seeing large sums of money transfer into a German business account under her control."

"Ooh – a mystery bankroller!" Ella said. "I like it."

"Source?" said Mason.

Ezra shook his head. "She shut the account down two weeks after we started monitoring it. I'm guessing whoever pulls her strings figured out we were poking our noses in there and shut the thing down."

"What sort of money?" Caleb asked.

"Fifty thousand US per week, so a hundred grand in all."

"So whoever's turning his key has wealth," Ella said.

Mason shifted in the comfortable leather seat and sipped some water. He'd relented and let the medic tend to his wounds, including pumping him with painkillers. "Tell me more about this Finn guy."

"He's a British national, and a highly intelligent former army officer who spent five years in prison for robbery and didn't like it. After that he turned to more complex, white-collar crime and he's wanted for a string of offenses by the British authorities. He's the ultimate apex predator. His codename is Tarantula."

Ezra turned in his seat and activated a small plasma screen on the aircrew cabin wall. Seconds later, several mug shots flicked on the screen.

"Woah," Zara said. "That's five people you don't want to meet on a dark night."

Ezra confirmed her observation with a shallow nod. "Finn's latest employee is a Latvian thief named Iveta Jansons, codename Hobo after the Hobo spider. The Latvian authorities suspect her of being the genius behind dozens of high society robberies. She uses her looks to persuade men to take her to exclusive parties all over Russia and Europe and then she gets to work cleaning out the cream of the crop. She has never been caught and some say she doesn't even exist."

"A ghost…"

"Next up is this man – Bjorn Brick. A native of Seattle. As far as armed robbery is concerned, he wrote the book. Calls himself Huntsman."

"Who's that guy with the spider tattooed on his neck?" Ella said. "I don't like that at all."

"Kyle Cage, Codename Wolf. He's the man who went into the university and physically snatched Dr Starling. Most members of SPIDER have the spider tattoo on their arms, but Cage opted to have his loyalty etched permanently on his neck."

Milo raised an eyebrow. "That could be a problem with future employers. Really."

"Thank you very much for that, Mr Risk," Ezra said. "But five years ago, Cage was convicted of killing nineteen people over a period of ten years, so I think that ship sailed already."

"Nasty," Ella said.

"He was busted out of ADX Florence supermax prison in Colorado a few months ago, almost certainly by the rest of SPIDER."

"Oh great," Zara said. "A free-range psycho."

"No," Ezra said firmly. "I want you to understand that Kyle Cage is no psycho, and he's no serial killer. The people he murdered were all hits ordered by whichever Chicago gang boss he was working for at the time. His skills were very much in demand – still are, in fact. He's highly intelligent, and very precise in his work. But he is no free-range psycho."

"If you say so," Zara said, raising an eyebrow.

Ezra fixed his eyes on Zara and for a second it looked like he was about to burn two holes through her with the look in them. "I absolutely *do* say so, Miss Dietrich. But don't get trapped in an elevator with him."

"What about the other girl?" Caleb pointed to a mug shot of a woman no older than twenty-five. Short, pale skin and bright red hair.

"Molly Cruise," Ezra said. "Another Brit, from Manchester, Codename Redback. She's a small-time hustler with some street smarts but her real skill is behind the wheel of a car."

"You're kidding?" Virgil said.

"Our very own little Lightning McQueen," Zara said seriously.

"I am not kidding. She's pretty much the best getaway driver there is. She has abnormally fast reflexes and her reaction time is considerably quicker than most people's. She can drive a car like you wouldn't believe, so don't let the pretty, young face fool you."

"Good to know," Caleb said.

"There's another man who has been known to work with the Spiders. His name is Alfredo Lazaro, a Cuban hit man. He went underground some time ago after a hit in Vietnam when he killed a double agent by the name of Elizaveta Compton. No one's seen him since then, so for now we're not considering him part of the crew."

"Also good to know," Ella said. "Sounds nasty."

"Where are the Spiders holding this Dr Starling?" Virgil asked.

"According to latest intel, they're holding her in Frankfurt, Germany."

Zara clapped her hands together and rubbed them. "Great. Who doesn't like a few inches of knackwurst – Milo?"

Milo gently passed his hand over his floppy hair as if he had all the time in the world. "You know why you're such an asshole, Zara?"

"Do tell, my eager young padawan."

"Because fuck off, that's why."

Zara clasped her hands over her mouth. "Oh my goodnesses! That was so *funny!*"

Ezra sighed. "If you successfully extract Dr Starling from the safe house where Linus Finn and the rest of the Spider team are holding her, you will learn more about why she was taken in the debrief."

"You mean there's more we don't know?" Mason said.

"A hell of a lot more, but I'm not prepared to go there until Dr Starling is safe. After that, it's up to you if you work with me or go your own way."

"It's up to us what we do right now," Mason said, looking each member of his team in the eye. "So are we doing this or not?"

The look in their eyes gave him the answer.

*

Katherine Addington lowered the collective on the R22 and brought the light utility chopper down on scrubland to the north of Istanbul. With the blades still whirring above her head, she leaped out of the helicopter and jogged over to a Fiat Doblo she had parked up on the side of the road earlier in the day.

She jumped in the driver's seat and pulled Mason's canvas bag onto her lap. She opened it, excited to see the asset with her own eyes.

No asset.

She turned her head up and looked through the windshield. Her eyes squinted with confusion and she plunged her hands back into the bag, eventually pulling it inside out in a frantic search for the steel tube. This can't be happening, she thought, and ran back to the chopper to search the cockpit. It must have fallen out of the bag when I was flying out of the city.

No luck.

She raised her hands to her head and screamed with frustration. That no-good son of a bitch must have double-crossed her. She felt the anger rise in her heart, a wild, hot pain that felt like burning gasoline. She screamed again and stomped back over to the Doblo. Kicking the side of it hard, she dented the rear door panel and cursed. "You bastard, Jed… I'll get that damned thing back from you and teach you about betrayal at the same time."

She turned the ignition and sped onto the road, leaving nothing behind but a cloud of gravel chips, diesel fumes and the low echo of her scream as it traveled down the valley.

## CHAPTER TWELVE

With so little time to prepare, Mason was less confident about this mission than any he had ever done before. Now, as they piled into a black Mercedes SUV and began their journey into Frankfurt, his mind was swimming with plans. Ezra's briefing about the location had been exactly that – brief. It was no Fort Knox because Linus and his team were not expecting any trouble but things could still go wrong and he didn't want his crew's blood on his hands. He knew what that felt like already.

The Spiders were holding Eva Starling in an old safehouse in Innenstadt just off Berliner Straße, one of the main streets cutting through the center of the city. It was a built-up area, with thousands of pedestrians, cars, cabs and lots more that Ezra was keen for the team not to trash.

Mason was well-versed in techniques of what those in the trade called 'building clearing', and the Raiders knew how to conduct a tactical raid better than anyone. Between them they had more than enough experience, and they liked to break the rules by using unorthodox weapons like Ella Makepeace and her uncanny methods of manipulating people's minds.

As they raced through the streets of Frankfurt, Mason turned the Mercedes SUV into a mobile office, and shifted in his seat to address the rest of the crew. "As ever, this is all about the details," he began. "After Ella works her magic, we go in as planned, breaching the two entry points and search the property room by room. Two two-man teams, one covers and one searches. Spiders to be taken out on sight and the target to be extricated under cover."

"Are they inward or outward opening doors?" Zara asked.

"Inward," Ezra said. "Already checked."

"We're not taking the whole bag of tricks then?" Virgil asked. "Sledge hammer, hydraulic spreader, j-hooks and t-bars?"

Mason shook his head. "That's why Ella's going in first. She'll get the front door open without so much as a punch, right?"

Ella nodded. "Just watch me."

"Looking at the floor plan of the safehouse," Milo said, "it looks like you want a buttonhook entry at the front because you can get two inside quicker."

"Got it," Mason said. "All right, we're good to go, and Virgil can keep Ezra company here in the Merc. Remember, it's not the first bullet that wins the battle, but the first accurate bullet."

"Your weapons," Ezra said, twisting in the front seat. From a small bag in the passenger seat footwell he handed each of them a gun and a box of ammunition. "I'd say try not to use them but I doubt the Spider crew will play it that way. They're trigger happy and like death for the sake of it. Also, it's highly likely they have several local thugs in there as well. Be prepared for that."

"Got it."

"With the exception of Miss Makepeace, Mr Risk and Virgil here, you're all former military or police so you know how the game works."

"How many years were you with the LAPD?" Milo asked Zara.

"Seven."

He gave her a smug look. "Is that all?"

"It's long enough."

"At least ten years on Call of Duty and GTA," he said proudly, crossing his arms behind his head. "That's all I'm saying, beeatch."

Zara rolled her eyes and the Merc pulled up outside a burger joint. Ezra opened his door first, and climbed out into the fresh air. It was summer and dusk. The tops of the highest buildings were sparkling with the setting sun but everything at street level was already starting to get dark. Birds sang in the trees on the sidewalks and people were milling around with smiles on their faces.

"All right," Ezra said, businesslike. "Don't forget – we need Dr Starling alive at all costs. She is an innocent party in all this. The Spiders will not kill her so long as she has the information they need. She will understand this and will have withheld critical information so they keep her alive, but I do not want her getting hit in the crossfire."

"And what about you?" Ella asked Ezra. "Aren't you joining in the fun?"

"As former DIA and NSA, I'm too close to the US Government. If I get caught shooting up a safehouse in Frankfurt I'm going to lose my pension for sure," he said with a smile. "I'll be monitoring radio chatter out in the SUV, and at some point after I know Dr Starling is safe, I have to return to the States. We'll talk about that at the debriefing."

The safehouse was up a side road to the north of the main street, nestled in a fold of boutique shops and kebab houses. They made their way closer to it, keeping on the same side of the road so they were well out of view. Mason ran through the plan one more time.

"Ella goes in first, remember?"

"Holy smokes," Zara said. "You only briefed us a half hour ago."

Mason gave her a flinty look. "You know the way I do things, Zara."

She raised her hands. "I'm sorry."

"Ella goes in first," he repeated. "She works her magic on whoever opens the door then the rest of us go in hard and fast from our positions. Me and Caleb are going in right through the open front door, Zara and Milo go in through the skylights. All good?"

"All good," Caleb said. "Ella wearing a wire?"

She shook her head. "No wire. I'd make less of a stir if I turned up in a pink tutu. And don't even think about asking how I know that."

Zara and Caleb shared a high five. "Last one to draw blood is buying the beer tonight," Caleb said.

Zara agreed. "You sure you can afford it, big man?"

"All right," Mason said. "Check weapons and then everyone into position."

\*

Zara Dietrich jogged around the rear of the safehouse with Milo at her side. When they arrived, she rapidly studied the form of the building in preparation for the climb to the top floor. Buildering was not an art form to take lightly, but her martial arts career had depended on the same agility and nerve when it came to learning the craft of climbing up buildings with no safety ropes.

Zara used the barest minimum to ascend any building, and now was no exception. In her bag of tricks were the usual array of sky hooks, camming devices and suction cups. She knew how to use them and she knew when to use them.

She made the ascent easily enough; the safehouse was only four storeys high and she had scaled skyscrapers in her prime. When she reached the roof she lowered an anchored rope down for Milo who promptly climbed up and joined her. Then she prised open the skylight and radioed through to Mason.

"We're in position."

"All right. Ella's in position. Everyone wait till I give the word."

\*

Ella Makepeace straightened her shirt and skipped up the steps to the safehouse. She knew what she was doing and she wasn't nervous. She had never been nervous. Confident and popular at school, cocky at college and never any stage fright. The only thing that frightened her was that she found it so hard to think about anyone other than herself. With the exception of her relationship with Ben, almost everything she had ever done had been all about her — her pleasure, her wealth, her power, her fame.

That was where the Raiders came in.

Working for Mason's world-class asset recovery crew had enabled her to give something back and help others in a way that being a c-list TV celebrity could never do, even if she was just a casual part of the team.

She knocked on the door and a second later a woman swung it open. Ella recognized her at once from the briefing: Molly Cruise, and she immediately started talking to her. A minute later, Molly walked out of the house in a daze and turned right on the sidewalk.

Ella radioed the rest of the team. "Molly's just going to get me a coffee from the place down the road," she said quietly into her mic. "I told her to wait there for me. She won't realize what's happened for hours."

'How the buggery fuck does she do that?" Milo said.

"That's confidential, Milo," Ella said. "You know that. I'm coming back to the SUV."

"Okay everyone," Mason said. "Ella's got the door open and sent Molly Cruise down for a latte. We go in three, two..."

*

Zara closed her eyes as she listened to Mason counting down. Even at sunset the heat in Frankfurt was still hot, and a heavy humidity was stifling the city. The hum of the main road traffic filled the air and the sound of laughter and mischief floated across from a café a few doors away. From their position on the roof she and Milo had an elevated view of the city. In the west, an orange ribbon divided the industrial skyline from the sky above. When the sun finally sank beneath the smog, the night, with all its pleasures and horrors, would begin for real.

A stark memory of her time in the Los Angeles Police Department burst into her mind. She had been tracking down a notorious serial killer called the Choker along with the rest of her team of detectives. They were a hard-boiled crew of men. There had been another woman on the team – Alice – but she was the Choker's latest victim. Now, they were all just about ready to burn the freak alive, but there was just one problem.

They had to catch him first.

When they tracked him down, it was to a crack house in Lincoln Heights. Once upon a time in the west, the place had been a former recording studio with twelve bedrooms but by the time Lieutenant Dietrich pulled up in her unmarked Ford Club Wagon it was a broken-down warren of danger and filth. Lurking somewhere inside was the Choker, and she decided she was going to scale the south wall and get in on the top floor.

The memory was cut dead by the sound of Jed Mason: "...One, all teams go!"

She lowered herself down through the skylight and touched down on the unpainted floorboards below like a cat. Pulling her gun, she slid a round into the chamber and silently crossed the loftspace on her way to the door. Milo was just seconds behind her.

She reached out to turn the handle when she heard gunshots coming from downstairs, and then Caleb Jackson's voice crackling through the earpiece. "Asset's not where she's supposed to be... sweep the whole house!"

She ran forward, joined now by Milo, and they reached a white-painted door. "We're on our way, Cal!"

Zara moved to open the door when Milo stopped her. "Wait – you hear something?"

"No, what?"

"Someone's coming!"

Zara leaned in and also heard footsteps outside the door. Reaching for a grenade on her belt, she turned to Milo and gave him a wink. "Put your mask on! This could get dangerous!"

# CHAPTER THIRTEEN

Snatching a CS Handtoss grenade from her bag, Zara kicked the door open with her boot and rolled the weapon out into the hall. The grenade exploded in a thick, white cloud of noxious gas and the next thing she heard were two men coughing and gasping for air. Milo was wearing his mask now, and peered into the gloom through the visor. "They're still coming!"

"Not for long." Coughing with the gas, Zara fired the Glock 23 into the cloud and killed the two men, and then quickly slid on her gas mask before making her way down the stairs. She pulled her wrist up and spoke rapidly into the palm-mic. "Just took out two of Ezra's local thugs up here. You got anything for me on the asset's location yet, Cal?"

"Nothing," he said. "We're pinned down by some heavy fire on the first floor."

"That means ground floor, Milo," Mason threw in.

She heard someone else pounding up the stairs. Heavy footsteps. A man. She guessed it was Bjorn Brick whom Ezra had briefed her about earlier. She watched as his enormous frame came bobbing up through the CS gas and saw he was wearing a gas mask.

When Brick's head was in the right place on the stairs, she kicked her leg out as hard as she could and caught the end of his mask's filter canister with the toe of her boot. The power of the unexpected impact smashed the mask into Brick's face and knocked it away from his mouth and nose. He fell back immediately with the force of the strike and them tumbled almost comically back down the stairs.

"Nice kick!" Milo said.

Zara heard his hefty frame crunch into the landing but he was obscured once again by the gas. He was going to be pretty pissed about getting belted like that without any warning, so she figured it made more sense to finish the job while he was still disoriented. If you're going to poke a bear, then better off do it in his eyes.

She leaped off the top step and flew through the CS gas like a ninja, landing with a controlled thud on the landing. She was on her own. Brick had come to his senses and rolled away, and now he was hiding somewhere for her in one of the mansion's other rooms. An angry bear with a score to settle.

She heard gunshots and realized Brick was firing on them. "Get down!"

They hit the deck and she fired back, emptying her magazine in the hope of taking out the Spider.

"You're firing at ghosts, Z!"

Milo was right. She tossed the gun and made her way down the next staircase. "Keep up, Miles!" she said, and swept her gun from side to side as she gave chase to the Huntsman.

*

Dr Evangeline Starling heard gunshots all around her, but thanks to the bag on her head she saw nothing but blackness. She was disoriented, scared and she felt sick, and when the shooting got closer she was certain she was going to die.

She didn't even know where she was. They had let her see the ankh, but that was in this windowless room and when she had done their bidding they had put the bag back over her head. The last time she had seen daylight was when she had stepped inside the Harvard Museum of Natural History and that was back in Boston. She had no idea where they had taken her but she knew it had involved a long flight.

She could be anywhere.

And now there was a gun battle raging around her and she was tied to a chair with a sack blinding her and preventing her from defending herself. She worked hard to control her nerves, but couldn't stop herself from jumping every time one of the guns went off. If she made it through this it would be a miracle.

*

In the kitchen, Mason and Caleb were still under heavy fire. Mason saw in the reflection of the chrome refrigerator that their tormentors were Kyle Cage and Iveta Jansons. He knew Zara and

Milo were hunting Bjorn Brick upstairs and Molly Cruise was trying to buy a latte without any money down the street, so that meant Linus Finn was guarding the asset.

Caleb took the brunt of the fire, keeping his head below the level of the kitchen units while he reloaded his weapon. Mason provided cover fire and managed to drive both the Spiders from the kitchen and back out into the hall. He could smell CS gas and knew Zara must have deployed it. It was a standard weapon they used on their retrieval missions when they ran into trouble.

Suddenly he heard the firing go silent, and peered over the counter to see both Cage and Jansons peel off and make a break for it. Linus had obviously ordered a retreat. The Raiders hadn't caused anywhere near enough havoc to force a man like Linus to back off yet, so that meant they had what they wanted.

He saw a door leading to the basement and blew open the lock with his gun.

"I'm going down, Cal! Cover me in case they come back."

"Got it."

Kicking the door open he made his way down the steps until he saw the asset. She was sitting in the center of the room with a bag over her head. He moved forward until he noticed others in the darkened space, and then he opened fire on them. They fired back. The exchange was short and he heard a cry in the darkness and something hit the cold tiled floor. He had hit one of them, but now Caleb piled in behind him and added more manpower, firing at them as they sprinted through another door into the dusk.

"Is she still alive?" Caleb asked.

Mason prayed she was, and ran toward her.

*

With Milo struggling to keep up, Zara saw Brick climbing out of a window and heading for the roof. She gave chase, slipped through the window and sprinted along the rooftiles in pursuit of him. It wasn't her first rooftop chase, and she was once again taken back to Lincoln Heights and the Choker. She had given chase to the serial killer, running with everything she had to keep up with the much larger man. He had vaulted over a low wall and approached what looked like the edge of the roof. She saw him jump over it again and from her perspective it looked like he had leaped off the roof and into the ether.

When she got there she realized he had leaped down to a lower roof and was now sprinting toward an empty rooftop swimming pool full of junk and surrounded by broken sun loungers. She guessed it had been pretty classy many years ago but since the crackheads moved in the pool had been turned into a giant landfill and was full of bottles, cans, old furniture and thousands of needles.

She had seen worse.

That was partly why she had tossed that life away and become a bhikkhuni.

Now Brick stood on the roof's edge and faced her, his chest heaving up and down with the effort of the chase. "You're good," he said.

Zara slipped her hand into her pocket and slid her fingers through her faithful knuckle duster. "And you're finished."

He started laughing. "Who's going to finish me?"

"Me."

"You? You and whose army, sweetheart?"

Zara charged forward and smashed the knuckle duster into the left side of his jaw. She heard the sound of bones breaking as his head rocked backward. Brick looked genuinely shocked and tried to move back but the wall stopped him in his tracks. Zara brought up her other hand, also armed with a knuckle duster but this time he was smart to her tricks and grabbed the hand. He squeezed it until she thought every bone in her hand was going to break. "Jesus..."

"Looks like sweetheart has a weak link," he said, laughing.

"We all do, right?" she said.

"No," he said flatly.

"Let me prove you wrong," she said, and brought her knee up into his balls. She drove her kneebone up into him as hard as she could and got the result she needed.

He howled in pain and released her hand. "Fucking bitch!" he growled, and delivered a meaty back-handed slap to her face.

It caught her off-guard and she tumbled backward and fell over onto the roof.

He padded over to her and snatched up a length of metal piping out of the detritus around him. "I'll teach you a lesson that you won't forget in a hurry."

She kept her nerve and waited until he was nearly over her, and then spun around in a circle and leaped to her feet ready for another round.

She heard gunshots and looked over her shoulder to see Milo firing on Brick.

The Huntsman dropped the piping, blew her a kiss and winked. "Another time, sweetheart." He fled like a panther, leaping off the wall and smashing down on the roof of the adjacent building. He was gone.

"Brick's out of here," she said into her palm mic. "I repeat, Brick's out of the building. We're all clear up here."

She screamed, turned and kicked the metal piping so hard it flew over the wall and spun out of sight over the rear garden.

\*

Mason breathed a sigh of relief when he saw Eva Starling turn in her chair. He'd just heard Zara reporting that Brick had fled, so that meant all the Spiders were gone, but at least the asset was alive. That was always the primary goal of an extraction and rescue squad like the Raiders.

"Who's there?" she asked.

He rushed forward and took the bag off. She had been crying, and mascara was streaking down her cheeks. A slight bruising under her right eye and a split lip also told him someone had gotten physical with her as well, but they were questions for later.

"Who are you?" she said, her voice hoarse and desperate.

"My name's Mason," he said. "Jed Mason, and I'm here to rescue you."

"Thank God!" she said. "I thought you were those weirdos again."

"Do you know where Linus went?" he asked.

She shook her head. "Sorry, no... and what the *hell* happened to your face?"

"Long story," Mason said.

As he spoke, Caleb snatched up a strange golden object from the floor. It was heavy, and covered in jewels. "This must be what they dropped when you hit one of the bastards."

Mason had no time to look. "You're coming with us. You're safe now."

"Wait a minute – you're not American."

Mason hacked at the cable ties binding her hands together and strapping her to the back of the chair. "An astute observation," he said. "I'm working with Americans."

"Are you SAS?"

"No. Let's just get out of here and then we'll talk."

She breathed a sigh of relief, and he saw hope flicker into her blue eyes for the first time since he'd removed the bag. "Whatever gets me away from these crazies faster!"

Holding her tightly by the hand, Jed Mason told her to keep her head down, and then he led her back to freedom.

## CHAPTER FOURTEEN

Mason stood with his hands in his pockets and studied the Frankfurt skyline. He was standing in a room on the top floor of another safe house across the city and this time, it was *their* safe house, arranged by Ezra Haven. The man himself was in the next room talking with Eva who was undergoing a full examination by the medic, an American named Mat Wills. Wills believed she was showing symptoms of PTSD after the kidnap and assault and had whisked her away the moment he saw her almost as fast as Ezra had taken the strange jewel-encrusted object away.

Caleb and Zara walked over with coffees and sat down opposite him at the little table.

"I told you we could trust him," Caleb said.

"What?" Mason said, knocked from his daydream.

"I said I told you we could trust Ezra. We go way back."

Mason gave another weary sigh. "The mission's not over yet."

"I think he's kinda cute," Zara said. "That whole Special Agent Dale Cooper thing going on and all."

Mason rolled his eyes. "Since when do we judge if we trust someone based on what they look like?"

She shrugged. "Just sayin'."

When Ezra entered the room, Mason's mind was still buzzing, but he worked hard to look cool and collected. Turning to the American, he said, "On the jet from Turkey, you told us that these Spiders were working for someone else. I want to know who, and now."

Ezra gave a brief nod. "All right everyone, gather around."

"How's Dr Starling?" Virgil asked.

"Dr Starling is still with Mat Wills next door. He thinks maybe she's been drugged."

"Drugged?" said Ella.

"I asked about who controls the Spiders," Mason said, louder this time and the frustration rising in his voice.

"And I'm going to answer you right now, just take it easy. As you know, SPIDER is a tight operation and they can be anywhere with very little notice. They're usually independent, but they're also for hire. Following the successful extraction and rescue of Dr Starling, my organization has now cleared you to know that we believe the Spider crew were hired by a kind of cult."

Everyone in the room stopped talking and all eyes fell on the man in the black suit.

Mason spoke for the whole team. "A cult?"

Another brief nod. "A secret order we know very little about. We think they hired the Spiders to snatch Eva Starling."

Mason's eyes widened. "That's who Eva described as weirdos! At some point, they must have been at the safehouse where the Spiders were keeping her."

Ezra nodded. "Looks that way. The plan must have been to meet there – Spiders bringing Starling and the cult bringing the item they wanted her to translate."

"That thing we found on the basement floor?" Caleb said.

"We'll get to that."

"Are these guys a bigger threat than the Spiders?" Milo said, shifting uneasily his seat.

"Without a doubt."

Caleb cleared his throat. "And what do we call this threat?"

Ezra sighed deeply and rubbed his tired eyes. "What I'm about to tell you might sound like the plot to a Mission Impossible movie, but it's true – every damned word of it. Their name is Occulta Manu. It means Hidden Hand in Latin."

"The Hidden Hand?" Zara said. "I don't like the sound of that."

"Me neither," said Milo. "I was freaked out enough by the Spider guys, and now this."

Virgil furrowed his brow. "You can't be talking about *the* Hidden Hand?"

"I'm afraid so, Mr Lehman. You're aware of them?"

"My PhD is in the classics. I speak Latin and Ancient Greek. If we're talking about anything from the ancient world, or any sort of esoteria, then I'm aware of it… but I thought they faded away centuries ago."

"They did, but now they're coming back to life. Someone, or *something*, woke them up."

"I've heard of them," Ella said. "But I thought they were only a legend, not some kind of dormant monster."

"I only wish they were a legend."

"What do we know about them?" Mason said.

"As I say, very little. I know a great many NSA researchers, and those guys have access to the best military intelligence on the planet and a free pass to go pretty much anywhere they want with their research. However, all they have – and all *we* have – is that OM have been around longer than any of the other organizations you've ever heard of, and even though they usually stay in the shadows, when they strike they strike hard. They have a strong interest in controlling the flow and direction of history and they kill easily and without conscience."

"Especially their own, yes?" Mason said.

"Yes," Ezra said, raising an eyebrow. "How did you know?"

The Londoner shrugged his shoulders. "Same as any other fraternity, gang, brotherhood – loyalty is powerful but if you betray your brothers they see it as the greatest crime of all. You see it with all the street gangs, Russian Mafia, you name it."

The American man gave a pensive nod. "It's interesting you mention gangs, because gangs usually have a pecking order. One of the few things we know for sure about the Hidden Hand is that they have a strict hierarchy. A newly initiated member becomes a Corax, or Raven, then a Nymphus or Bride – male or female, then a Soldier, or Miles and then a Leo, or Lion. These are the rank and file members of OM. After these levels is what you might call the officer class when a member becomes a Perses, or a Persian, and then finally a Heliodromus, or Sun-runner. These ranks each have their own special symbols based on the old Cult of Mithras – raven, diadem, lance, lion, crescent moon, and the sun-god."

"And the Sun-runner's the boss?" Zara asked.

"No. The top man is called the Pater, or the Father. His symbol is the patera, what the experts call a shallow libation bowl but you or I would call a kind of cup without handles. We estimate there are thousands of Ravens, Brides and Soldiers and probably hundreds of Lions. We really have no solid idea but our best guess is that there are probably only a few dozen Persians and around twelve Sun-runners." He looked at them and offered an apologetic shrug. "For certain, there is only one Occulta Manu Father."

Zara gave a grim laugh. "So in other words we know there's a weird bunch of men running around in robes calling each other Ravens and Brides and they have lots of money and power?"

Ezra frowned. "The idea of these guys going around in robes is ridiculous. The Hidden Hand might be some kind of secret cult following ancient pagan rites, but they exist in the modern world. And it's men and *women*," he said. "As I just mentioned, OM uses the rank system of an ancient Mystery Cult called the Cult of Mithras, but there's a big difference – the Mithrians were strictly men only – we know for a fact that the Hidden Hand actively recruit women from all over the world."

"An equal opportunities secret society," Zara said. "They don't sound so bad."

"They are seriously bad, Miss Dietrich," Ezra said, a note of fear in his voice. "Occulta Manu are something no one in the NSA, or any other branch of US government intel for that matter, know very much about. Most of our enemies are easy to understand and monitor – other states, foreign spy agencies, international terrorist cells, and so on. But OM is different. Very different. Frankly, there are many in the intelligence community who are just plain old-fashioned scared of them. Not even Titanfort has a handle on this organization yet."

Mason gave him a sharp look. "Titanfort? I've heard of Titanpointe – that's the NSA's spy hub, but what's Titanfort?"

Ezra paused a beat while he scanned their faces. Again, the man in the black suit was processing countless thoughts and calculations. "Titanfort is the spy hub owned by the private agency that employs me, and maybe you, too. Don't confuse it with Titanpointe."

"What's the difference?" Mason asked flatly.

"Titanpointe is government. They're south of us in Lower Manhattan. Titanfort is ours, and it's private. It's different."

"You already said that, but what makes it so different?"

"The world knows about Titanpointe. No one knows about Titanfort." He lowered his head and stared at them, unblinking.

A look of menace crossed his face. "And that's the way it's staying."

Jed Mason frowned. The last thing he wanted to hear was that one of the world's best funded intelligence agencies was scared of something, and now he had to process the Titanfort revelation on top of everything else.

"Who controls Titanfort?"

"Classified."

Mason sighed, but managed a grin. "All right, fine. Let me try this instead: you said this secret order vanished for a few centuries, but now they've woken up – what did you mean by that?"

"For a long time they went silent, and for centuries we thought they were gone, but a few years ago the NSA and other agencies started picking up chatter. Both they and Titanfort began to have concerns they were coming back, getting stronger, adapting to the new world – undermining civilization and reshaping it in their own image. They're like a pathogen."

Ezra let the words sink in before continuing the briefing. "Reges Chao – Latin for the Kings of Chaos. This is another name they go by, and it's an accurate description because of their habit of infiltrating institutions and creating mayhem inside them."

Mason sighed. "I'm starting to get the picture."

"In a word, they are unknowable. Their acolytes are in every government in the world and yet the infiltrations are anonymous. It's Titanfort's speculation that every institution on earth probably has at least one Hidden Hand acolyte inside it, usually at the top somewhere and protected by what they call drones."

"Drones?" Milo asked.

"People who do their bidding without knowing it."

"A touching description," Ella said.

"Quite," Ezra continued. "Once on the inside they shape things for the advantage not of the institution but for their own mysterious cult. They direct whole governments for the benefit of themselves and have zero regard for the average man or woman in the street."

"Are you sure you're not just talking about regular politicians?" Zara said.

It raised a low laugh, but everyone was starting to feel more than a little freaked out by what they were hearing.

"As I say," Ezra pressed on. "The long-term stated goal of Occulta Manu is to destroy the existing power structure and create the world in its own image."

"They want to control the world, then," Caleb said.

"Yes," Ezra said bluntly. "To do this they need to control the future, and to do that they must control the past. Along with their work infiltrating governments and institutions around the world, they are obsessed with the control of history, particularly the history of the ancient world. From what we can work out, they figure that if they control the flow of information and knowledge relating to our most distant past, they can shape future minds any way they want."

"Stop the plane… I want to get off," Ella said.

Ezra sympathized. "I'm sorry, but OM is the big boy holding all the strings, Miss Makepeace. There's no getting away from them, on or off this aircraft."

Zara sighed. "Still don't get why most of us has never heard of them."

"Like I already explained, if you've heard of them, they're not secret societies. The ones you've heard of or read about on the internet are publicly recognised institutions that give to charity. Occulta Manu does not give to charity."

Ella shivered. "This is all starting to sound kinda creepy."

"You can say that again," Milo said. "Remember the good old days when we thought Kyle Cage sounded scary?"

Virgil crossed his hands behind his head. "Ah, the good old days…"

Ezra frowned. "And he still *is* scary, Mr Risk. If you underestimate a man like Cage you'll live to regret it, but not for long, I assure you."

Another grim rattle of laughter rippled around the small room but everyone knew it was just nerves.

"Jesus, talk about getting red pilled," Zara said. "When I woke up this morning I thought the worst thing that could happen was another Ed Sheeran song at Number 1. How fucking wrong was I?"

"Very wrong," Ezra said. "And it gets a lot worse."

"We can take it," Mason said.

Caleb brushed his jaw and gave a confident nod. "Yeah, let us have it, Ez."

"Okay – but don't say you didn't ask for it."

## CHAPTER FIFTEEN

Far across the city, Mason watched a large jet plane push up into the sky and disappear in a bank of low, gray clouds. "Gets a lot worse, you say?" he asked.

Ezra gave a resigned nod. "As I have indicated, after the Athanatoi, the Hidden Hand is the highest of all secret societies."

"The Athanatoi?" Virgil asked. "Now they really are just a myth, right?"

"Wrong," Ezra said bluntly.

"Who are they?" Ella asked.

"They're someone else's problem. Our problem is the Hidden Hand, and they sit at the top of an unimaginably vast network of less powerful societies. These lesser societies operate all over the world, but it's from the Hidden Hand that these societies get their orders."

"You mean secret societies we've actually heard of?" Zara asked.

Ezra's tone grew weary. "If you've *heard* of a secret society then they're not a secret society any more. That's not the way these guys roll – they demand total secrecy, loyalty and anonymity and traitors are extinguished without mercy. When the world hears about a society that's because they're done with it and they've moved on. Skull and Bones, Priory of Sion, Carbonari, Bloodline of the Snake – all of them now just mere shells compared with what they once were as the power goes elsewhere."

"Like the Illuminati?" Ella asked.

Ezra laughed. "The Hidden Hand is the ultimate Mystery Cult. The Illuminati was created by men who were ordered to do so by the Hidden Hand. They come from Masons and Masons come from ancient Mystery Cults. This is very well-documented. Like the Skull and Bones and the Priory of Sion, they're just another creation of the Hidden Hand; just one of many cogs in Occulta Manu's vast, hungry machine. It's there to deflect from the real deal, like a simple façade in front of a house of horrors."

Milo was frantically scrolling through pages on the internet. "Shit, he's right – but there are so few references to the Hidden Hand it's almost impossible to know anything about them."

"As I said," Ezra said, "OM are not in Show Business. These are the big boys, pulling the strings of organizations like Skull and Bones, Rosicrucians, Illuminati, Bilderberg, Carbonari…"

Zara leaned forward in her seat. "Wait, that's the second time you said that, but isn't that a pasta dish?"

"That's *carbonara*," Ezra said with a weary sigh. "The Carbonari were a group of revolutionaries operating in Italy during the early part of the nineteenth century during Napoleon's rule."

"I'm just yankin' your chain, Ez."

"Sure you were. And it's Ezra."

Before Zara responded, Mason said, "What was that about Napoleon?"

"History records the Carbonari's original purpose as resisting the French occupation under Napoleon, but the truth is somewhat darker. The truth is that they were ordered by their masters in the Hidden Hand to resist Napoleon as a punishment for his Egyptian expedition."

Virgil shook his head. "So they really *have* been controlling history since way back then."

"To the members of the Hidden Hand, the time of Napoleon was five minutes ago. They go back way further than that. Anyway, all of these organizations that I've mentioned were all created by the Hidden Hand at various times in its long history, and each time there was a specific reason for doing so – a specific place or institution that had to be infiltrated or controlled. Occulta Manu is the dark secret that no government wants you to know about – believe me."

"Sure sounds like it."

"When an initiate in other lower societies gets an order from OM they will usually have no idea why they have been ordered to do it or even where the order originates from. The only people in the know are those at the heart of the movement – those men and women who have vowed to follow the ancient mystery religions."

"Which is where all this Raven crap comes from, right?" Zara said.

"Correct. That is why they hold the ancient symbols in such high regard – with reverence, actually. These guys are the real deal. They carry ideas and beliefs older than Egypt itself – maybe even Sumer. Stuff so ancient we couldn't begin to rationalize it but to them it's a code to live by. If you screw with these people you will die. The only way to handle them is with the utmost respect."

"Has anyone ever gotten close to them?" Caleb asked.

Ezra looked doubtful. "Not really, but last year a man named Morton Wade was killed by the ECHO team. We were monitoring Wade for a number of reasons, not least his connections to the Hidden Hand. He had been part of them once. That may or may not have been where he'd gotten his bloodlust for human sacrifice."

"Human sacrifice?" Ella asked, horrified.

Ezra nodded. "As I've already briefed you, Occulta Manu descends from the ancient Mithras Cult and while there's no modern evidence of blood sacrifices to Mithras, ancient writers like Socrates described how the mystery religions sacrificed people. I warned you that things were going to get a lot worse."

"Never mind getting off this plane," Zara said. "Stop the *world*, I want to get off."

"I know how you feel," said Milo. "Anyone else starting to feel a little sick?"

"What did Socrates say?" Mason asked.

"He described how the Greeks killed men during the observance of religious rites. Not only that, but during an excavation in the Saarburg mithraeum in 1895, a skeleton was found with its arms chained behind its back in a face-down position. This is how victims of Mithraic human sacrifice are usually found."

"Mithraeum?" Zara asked.

"A Mithraic temple," Virgil said casually.

"Thanks for telling me this, guys," Zara said. "I feel I can sleep much more peacefully tonight."

"Sorry, but this is nothing new. It's well-documented that such things have gone on right back into antiquity. Wade was part of that, but he started to show signs of insanity and egomania and the Hidden Hand rejected him from their fold. That's when he created his own death cult and started sacrificing humans in Mexico. It's not evidence that his masters in OM are still practicing sacrifice, but it's a possibility."

"And you say some of the most powerful people in our world are in the Hidden Hand?" Milo said.

Ezra nodded. "Sorry, but yes. Some of the most high profile people are inside their ranks."

"I refuse to believe this," Ella said.

Ezra gave her a look of understanding. "I'm sorry but it's true, and there's more you need to know."

The silence said everything.

"Go ahead," Mason said finally.

Ezra sighed. "We think they're on the cusp of being able to process specific algorithms to form one cybernetic hive mind," he said grimly. The gravity of what he had just said was lost on no one, and now a grim, heavy silence filled the air.

"You're joking, right? Mason said.

"No joke."

"A hive mind?" Caleb said, dumbfounded. "I can't believe it. I knew DARPA was working on stuff like that but last time I checked in it was pretty basic. You're trying to tell me that this Hidden Hand society has already perfected the technology?"

"I wouldn't say perfected it, no," Ezra said. "But according to the small amount of information we've been able to get hold of, it looks like they're ahead of the US in the field on this one."

"How can that be?" Ella asked.

"I can put two and two together," Caleb said. "And ethics is the four, right?"

Ezra nodded. "That's about the size of it. Any US Government agency like DARPA has to work inside very specific ethical guidelines when it comes to testing technology like this out on people. I'm guessing the sort of people running Occulta Manu have no such problems, as such, they've gotten ahead of us."

"But what does this even mean?" Zara said. "A hive mind?"

"It means anyone inside the hive mind will be able to share thoughts, to a certain degree," Ezra said. "The science is in its infancy right now, and as I say, we have no idea what level OM has taken it to, but we can surmise that anyone inside the cybernetic hive mind will be able to communicate with anyone else inside that framework to a certain degree. It means they can communicate at the speed of thought. They blend ancient magic cult with high-tech hive mind – the ultimate enemy."

"Well, shit in a paper bag and set it on fire," Milo said.

"This is just great," Caleb drawled. "Ancient human-sacrifice cults, insane billionaires, hive mind Matrix warriors and plots to take over the world; I liked life when it was simple – just the Raiders getting people their loved ones and precious things back."

"If you're going to work with me, then get used to it."

Mason was not satisfied. "If we're going to work with you, then the first thing I want to know is precisely why Eva Starling was kidnapped."

Mat Wills poked his head around the door. "She's fine, but pretty badly shaken up. I can do some more blood tests on her when we're back on the plane."

"Plane?" Zara said. "Going somewhere?"

Ezra looked at his watch and frowned. "We leave for London in less than an hour so we have to get to the airport."

"London?" Ella asked. "Why London?"

"The rest of the reason you were hired," Ezra said. "And the whole reason they kidnapped Dr Starling. The Hidden Hand wants something that's in London, and we're going to get it first – with your help."

# CHAPTER SIXTEEN

With the Titanfort Citation racing into the sky and leaving Frankfurt far behind, Mason peered out of the window. Seconds later the world below was nothing but a sea of black, and he pulled down the shade, took a deep breath and sighed. When all this was over he was going to take long break beside a very quiet lake.

Or maybe climb Kangchenjunga. He'd always wanted to do that.

He leaned back in the leather chair and allowed his thoughts to drift. The enigmatic Eva Starling had ridden with Ezra Haven in a separate vehicle on the way back to the airport, and now she was with Ezra and Wills at the rear of the plane undergoing further tests.

Zara sat beside him. "Has anyone spoken with the Sainted Doctor Starling yet?" she asked, peering toward the back of the jet. Ezra and Evangeline Starling were now deep in conversation.

"Not yet," Mason said.

Ella took a look and said, "She's apologizing to him."

"How do you know that?" Caleb said.

"Body language, the way she's moving."

Mason was just beginning to wonder if he would ever get to talk to her when Ezra and Eva finally walked over and joined them in the main part of the aircraft's cabin.

"Maybe it's time you gave us the rest of the picture," he said firmly. "We're all here on your plane, after all."

Ezra ignored him with a polite smile. "All right everyone – listen up. Mat Wills has declared Dr Starling here fit and ready to brief you on the rest of the mission."

Eva was moving cautiously, but she looked better now, and calmer. Earlier, the medic had given her a mild sedative, and now she sat down among them all and gave a weak smile. "I never thanked you for getting me out of there."

"Think nothing of it," Mason said.

"Sorry if I'm out of it, but Dr Wills says it looks like they pumped me with oxytocin."

"Oxy-what-now?" Zara said.

"Oxytocin," Wills said. "It's being used more and more as a kind of truth serum. I suspect they gave Eva a dose to check if she was making a truthful translation."

Ella looked concerned. "Jesus, are you all right?"

"I think so…"

Then Ezra spoke. "Mat says she'll be fine, so now to business. You know about the Spiders and you know about the darkness that is Occulta Manu, but what you don't know is why Eva was kidnapped."

"About bloody time," Mason said.

Caleb passed a weary hand over his eyes. "You said something about this secret order wanting something translated?"

"We'll get to that, but let's start at the beginning. A few days ago the director of the Vatican Secret Archives was murdered."

"Wait," Milo said. "I read about that."

Zara turned toward him and opened her mouth theatrically. "You can *read?*"

"Sod off, Wonder Woman."

"You think I'm like Wonder Woman?" she said, smiling with pride.

"Sure I do, because everyone wonders why you're such an arsehole."

"You wound me, Milo," Zara said. "You wound me with this talk. Get me another coffee, would you?"

"Why me?"

Zara shrugged. "Shit rolls downhill, I guess."

"Nice attitude," he said. "You should be more respectful to your elders and betters."

"Yeah, about that, Milo. 1993 called, and they want their waistcoat back."

Milo exploded into a peel of fake laughter. "Oh, my sides; please stop before they split wide open."

"And you're about a year older than me, Milo, so shut up."

Ezra cleared his throat and recaptured their attention. "As I was saying, Signor Scala was murdered."

Virgil frowned. "But the newspapers said he died in his sleep."

"Sure they did, but that's not what happened. That was a cover-up ordered by the Pope. The reality is that Monsignor Bruno Scala was brutally murdered on the rooftops of the Vatican. It looked like he had been stabbed or sliced to death. The Italian Secret Service report concludes that his injuries are consistent with those caused by shuriken stars."

"Holy shit floating in a punch bowl," Milo added.

Ezra frowned. "Monsignor Scala's death is directly connected with the kidnapping of Dr Starling here the next day. I'm going to stand aside now and let Eva fill in the rest."

*About fucking time...* Mason considered.

Evangeline Starling stepped up and looked at each of the Raiders before starting to speak. "As we all know, Kyle Cage kidnapped me from the heart of Harvard University and before I knew it I was in the back of a van with a bag over my head. I hope I never see that man ever again."

Eva said this with a visible shudder. "Kyle Cage is one angry individual. I saw him up close and personal and there's nothing in his eyes except a cold, calculated cunning. Evil, I guess. They told me I was safe and would stay that way so long as I cooperated. Then they drugged me. I woke up in Frankfurt to see Linus Finn and some strange individuals dressed in black standing in front of me."

"They would be the Hidden Hand," Ezra said.

"Quite," continued Eva. "Anyway, Finn was holding an ancient artefact and demanded that I translate it for the weirdos."

"What sort of artefact?" Caleb asked. "The one we found, right?"

"Right – it's the object taken from Scala after his murder," Ezra said. "The Vatican has been guarding it for centuries."

"What was it?" Mason asked. "I'd never seen anything like it before."

"It was this," Ezra said, and pulled it from his pocket.

"Woah!" Zara said. "Who needs the lottery?"

Eva's eyes came to life when she saw it again. "It's an ancient Egyptian ankh, a very rare relic from the Thirtieth Dynasty, specifically during the reign of Nectanebo II."

"I failed history," Zara said, crossing her arms over her chest and blowing a bubble with her gum. "Humor me."

"Nectanebo II was the last pharaoh of the Thirtieth Dynasty, which was around three hundred and fifty B.C., so nearly two and half thousand years ago. I'd never seen anything quite like it before. As a piece of religious iconography it's not special, but what makes it so significant is two things – first its condition. It's damn near perfect, like it's been made yesterday, and the second thing is the symbols."

Mason leaned forward in his seat. Despite his earlier resistance to the mission, he was now totally absorbed by what the American archaeologist was saying. "Symbols?"

Eva nodded. "Yes, along both the front and back of the flat part of the ankh are a series of symbols – look."

Ezra handed it around. The jewels sparkled in the low light.

"They're very strange hieroglyphics that are unlike anything I've seen before. It soon became clear that the weirdos in black had hired Linus Finn and his thugs to kidnap me and force me to translate these symbols."

The jet shook slightly as it plowed through a stretch of turbulence. For a moment the only sound was the gentle hum of its two powerful engines roaring away outside the cabin.

"And could you translate them?" Milo said.

"Yes, she could," Ella said.

"How do you know that?" Eva said.

"She's a mentalist," Zara said. "She can read micro-expressions as easily as you can read a newspaper."

She gave Ella a wary glance. "Well, I could translate them, yes."

Mason saw she had started to pale. "What do they say?"

"They say that the Book of Thoth is real."

"The Book of Thoth?" Ella asked. "What's that?"

Eva raised an eyebrow. "You mean you can't tell by reading my micro-expressions?"

"It doesn't work like that," Ella said sharply.

"*Shame,*" Eva said smugly. "Anyway, up until today I believed the Book of Thoth referred to a series of ancient Egyptian texts all written by Thoth, the Egyptian god of knowledge and writing. Right from way back in the Ptolemaic period, there have always been rumors of a single magical text called the Book of Thoth which is supposed to exist and contain two specific spells. The first is supposed to let the reader of the spell communicate with animals."

Zara turned in her seat. "Shit, Milo – we could use that to understand you."

"Oh Lord," Milo said. "The Raiders' gain was stand-up comedy's loss."

"You said there were two spells in the book," Mason said. "What was the second?"

"The second spell is supposed to contain magic that will allow whoever reads it to see the gods. It may be that the Book of Thoth is a kind of ultimate Book of the Dead, or Book of Spells, but whatever you call it, it's supposed to contain magical texts and pictures."

"To help see the gods?" Virgil asked.

Eva gave a non-committal shrug and Ezra slipped the ankh back into his jacket pocket.

"Do you know who carved the symbols?" Mason asked.

Eva nodded. "I think so. His name was Parennefer. He was a priest, vizier and prophet in the first century, most probably named after the famous High Priest of the 18th Dynasty who advised Akhenaten."

The short silence was ended by Zara Dietrich. "What a load of bull crap."

"Maybe," Ezra said, "but maybe not. As I said, we have always understood the magical Book of Thoth to be nothing more than a fictional idea, but since the discovery of the ankh we now think it's worth pursuing. Remember, the Vatican has been sitting on this for centuries, but now the secret's out, and worse than that Linus Finn and his puppet masters in the Hidden Hand are onto it. If they want it, I want it."

Mason closed his eyes and ran through everything he had just heard. Ancient spells and Egyptian magic and secret orders… it was a far cry from his normal meat-and-potatoes work of asset recovery. Kidnapped people, stolen jewellery yes; mystical texts that allowed you to see gods, a big no.

"I refuse to believe in magical spells," he said at last.

"And you're probably right to," Eva said.

"So why is the Hidden Hand after it?" Milo said.

"Just about everything in our Western society is based on ancient Rome and before that, ancient Greece. Much of these cultures was shaped by ancient Egypt so if there really is a Book of Thoth, or Book of Spells, it might contain information that could change everything we know about our history."

"And that's why OM want to get their hands on it," Ezra said flatly. "They want to control the flow of history and shape everything to suit their agenda."

"And where do we find this ancient book?" Mason said.

"The Book of Spells itself should be in Egypt somewhere, but Egypt's a big place. Beyond that, this is where the ankh became cryptic," Eva said. "It made a reference to Nectanebo II and how he would take the secret into the heavens via a mystical codex. My speculation is that Parennefer detailed the location of the Book of Thoth in some kind of codex, and that this codex is hidden inside the old king's sarcophagus. I think the ankh is some kind of key to access it."

"And that's why we're going to London?" Caleb said.

Eva nodded. "Indeed – the sarcophagus is in the British Museum. It was taken there in 1802 as a condition of the Treaty of Alexandria. Napoleon had already taken the sarcophagus during his famous expedition to Egypt, but it was handed over to the British after the capitulation of Alexandria when they besieged the French troops there. After that it went to London and it's been there ever since."

After a long pause, Ezra said, "So are you in on it or not?"

"I don't know," Mason said, his words heavy with a genuine uncertainty.

"Things have been getting kind of stale recently," Ella said.

"That's true," said Milo. "And we're not just talking about Zara's t-shirts either. Work has also been getting kind of boring."

Zara shook her head and smirked. "Oh, Milo – one day I'm going to use your ass as a free-standing punch bag until my goddam foot falls off."

"Please, Zara," Caleb said. "There's no need to tell them about what foreplay you two engage in. This is private and between you and Milo."

"Oh, funny man makes funny," Zara said. "You want your butt kicked too?"

Mason looked at Ezra and Eva Starling and how they were watching the Raiders as they sparred. "I bet you're regretting asking us to do this right about now, right?"

"Not at all,' Ezra said. "I've seen you scale the Istanbul Sapphire and now break into a safehouse in Frankfurt. I know you can handle this."

Mason couldn't resist smiling. "Fine, count me in."

## CHAPTER SEVENTEEN

As the aircraft raced toward England, Mason allocated jobs and checked everyone was up to speed with the plan: Caleb looked into the Spiders and their back stories; Virgil tried to look into the Hidden Hand; Ella and Milo helped Eva look into the sarcophagus in more detail while Mason made the painful decision to start looking into Kat's past a little more closely. Zara spent her time checking the weapons inventory and chatting to the Titanfort pilots.

The fruits of their collective labor weren't promising. Caleb found nothing more on the Spiders than they had already learned at Ezra's initial briefing. They were a dangerous group of highly trained individuals, mostly former military and all criminals and thieves of one kind or another.

Virgil drew a total blank on the Hidden Hand, just as everyone had suspected he might. After a good deal of time trawling through every internet forum and conspiracy site he could find he was left with almost no more than when he started.

Occulta Manu was nothing more than a rumor, and not a very convincing one at that. Just about no one had ever heard of them and those who recognized the name remained convinced the organization was nothing more than a myth fabricated by trolls in the darker corners of the internet. If Ezra was right and the Hidden Hand was real, then the Raiders were going to be chasing phantoms.

Ella, Milo and Eva made much better progress. The sarcophagus was still in the British Museum, where it had been since the day the British seized it from Napoleon and his army. They quickly found its location inside the museum and even managed to speak with the museum's director, a woman called Dr Iris Hamilton.

After a short conference call between Ezra Haven, the US Embassy and the British Home Office, Dr Hamilton agreed to meet them at the museum. She would show them inside so they could see the sarcophagus even though the entire building would be shut by the time they landed in London. They were all relieved to hear that there were no problems at the museum and no one had attempted to break in or access the sarcophagus even though OM now had the information they wanted.

As for Mason, he was almost too frightened to dig into Kat's past for fear of what he might find hiding there. Katherine Addington was born on her aristocratic father's vast estate in Norfolk less than five years after Mason was born in London. She excelled at school and went to the London School of Economics before joining the Metropolitan Police Force. From there she transferred into the Counter Terrorism Command. Recruiting her into the Raiders had been a coup, and shortly after they became a couple.

He knew all this. They had been together for several years. They had shared good times and bad; traveled the world together and even discussed getting married, although she had always killed the idea of having kids with him stone dead whenever the subject arose.

Why would she just turn on him like this? Even after what had happened in Istanbul he still found it impossible to believe that she would betray him without a reason. Maybe someone was blackmailing her? Maybe she was in trouble. He didn't know anymore – seeing her flying away from the Sapphire made his stomach turn over and he forced himself not to think about it.

\*

They landed at London City Airport and Ella watched silently as their aircraft parked up beside a brand-new Gulfstream with ECHO written along the side of it in large black letters. The pilots opened the door and they stepped out onto the tarmac as the engines were shutting down.

"ECHO," she said, casually pointing up at the Gulfstream. "You think they're trying to get in on this mission, too?"

Mason shrugged. "Doubt it. This stuff is pretty hush-hush."

Ella Makepeace recalled a story she read in the newspaper about the Texan billionaire Ezra had mentioned – Morton Wade, and how the notorious ECHO team had ended his insane human sacrifice cult in the Mexican jungle a year or so earlier. She thought of Ezra Haven and his warning about the Hidden Hand's rumored penchant for the same terrifying rituals, and for a passing moment, she wondered if the Raiders might collide with Joe Hawke and the rest of his team while on the mission.

"We could use their help on this though," she said. "Joe Hawke, Lea Donovan, Cairo Sloane..."

"Cairo Sloane?" Zara scoffed. "I could kick her ass up one side of her bad attitude and right down the other."

"Josiah Hawke," Caleb said with respect. "I heard a lot about that guy."

"Josiah and Jedediah?" Zara said. "It's starting to sound like the Old Testament around here."

Mason gave a weary sigh. "How many more times? My mother was from New York and I was named after Jedediah Smith – the American frontiersman and hunter."

"I'm just yanking your chain, Holmes," Zara said with a friendly smile.

"And this is *our* mission, not ECHO's or anyone else's," Mason said. "So let's get on with it."

Emerging from the arrivals lounge they climbed into an SUV and hit the road. They crossed the river and exploited the late hour to make good time getting across the city. Exiting the SUV they jogged up the stone steps to the British Museum.

Everyone recognized the building's famous Greek Revival façade as they made their way up the steps beneath the temple-style portico that housed the entrance. The weathered Portland stone had faced the elements for nearly two hundred years, and high above it all the Union flag flapped in the Bloomsbury breeze.

They saw a small group of people at the top of the steps – a woman in a smart, charcoal-colored suit stood beside a smartly-dressed man, two security guards and two policemen were armed with Heckler & Koch submachine guns. Taking note of the weapons, Mason focussed on the mission at hand and aimed for the woman in the suit.

Dr Iris Hamilton met them at the entrance with the two armed police officers. Ezra approached the man in the suit and they spoke for a few seconds. It turned out his name was Dunford and he was an old friend of Ezra's from the US

Embassy. Telephone calls had been made, and people were getting nervous.

"This your team?" Dunford asked Ezra.

The man in the black suit nodded once. "Best asset recovery team in the world."

Dunford turned to Eva. "You have the ankh, Dr Starling?"

"We do, and I've translated it."

Dunford looked anxious. "All right. Let's get on with it. This stuff creeps me out."

Iris Hamilton cleared her throat and craned her neck toward Mason. "We don't usually open the museum after hours."

"But needs must when the devil drives, right?" he said with a smile.

Zara scanned the street for any sign of trouble, but there was nothing. "Looks like the Spiders had enough and went home," she said.

"Don't count on it," said Caleb.

Mason checked his watch. "Milo, you're going to the museum's CCTV station. You're my eyes in the sky and I want to know if anyone comes anywhere near us, all right?"

"Got it, boss."

Dr Hamilton looked confused. "The Spiders?"

"Don't mind us," Ella said. "Shall we go inside?"

# CHAPTER EIGHTEEN

Eva Starling stared at the heavy sarcophagus and realized as Ezra handed her the ankh that her hands were trembling. The draining holes in the base of the thing were clear enough. They had been drilled countless centuries after its original use so someone could use it as an ablutions tank, but the one at the head of the sarcophagus was a slightly different shape to the others.

"It's different – can you see?"

Mason leaned in. "Not really."

"What are all these markings?" Ella asked.

"They're hieroglyphics describing part of what we call the Amduat. It's a funerary text and means the Book of What is in the Underworld."

Zara whistled. "Catchy."

"In this case here, the glyphs referring to the Underworld are directly above the odd-looking drainage hole. It's a play on words because it's describing the underworld and the key-hole is directly beneath the glyph referring to under."

"Who says the ancients didn't have a sense of humor?" Caleb said.

"I guess this is it, then," Mason said.

"You really think Parennefer's codex is inside this thing?" Ella asked.

"The ankh was very clear about it," Eva said. "It said the codex was sent into Sekhet-Aaru with Nectanebo. Those are the reed fields, or their conceptualization of heaven. There was only one way to send the codex to heaven with the king, and that was by putting it inside this sarcophagus."

"So, yes, in other words," Zara said.

Ella sighed. "That's what she said."

Zara raised her palms. "Hey, no harm no foul. She's an academic, right? That means she has to use fifty words when one will do."

Eva didn't respond. Her mind was focused on the jewel-encrusted ankh in her hand and how heavy it had started to feel. Not just gold anymore, but the weight of the world.

She knelt down on the hard tiled floor and pushed the ankh inside the hole directly beneath the Underworld glyph. The other holes were perfectly round, but this one had a vague octagonal shape that matched the styling of the ankh. She felt a clunk and then realized the key had slotted into whatever ancient lock mechanism was inside the base of the sarcophagus.

"It's in," she said.

"Those dudes from the Young Guns can't be far behind us," Zara quietly pointed out. "So, maybe time to crank this up a notch?"

Mason's eyes flicked from Zara's calm, confident face to the trembling hands of Dr Eva Starling. "She's right, Eva. We need to move this along."

Eva's reply was to turn the ankh in the hole. She felt an immediate clicking sensation travel up the golden key, and then they all heard a loud *clunk*.

"What?" Zara whined. "No fireworks?"

"Not yet," Ezra said.

"Now what?" Virgil asked.

Eva looked crestfallen. "I'm not sure."

"Let's have a look," Mason said, crouching down beside Eva. He moved his hand to the key, brushing the back of her hand. "May I?"

"Be my guest."

Mason took a firm grip of the ankh and pulled it as hard as he could. The key came out of the hole easily, but pulled behind it a long copper tube around an inch in diameter and twelve inches long.

"Woah!" Zara said. "Now we're cooking with dynamite, baby."

"What is that thing?" Ella asked, taking a step closer.

Mason handed it over to Eva. "All yours. Something tells me you're going to have a better idea about what to do next than me."

Eva took the copper tube in her hands and blinked as the emergency fire exit lights flashed on its smooth curved surface. She tapped it with her fingernail and a metallic ping echoed in the room. "The codex must be inside."

She turned the ankh in the hole and it pulled out to reveal an open aperture. "There's something in here," she said, her voice growing in excitement.

"So don't keep us all in suspenders," Zara said. "Get it out."

Eva pulled out a single piece of yellowed rolled-up paper, and then they heard the sound of Milo's voice in their earpieces. "We got company."

Zara sighed. "Spiders or weirdos in trench coats?"

"Oh, it's the Lost Boys, all right," Milo said. "Sorry."

Mason pulled his Glock 17 from a shoulder holster and pulled a round into the chamber. "Everyone here is going to do as I say, and that way no one gets hurt."

"Oh *my*..." Dr Hamilton nearly passed out, and the two security guards took a step back.

"You can't have that in here!" said one of the guards.

The other spoke up, and extended his hand. "Come on, hand it over."

They all heard the sound of gunfire.

"What's going on, Milo?" Mason asked.

"The two policemen at the entrance are down, Jed. I repeat, they're both down, and so is Dunford."

"Ken's dead?" Ezra said. "I don't believe it."

The two security guards rushed back toward the main entrance.

"What do they want?" Hamilton asked.

Eva held the rolled paper to her chest. "This," she said coldly. "And they'll kill anyone to get it."

Hamilton fumbled for her phone, but dropped it to the floor with her trembling hands. "We have to call the police!" she said meekly as she picked it back up again.

"No time for that," Caleb said gruffly. "These guys will be in and out of here long before even the fastest response unit can arrive."

"Caleb's right," Ella said. "We have to deal with them ourselves."

Mason nodded. "Milo, you still got these guys on the monitors?"

"Sort of."

"What the hell does *sort of* mean?" Zara said.

"They're shooting the CCTV cameras as they make their way toward you."

"Toward *us*?" Dr Hamilton fainted and crashed to the floor.

Caleb sighed and picked her up with a fireman's lift. When she was safely over his shoulder they started to make their way to the exit. "Time to live free or die."

"Okay, Milo," Mason said. "We need you to direct us toward you and then we're all out of here. We need to get out of here and it's better for everyone if we can do that without a fight."

Zara looked at him in the dim glow of the museum's emergency night lighting. "You know, as you get older, Jed…"

"I get more rugged?"

"No, your testosterone levels are dropping, old man," she said with a shake of her head. "Better without fighting, indeed!"

"I hate to break things up," said Milo. "But the Lost Boys are nearly on top of you. You guys need to take the exit to your left and start moving or you're in a war zone."

"Let's get out of here," Mason said.

## CHAPTER NINETEEN

Moving toward the security office things got real in a hurry. The two security guards who had headed back to the entrance now lay dead on the floor in the corridor; blood and brain matter splattered over the polished white tiles.

Ella raised her hand to her mouth to stop herself being sick and turned away; Mason knew at once that they were in grave danger and had to act fast. The murders had been professional and quick. He was certain the killers had mufflers on their guns so they didn't attract the attention of any of the other guards in the museum. What made it particularly vile was that these guards were all unarmed.

The clock was ticking. Mason knew time was running out. The wounds on the dead guards were fresh, and it was clear they had been killed within the last few seconds. "Where are they, Milo?"

"In the room you guys were just in. They're looking at the sarcophagus right now and they don't look very happy to be honest."

"Neither do the two dead guards in the corridor," Ella said.

"I saw them die on the monitor," Milo said. "These guys are quick, everyone. They moved like they were on fast-forward or something."

Milo kept one eye on the Hidden Hand as he guided his friends away from the enemy and toward the security office. Safely inside, they gathered around the CCTV monitors and watched the Bride and her Ravens sweeping through the empty museum in pursuit of them. "They're hunting the codex," Mason said. "Look at how they move and communicate with one another."

"You weren't screwing around when you told us about these guys, Ezra," Zara said.

Caleb let out a deep, knowing sigh. "He never screws around, believe me."

"True story," Ezra said.

Mason watched the CCTV covering the Egyptian department closely for a few seconds and then he saw the Bride up close for the first time. She was standing in front of the sarcophagus. Flanked on either side by two powerful looking men dressed in black, her beauty was almost bewitching.

But she was the enemy.

"Is that her?" Zara asked.

Ezra nodded. "That's her."

"What about the guys in leather trench coats?"

"They're her Ravens. Utterly loyal to their Bride. It's an order of loyalty right out of the ancient world and not something most modern minds could understand. They will happily sacrifice themselves if it means she survives. She would do the same for her Lion and so on up the line."

"Like some kind of crazy suicide cult?" Milo said.

"No," Ezra said firmly. "Nothing like that at all; as I said, their loyalty to the Hidden Hand is a kind of commitment that just doesn't exist in today's world. It's not suicide. They are warriors in a global order that goes back further than any other we know. To betray that order is worse than suicide."

Eva leaned into the screen. "Now they're working out that the codex isn't where it's supposed to be."

They watched the shadowy figures discuss the situation. The woman in particular looked highly agitated. After a few seconds they turned and made their way out of the Egyptian Department.

Ella felt a shiver go up her spine. "Now they're hunting *us*. They know we have the codex."

"We have to get out of here," Milo said nervously. "We've been up against some rotten scumbags in our time but these guys are from another dimension."

"Agreed," Mason said. "Dr Hamilton – what's the fastest way out of the museum from our present location?"

Still drowsy from passing out, she took a few seconds to think. "At the end of the corridor outside this room there's a lift which will take us back down to the ground floor. From there it's only a short walk to the Great Court. We'll come out on Great Russell Street."

"You stay here, Dr Hamilton," Mason said calmly. "They want us, not you. We'll draw them away." He looked at his team and felt a sudden burst of pride in them. "Let's get on with it, and keep that codex safe because right now we're ahead of them."

\*

Kiya felt the anger flood her body alongside a rush of adrenalin. She had gotten to the British Museum minutes too late and now the enemy had the codex in their hands. The Lion would not be happy but maybe if she could retrieve it fast enough he would never have to know about her error.

As she slipped through the shadows of the museum she swore she would not only hold the codex in her hand, but execute whoever had tried to take it from her.

"How do we find them?" Dariush said. His breathing was hard as they pounded through the darkened corridors.

"We go back to the main entrance," Kiya said. "They will call for back-up and that is where it will go. That's where our enemy will head next."

"There will be many armed officers," Tekin said. "We must ready ourselves to fight them."

"I am always ready to fight," Kiya said without emotion. "And you should be too."

She and the two Ravens entered the Great Hall and then she saw them. As Tekin had mentioned, there were several armed policemen holding Heckler & Koch submachine guns. With the terror threat so high in London their incredible reaction time was no surprise. They must have been here within minutes of their colleagues being shot.

Kiya stopped in her tracks and the two Ravens immediately halted either side of her. She heard someone cry out: "There they are!"

Fearing they had been seen by the anti-terror police, they darted back into the shadows only to see their enemy appear in the Great Court. They were walking in a group now and the American woman was holding a copper tube in her hand.

"There it is!" she whispered.

"What's our next move?" Tekin asked.

"Take out the law, then we kill our new enemy and we have the codex."

They stepped out from the shadows and opened fire without warning on the anti-terror police officers. Their M6 carbines spat fire and wrath across the Great Hall and mowed down four of the six police officers before they knew what had happened. The two survivors dived for the cover of an information board as they desperately radioed in the attack.

*

Mason and the other Raiders sprinted for one of the enormous circular help desks and skidded to a halt behind the relative safety of a large central island covered in tour guidebooks.

Zara checked her weapon was loaded and gave Mason an anxious look. "Holy shit, they're already on us, Jed!"

Milo was almost speechless. "Fucking hell, did you see what they did to those coppers?"

"It's not over yet," Mason said. "The ugly one's got an HK compact grenade launcher – check it out."

Milo peered over the desk and watched as Dariush opened fire on the two remaining police officers with the grenade launcher. He fired three of the grenades in rapid succession and they blasted the information board and both the counter-terror officers to pieces.

"Looks like we're next!" Ella said. "They're heading this way."

Unprepared for such a heavy gunfight, both sides had emptied their mags within minutes of the exchange and now the battle would get more personal. Kiya was first into the fray, leaping without fear over the help desk and grabbing hold of Virgil. With one devastating downward elbow strike he was out cold, but what unsettled Mason the most was how fast she had assessed Virgil as the weakest link. A heartbeat later she spun around and struck Milo in the head with the heel of her boot, knocking him out cold beside Virgil.

As Milo and Virgil slumped to the floor, the Bride pulled away and took stock of the new situation as it was unfolding around her. The two Ravens were now engaged in a furious battle with Zara. Mason thought that two on one didn't seem fair – to the Ravens – and now Zara was a whirlwind of kicks and punches as she worked some of her aggression out on the two men.

Mason moved forward and approached the Bride. She looked at him with a simmering hatred in her eyes; eyes that were almost mesmerizing in their beauty – a devastating beauty that would lure him to his death if he didn't back off and snap out of it. He moved in for the kill, but then she ordered Tekin to attack Caleb.

Tekin spun around to increase the momentum of his kick. He was a big man to start with, and now his boot smashed into Caleb's thigh and almost broke it. The Arizonan recoiled in pain, desperate not to show it to his enemy, and mustered every fiber of strength in his body to deliver a counter-strike. The Raven took the blow to his jaw with little sign of distress and then effortlessly swept Caleb's striking hand away before aiming a high-speed tiger punch at his throat.

Caleb saw it coming and ducked to the side, narrowly avoiding a crushed windpipe and an agonizingly slow death as he suffocated on the floor, but as he went down he struck his head on the side of the desk and passed out.

Now, Mason stepped up and fired a volley of hefty jabs at the Occulta Manu Raven. He threw punch after punch at the man but he blocked them all with ease before lunging forward and piling the back of his hand into Mason's face, knocking him on the back foot.

"Shit, Jed," Ella said. "Are you all right?"

Mason spat a wad of blood on the tiled floor. "Feeling just fine, Ellz, thanks for asking."

Ezra jumped in, landing a solid punch on the Raven's temple, but the OM man easily repelled him with a backwards sweep of his arm, bowling him over onto the floor.

"Even Zara's getting her arse kicked!" Ella cried out.

Mason glanced to his right to see Zara struggling with Kiya. The Bride had now pinned his old friend to the help desk by her throat and was smashing a series of punches just below her ribcage. The former cop and Buddhist *bhikkhuni* usually used hand-to-hand combat to work out and sharpen her skills, but not today. Right now she was working harder than ever just to stay alive.

"Ella!" Mason yelled. "Get Eva and the codex out of here, for fuck's sake!"

Ella nodded and grabbed hold of Eva Starling. "We're out of here."

"No," Kiya said, turning from a barely conscious Zara and facing her and Eva. "You are not."

Before either of them responded, Kiya attacked them both, easily knocking Ella to the floor with a windpipe-bruising side-slap. As the Englishwoman gasped for air like a landed fish, the Hidden Hand Bride moved behind Eva like lightning and quickly placed her in a choke hold. Deftly taking the codex from the American's pocket and slipping it in her own, she spoke in a language no one understood. Dariush and Tekin withdrew from the fight and joined her.

Mason watched her and the Ravens walk slowly backward away from the desk.

Kiya's eyes narrowed. "You follow us and I will kill her."

Mason heaved his breath back into his body and surveyed the carnage scattered all around him: Virgil, Milo, Zara and Caleb out cold, Ella half-dead and gasping for breath on the floor, and he could barely move. Ezra was only just crawling to his knees. To think all of this destruction was done by just three of these people didn't fill him with confidence about having to fight any more of them.

Zara came to, slid off the desk and winced in pain as she rubbed her throat. "Did I try and swallow a motorbike or what?"

"You got choked by Kiya."

"What happened?" Virgil said groggily.

"Otoshi empi uchi," Zara said.

"What the hell?"

"Downward elbow strike delivered to the middle of your face is what happened," Zara said, checking the young man's eyes. "Follow my finger."

Virgil did as he was told and Zara was satisfied he was okay. Her LAPD training had included first-aid, and she'd had plenty of opportunity to use it on the streets during her time on the force. "You're going to be fine," she said, getting to her feet. "Still ugly, but fine."

"Thanks, Zara."

But Zara had already turned to see the enemy. "Over there – they still have the codex and they're getting away!"

# THE RAIDERS

Kiya and the surviving Ravens gave no indication of what they were thinking as they dragged Eva toward the fire exit. Tekin was holding her now, and Kiya was in the lead.

"Freeze!" Zara yelled, and raised her freshly reloaded weapon.

Neither the Bride nor the Ravens paid any attention, and the only response was when Tekin spun around and fired his M6 at her while his free arm was still gripping Eva around her neck.

"Dammit," Zara said. "No clear shot with Eva in the way."

Ahead of him, the woman, the one Ezra had called Kiya, was clutching the codex in her hand as she booted open the emergency exit's panic bar and vanished in the night air. Seconds later Tekin and Dariush made the same escape, releasing Eva at the last second before fleeing into the night.

# CHAPTER TWENTY

Kiya looked back at the American archaeologist for a second and turned and fled. She had what she needed – the Nectanebo Codex. All she had to do now was deliver it to the Lion, and with luck she would never see these people again. But who were they? Their fighting and persistence was impressive. Perhaps the Hidden Hand would reach into their lives and find out everything about them.

"Venite!" she whispered urgently, and without warning she turned on a dime and walked with purpose toward the street, a gun held tightly in her right hand. Walking in the rain-soaked London night, the cool rain felt good on her face as she filled her lungs with the damp air and decided what to do next.

They fled through the London crowd, bobbing and weaving as she went but never drawing attention to her presence. With each step she took, she brought the future that Occulta Manu wanted for the world a little bit closer to reality.

With the codex in her pocket, Kiya looked over her shoulder and watched the chaos unfolding back at the museum. Turning into Oxford Street, she saw a police car screech toward her and pull up on the sidewalk.

She saw her two Ravens in their long black trench coats reaching for their lethal M6s and lifting them into the aim. The policemen fired first, but the Ravens ended the gunfight in seconds. They all heard the screams of innocent pedestrians now running for their lives on the sidewalk and then she saw a cab driver who was distracted by the sight of the gunfight; the taxi mounted the sidewalk and crashed into a bus stop.

Havoc exploded all over the street now. People whipped out their phones and called the police, others ran for cover wherever they could find it. One party of Chinese tourists on the top deck of an open-top bus leaned over the side and started filming it as if it were a movie.

# THE RAIDERS

*

Leaving Ezra and the others back at the museum to deal with the authorities, Mason, Zara and Caleb sprinted after the thieves, stumbling out into the night to find the corpses of the dead anti-terror policemen and Dunford sprawled on the steps of the British Museum. Somewhere in the distance they heard the sound of car alarms and panicked people screaming.

"Bastards must be over there," Mason muttered, and he knew he had only seconds before they would be gone forever. "This way."

They moved faster now, speeding up the pace until they were almost at a jog. As they reached the bottom of the steps they saw several more armed policemen outside the entrance. They crossed the road and ran toward the sounds of chaos. Turning a corner they found themselves on Oxford Street in the middle of a scene of terror – a cab had smashed through a bus stop and its crumpled, smoking wreckage had come to a stop inside a store's window display.

Passing a bus, he kept his gun raised as he cut over the road and hit the other sidewalk. Caleb and Zara were now crossing the road ahead of him, each keen to be the first into the fight.

"You see them?" he called out.

Zara shook her head as she scanned the mayhem. "No sign of the assholes yet."

"Dammit!"

"Over there!" Caleb said. "They're heading toward the underground station – and I see the codex!"

Mason saw it too, clutched tightly in the hand of the man the woman had called Dariush. "It's now or never, guys. Let's end this."

*

Walking faster now, Kiya turned her head and located the tall man with the black hair and blue eyes. He seemed to be their leader – or was it the thin man in the suit with the American accent they had left back at the museum? She had to know more about them.

"Keep them busy!" she yelled and then snapped pictures of the three of them on her phone as Tekin and Dariush unleashed a savage volley of automatic fire from the two weapons.

Tekin aimed at the front tire of another bus and blasted the rubber to shreds. The bus collapsed down like a wounded dog and swerved into the center of the busy road. The driver struggled with the steering wheel but it was too late and the enormous vehicle struck the front of a black cab, shunting it around in a circle and pushing it in the path of more on-coming traffic.

A bright yellow Ferrari F12 raced into the mayhem. Aimed straight at the carnage in the middle of the road it was going too fast to stop. The driver spun the wheel hard to avoid a collision with the black cab but crashed into a Suzuki motorbike who was pulling out wide to avoid the same fate.

The smash was fast and hard; the motorcyclist sailed over the top of the sports car and landed on his back with a sickening cracking sound. The Ferrari crashed into the front of a shop with the Suzuki wedged under its front grille.

Kiya was satisfied that Tekin and Dariush were performing properly. They were defending their Bride at all costs and doing everything they could to make the mission a success. She was optimistic the Lion would also be satisfied. Chaos from order was the Hidden Hand's precious gift to the world, and the high-ranking members of the order thrived on it. The mayhem was their sustenance. It gave them life to see others struggling to survive, and Kiya wanted to feel it more than anything; breathe in that sensation of total power that only the highest members knew.

She sprinted and jumped on to the roof of the Ferrari to get a better view of the assault. The confused and dazed driver pushed down his window and pulled himself half out to yell at her.

"What the fuck do you thi…"

She powered her knee-high boot into his face and knocked him out cold. She hadn't even looked at him, and as he slumped back down inside the luxury car she kept her dark eyes fixed on the battle raging across the street. The Ravens were forcing the enemy back toward a newly formed police cordon.

"Nunc, imus!" she said.

Tekin and Dariush heard the sharp, almost metallic voice and obeyed at once, turning in their coats and running back toward the Bride.

Kiya turned and leaped from the roof of the Ferrari. The tails of her black trench coat flicked up into the air as she landed with a gentle thud on the oil-soaked sidewalk.

Flanked by her Ravens, she slid her unused gun back inside her holster and marched swiftly through the crowd. She ordered the men to knock out the CCTV as they weaved in and out of the panic, and they followed the orders to the letter, each choosing a different side of the street.

In perfect synchronicity, they blasted out every CCTV camera in their vision, and then, unseen, they followed their Bride toward Tottenham Court Road underground station.

# CHAPTER TWENTY-ONE

Mason, Zara and Caleb charged into the station's entrance and scanned the crowd for any sign of Kiya and her Ravens. After the commotion back on Oxford Street, there was a heightened state of alert, and now a van of armed policemen raced past the station on its way to the chaos.

"There!" Zara said.

"I see them," said Caleb. "Assholes at twelve o'clock."

Mason looked ahead and saw the three OM acolytes slowly descending the escalator, like vampires returning to their lair after feeding on the blood of innocents.

Mason led the way through the slowly moving crowd, weaving through the commuters and tourists as he tried to draw closer to the enemy without alerting them of his presence. They were at the bottom of the escalator now, and turning a corner to get to the westbound platform.

"We have to get to them before they get on the train."

"Can't we just have the train stopped?" Caleb asked.

Zara shook her head. "I know cops, Cal. Even if they believed us it's going to take too long, plus it'll give them a heads up that we're onto them."

"Zara's right," Mason said. "Better we handle it ourselves, and don't forget Ezra asked us to keep a lid on things. Bringing a major terror alert to the London Underground is probably not what he had in mind when he said that." He turned to Caleb. "But he's your friend – am I right?"

Caleb nodded. "You're right."

They made their way down the escalator. When they reached the bottom they heard a train pulling up, and by the time they turned the corner onto the platform Kiya and the Ravens were nowhere in sight. The platform was full of people exiting the train and heading in their direction toward the exit.

"They're on the train," Mason said. "They have to be."

Mason led the team onto the rear carriage of the train and they started scanning for any sign of the thieves. "We'll work our way to the front, but we have to work fast. If they get off at the next stop we could lose them."

They made their way to the front of the train. They were building speed as they moved through the tunnel, and as Mason opened the door to the next carriage, he saw the woman and the men they had fought back at the British Museum.

And the codex.

Dariush was still gripping it in his hand. "Let's take them out," Caleb growled.

They charged toward them, knowing they had nowhere to run.

The three Hidden Hand cultists also knew they had nowhere to run, and it was time to make a stand.

Mason headed for Dariush, and Caleb took Tekin. Zara went for Kiya.

The former British soldier grappled the hulk of a man to the floor in the aisle between the rows of seats and started pummelling him with every boxing trick he knew. For a few seconds he thought it was going to be easy, but then everything Ezra had told him about the secret order was confirmed with grim accuracy and power when the man started to fight back.

As Dariush delivered a hefty smack with his boot right in the center of Mason's face, he scrambled away and got to his feet. By now, the passengers were screaming and clearing out of the way, giving them room to fight. Many of the travelers whipped out their smart phones and started filming the brawl, and one man even yelled at them to keep fighting.

Mason heard none of it, but focussed totally on the Raven and the codex he was still gripping in his massive, tattooed hands. The man's chest heaved up and down with adrenalin-charged hatred, and then he spoke, his lips barely visible through his thick goatee beard. "If you want it, come and get it!"

Mason stared at the man and realized that far from a mindless thug, a tortured, agonized soul was staring back at him. The man ended the tension by pulling a compact push dagger from his belt and pointing its blade at him. Mason reacted immediately, snatching a Styrofoam cup of steaming coffee from a commuter behind him and hurling it in his face.

The Raven's instinct was to raise his arm but even his lightning reaction wasn't fast enough to stop the scolding liquid spraying into his face. He screamed with pain and whipped his hands up to his face to wipe away the smoking-hot coffee.

The woman screamed but the man next to her took one look at Mason and the Raven and decided to keep a low profile. The other passengers did nothing except take another step back. Some were trying to send texts to the police while others continued filming the violence unfolding before them in the hope of racking up some hits on their YouTube channels.

Mason took advantage of the moment and lunged toward him. He smacked the push dagger out of his hand with a Krav Maga disarming strike and slammed a fist into his face. The Raven rolled with the punch and struck back with a destructive blitz of punches and forced Mason onto the defensive.

At the other end of the carriage Zara was fighting with the woman. The Bride was almost inhumanly fast and agile, but her incredible fighting prowess didn't faze Zara Dietrich for a second. She threw herself into the battle with her usual courage, desperate for another notch on her belt.

She ducked a savage Shaolin tornado kick that would have knocked her out if it had struck her in the head, and responded with a barrage of low kicks aimed at the Bride's knees. She made contact with the woman's shin, and she grunted as her bone absorbed the blow and took a quick, defensive step back.

She moved into the path of a young man in a Metallica t-shirt who had moved around behind her. Metallica grabbed her around her neck and squeezed but Zara knew at once it was a tactical error. The Bride took half a second to bring her elbow into his ribcage and forced him to release her. He doubled over in pain and without looking, Kiya flicked her arm up and brought the back of her right hand into his face, smacking him backward into the window.

The woman who was standing next to Metallica snatched a laptop off the seats and tried to bring it down on the Bride's head, but she easily sidestepped her and smashed the computer out of her hand with a high-powered butterfly kick.

Silently impressed, Zara moved in for another attack and this time gained the advantage, forcing her back toward the door. The fighting was tough and she knew it would go right down to the wire, but a part of her was enjoying the challenge. Turned out

Ezra Haven wasn't kidding when he said these people possessed unmatched skills, but none of it frightened her — how could it with a past like hers?

At the other end of the carriage, Mason was dimly aware of Tekin falling to the floor. He was clutching a smashed, bleeding nose that had been delivered by his old friend, Caleb, who was now piling into the brawl with Mason and Dariush. The heavy-set American body-builder wasn't in the mood for screwing around, but he knew he was no match for this guy's martial arts skillset so he had to go easy and do it his way.

Mason was ducking and diving like a true cruiserweight, but even with his red, scolded eyes the Raven was slowly grinding him down with a brutal bombardment of kicks and punches from dozens of martial arts. He moved so swiftly it was like watching a Bruce Lee film on fast-forward.

"Need a hand there, buddy?" he said.

Mason ducked another tiger punch. "Wouldn't say no, my old friend."

"Should have asked," Caleb said as he crashed into the Raven with his mightiest NFL shoulder barge and crushed him against the carriage door.

Mason looked shocked. "Nice job."

"Linebacker in college," Caleb said, almost apologetically.

Before he could respond, the darkness of the tunnel dispersed as the train pulled into Oxford Circus. Enraged and driven by revenge, Tekin delivered a savage head butt into Caleb's face and pushed him away as he scrambled for the doors.

Seeing Mason still grappling with Dariush, Kiya called out to him. "Throw me the codex!"

Dariush tried to obey, but Mason smacked the ancient document from his hand before he had a chance to throw it to the Bride. It hit the floor of the carriage and skidded away toward the central doors.

Kiya stared at the codex, and distracted for half a second, Zara hammered a speedy palm strike into the woman's chin, striking her head back and knocking her clean out of the train. She hit the platform hard and for a moment they all thought she was out cold, but then she scrambled to her feet. She called out to Tekin and they started to retreat into the crowd on the platform.

"Get after them!" Mason yelled.

The doors started to close but Caleb and Zara jumped clear with a second to spare and then started their pursuit of the enemy.

Mason turned to Dariush.

Both of them knew only one man would walk away with the codex.

# CHAPTER TWENTY-TWO

With Caleb and Zara giving pursuit, Kiya and Tekin were almost out of sight now, fleeing into the crowd of people on the platform. The doors closed and the train started to move away. Mason cursed as he watched them disappear, but he knew they had at least failed in their mission to snatch the codex from the museum. The offending article was still firmly in the grip of his opponent, and he was determined to get it back.

Mason grabbed the man by the throat and piled another hefty punch into his face. The man grunted as his head cracked against the carriage floor. He was getting tired and hoped the Raven would buckle soon. "Give me the fucking codex!"

Dariush responded by bringing his knee up and driving it into Mason's ribs, winding him and forcing him back. Mason hit the carriage floor with a smack but quickly scrambled back to his feet. The enormous Raven rushed forward and swung a meaty fist at his face. It missed by millimeters and made Mason jolt his head back to avoid the blow, but the Raven was too fast. Before the Londoner could regain his balance, his opponent had swung his left foot out in an impressive arc and hooked Mason's feet out from under him.

He went down again, this time striking the carriage door with a heavy smack. The pain seared through his back and neck, and nearly knocked him out, but he shook it off and got back to his feet once again.

By the time he had his balance back, Dariush had decided to retreat and was turning toward the doors. The train was fast approaching Bond Street and Mason guessed he was desperate to rendezvous with his associates.

As the man made a break for it, Mason scrambled toward him and gave chase in a last, desperate bid to get the codex back. Catching up with him a few meters down the carriage he leaped at his legs and brought him crashing to the floor with a powerful rugby tackle.

Still clutching the codex in his hand and desperate not to let go, Dariush howled in pain as his chest and face smashed down into the floor. Holding the codex out in front of him, he had cushioned the blow a little and stopped himself from breaking his ribs, but his chin and mouth were now crushed into a bloody pulp.

Spitting a broken tooth into the air, he kicked and squirmed to break free of Mason's grip, all the time trying to keep hold of the precious codex in his hands.

"You bastard!" Mason yelled.

"Release me!"

"You're wasting your breath, mate," Mason said. "Your arse belongs to the cops and that codex belongs to me!"

"Never!"

Mason saw the coldest, darkest fear flash through the other man's eyes. Then, in a heartbeat, Dariush slipped a tiny glass vial into his mouth and crushed it with his teeth.

Mason gasped and leaped back, already knowing what had happened and that there was nothing he could do. The man had taken cyanide, and not even blinked while he was doing it. The automatic and immediate way he had swallowed the poison had shocked Mason to his core. Now, he watched helplessly as the Raven gasped and choked and foamed at the mouth. His eyes bulged, red and painful, but then it was over, and he collapsed back on the carriage floor, dead. Clearly, this Raven feared a painful death less than reporting his failure to secure the codex back to his superiors in the Order.

As the train slid into Bond Street station, Mason gently lifted the dead man's arm and peeled his fingers away from the stolen Nectanebo Codex. He shook his hand in pity, and calmly closed the dead man's eyelids as a sign of respect. Whatever he had been in life, he was gone now, and Mason wasn't the kind of man to disrespect the dead.

He was shaken from his thoughts by the familiar sound of his old friend Zara Dietrich as she ran up beside him, a policeman at her side. Caleb was there too, and the shrug he gave told him that Kiya and Tekin had slipped the net.

"Please tell me he didn't get away with the codex?" Zara said.

Through the pain, Mason gave a cocky smile, shook his head and waved the dented, copper tube at her. "What do you take me for? It's right here."

"Where's the Raven?" Caleb asked.

Mason indicated inside the carriage and his friends saw the dead man sprawled on the floor beside the main exit.

An armed police officer ran to Dariush with his weapon aimed at his head. "Stay down!"

Mason rolled his eyes. "He's dead, for Christ's sake."

The policeman ignored him, and wedging the toe of his boot under the dead man's chest, he kicked him over onto his back. Aiming the muzzle at him at all times, he leaned forward and checked his wrist for a pulse. Finding none, he stepped back and clicked the safety catch on his Heckler & Koch and rubbed the sweat from his face. After surveying the trashed carriage and faces of the terrified passengers, he said, "And you clowns do this for living, am I right?"

Mason managed a sheepish grin. "Well…"

"You did a good job," a tall man said. He flashed a warrant card that identified him as Inspector Henderson, and then he turned to his sergeant and nudged his chin in the direction of Dariush. "Get an ambulance over here right away. We're going to need a post-mortem on this one as fast as we can."

\*

Kiya stepped silently from the shadows and watched Tekin drag the dead body out of sight. Her Raven had just murdered a man returning to his BMW on the top floor of a multi-story car park not far from Oxford Street. The man had done nothing more than be in the wrong place at the wrong time, and now he was dead.

They climbed into the Beamer and Tekin used the dead man's keys to fire up the powerful engine. Slamming into reverse, he was out of the parking space in no time. The wheels spun and smoked as he hit first gear and stamped on the throttle, speeding along the down ramps without wasting a second.

Were it not for Dariush, Kiya might have smiled. It was a mistake losing the ankh in Frankfurt because of a simple flesh wound, and letting the enemy get to the sarcophagus first was unforgivable, but now she had the advantage. Their next destination was not far, and then she would have her prize. Whoever had been trying to stop them was tougher than the police, but still no match for her. If they crossed her path again she would be forced to kill them.

She closed her eyes and leaned her head back on the seat. The gentle motion of the luxury car rocked her. It felt soothing. She imagined there would be a lockdown back at the sight of the battle, but that was of no consequence.

Dariush had done well to sacrifice himself in the way he had done. He had brought great honor on his rank and bought Tekin and her several much needed minutes; precious minutes that would allow them to slip out of the city and into the peace of the night. She would report his bravery to the Lion and he would be honored.

"Why Oxford?" Tekin asked as he steered the car west.

"It's obvious," Kiya replied, crossing her long legs. The diffused overhead lighting of the instrument panel shone on her leather trousers. "The only man who can lead us to the codex lives there."

The confusion on Tekin's face was almost endearing. "But those people we fought... they have the codex."

"Wrong. I had time to unroll the paper they found in the sarcophagus. It is not the codex, but it will lead us to it."

"Then we shall have it," Tekin said.

*Yes*, she considered, *we will have it.*

As the car cruised through White City, she studied the pictures of the team who fought her on Oxford Street and back on the Underground. She felt a surge of hatred for them all, especially the man leading them. He looked cocky, and she wanted to break him down in front of his friends and show them all who called the shots.

But first, she needed to know her enemy.

She sent the pictures to the Lion with a request to make an ID search on him. There could be few people in this world that had the ability to run from the Lion, and even fewer who could hide from him. She was confident that she would soon have all the information she needed on this crew of rogue fools.

## THE RAIDERS

Tekin started to speak but she hushed him with a dismissive wave of her hand. In the new silence she had created she closed her eyes and saw the sun once again as it crawled toward the horizon and the desert went black. The pipes played once more; their hoarse, reedy notes danced over the dunes as the woman was dragged toward the fire and they made her kneel. The man in robes was here again, moving through Kiya's imagination like a spectre. He raises his sword and pushes the tip into the bound woman's chest. She screams. Those observing the killing scream and whoop like crazed animals as the man runs the sword through her and catches her blood in the cedar wood bowl.

Her eyes flashed open.

She was in a car in London and her heart was beating hard in her chest, like a caged bird trying to fight its way out of her. She slowed her breathing. The Augur had told her she was safe, and she believed him. No one in Occulta Manu ever doubted the Augur and his prophecies.

Still flanked by her remaining loyal Raven Tekin, she squeezed her eyes shut tighter and considered her next move as they slipped out of London. The sound of the car driving on the asphalt and the chit-chat on the radio talking about the terror attack on Oxford Street was replaced by the gentle, reedy call of the ancient pipes. The sun rose over the desert and she almost gasped when its rays struck her eyes.

The ancient order would always win.

Sacrifice, honor, death, eternal life.

But first, she had to get to Oxford because that was where her enemy was going – even if they didn't know it yet.

# CHAPTER TWENTY-THREE

Deep in Paddington Green Police Station, Eva tipped the ancient copper tube up and the piece of old, yellowed paper slid into her hand. The building is the most high-security police station in the United Kingdom, infamously known as the interrogation center for the most dangerous terror suspects, but today it was hosting a very much older and more dangerous threat.

Checking the tube was empty she set it down on the side of Inspector Henderson's desk and carefully unfurled the paper. It felt fragile in her hands, but she was very familiar with ancient documents and how to handle them, which is why she had requested a pair of latex gloves from the police. They weren't optimal, like the nitrile gloves she usually wore, but they were better than nothing. God knows how much damage had been inflicted on it since the Hidden Hand stole it.

Mason spoke first. "Is it okay?"

Eva looked at him and sighed heavily. "Hope so. Looks like some idiot has slopped coffee on it."

Mason shook his head with disappointment. "Some people…"

Ezra stepped in. "What does it say?"

"Yes, what's this all about?" said Inspector Henderson.

"Is it the map?" said Milo.

Eva read the words on the old, yellowed, paper and shook her head in disbelief. "I *cannot* believe this."

"Come on, Eva," said Mason. "Put us out of our misery."

Eva handed it to him, a look of consternation on her face. "Take a look for yourself."

Mason took the paper and his eyes danced over the neatly written words. "What the hell is this?"

"Not the codex," said Ella with a frown. "That's for damn sure."

"Check out who wrote it," Eva said. "It's signed right at the bottom."

She watched Mason look down at the signature. A vague smile played on his lips and he slowly shook his head in disbelief. "Is this for real?"

"Is *what* for real?" Zara said. "Someone needs to tell me what's going on or I'm going to start practicing cat kicks on Milo's swamp nuts to pass the time, dammit."

Milo looked horrified. "Hey!"

"It's a note," Mason said. "Written by one Napoleon Boneparte."

Zara looked over at them both. "As in the French dude with the big hat?"

"Your grasp of history is astonishing," Virgil said. "But yes, the French dude with the big hat."

Caleb gave them a concerned look. "And what does it say?"

Eva shrugged her shoulders apologetically. "Search me," she said. "It's not written in any language I understand."

Zara sighed. "I thought you were supposed to be some kind of walking brain or something?"

"It's impossible to know *everything*," Eva said, looking the former LAPD cop up and down. "Or in your case, *anything*, I suppose."

Zara fronted up to her. "You wanna say that again, sister? I dealt with more shit before I was ten than you'll get in your whole life."

Eva looked aghast, but Ezra broke it up and smiled at them to diffuse the tension. "Eva, if you're unable to translate it, *please* tell me you know a person who can."

"As a matter of fact, yes. Napoleon was very interested in secret codes and cryptography," she said, almost talking to herself. "No one knows more about the subject than Ambrose Lloyd in Oxford."

"And you know this man?" Ella asked.

It was obvious she did, but she explained that the relationship was only professional. They had met at a few conferences over the years.

Mason looked at his watch. "Oxford – they have an airport there. If we can get back to London City we can be there in an hour or so. That way we can get to wherever's next without coming back into the city."

"Sounds like a plan," Caleb said.

Mason took the lead at once. "First, we need to call this Ambrose Lloyd bloke and warn him that his life's in danger. Although they only had Napoleon's note for a short time, we have no way of knowing what they got from it. It's perfectly feasible that they read it and if this Ambrose Lloyd really is the leading expert on him and his codes, it's only a short step from this note to his front door."

Caleb nodded as he flipped out his phone. "Jed's right. I'll get on it."

Eva spoke up. "Ask him to get out of his house and go somewhere neutral where we can meet him and show him the note. I know Ambrose and he'll probably suggest the Ashmolean."

"Does he work there?" Milo said. "That could be just as dangerous."

"Not any more," Eva replied. "He retired last year – early, too. Wife inherited a fortune."

"All right, Ashmolean it is," Mason said. "And Cal, make sure to tell him to check he's not being followed."

Taking the lead came as second nature to Mason, but he was starting to feel out of his depth. Having a crew like the Spiders to deal with wasn't a stretch for any of them – their line of work had pulled them into the orbit of men and women like Linus Finn and his team many times, but Occulta Manu was another kettle of fish altogether.

What Ezra Haven had said about them had chilled Mason and the other Raiders to the bone, and he'd felt the weight of their organization on his shoulders since the start of the mission. Every stranger he saw had the potential to be an agent of the Hidden Hand, watching them, stalking them.

After the army he had built a solid international reputation in asset recovery and everyone in the business knew who to call when something, or someone, needed extracting and rescuing. But that was dealing with thieves, smugglers and kidnappers, not a force as deep and dark as this. This was different.

This wasn't famous art works or the kidnapped sons of billionaires being held for ransom. This was something more sinister than any of that. He could just about get his head around SPIDER but the Hidden Hand crew was something altogether different – a bunch of freaks with some pretty shady ideas about world history and politics.

Caleb stepped over to Eva and cupped the phone in his hands. "He wants to talk to you. Says I sound *dodgy*, apparently."

Eva took the phone and talked with Ambrose Lloyd for a few seconds. She cut the call and handed the phone back to Caleb. "He's fine. Wherever Kiya and the Raven are, they're not in Oxford yet. He says everything's quiet there and no one's contacted him. He's going to cycle down the hill from his place in Headington and meet us at the Ashmolean. He took some convincing to leave the house. Says he just sat down for his dinner."

"Is he freaking kidding?" Zara said. "He's about to get hunted down by the world's most dangerous secret society and he's worried about his goddam roast beef getting cold?"

Eva shrugged. "That's Ambrose. And it was lamb."

"I think we're going off on another tack here," Mason said. "It's good that he's safe and leaving the house. There's no reason for Kiya to track him to the Ashmolean. He retired there last year and it's shut right now anyway, right?"

Eva nodded.

"Good. Then let's get to the plane. Milo, get onto the pilot and make sure he gets a flight plan scheduled to Oxford. It's a short flight but I don't want any delays – and I want a car for the eight of us ready when we land."

"On it, boss."

"Seven," Ezra said coolly. "Titanfort has recalled me back to New York so count me out."

"You're leaving us?" Zara said.

He nodded.

"And just when things were getting dangerous, too," Mason said.

"I'm sure a man of your abilities and experience can handle it," Ezra said firmly. "It's important that I go back, and I'll coordinate from there."

"How kind," Milo said.

"Take it or leave it."

"Let's get to the plane," Mason said. "We have to get to Oxford before OM or Lloyd's a dead man."

# CHAPTER TWENTY-FOUR

After a long delay at London City, the tower cleared their flight to Oxford and seconds later the Citation was screeching into the sky over the Isle of Dogs. Banking 290 degrees starboard, they were on their way. They were scheduled to spend just thirty minutes in the air before landing, and with Ezra on a flight back to New York, Mason suggested everyone take the time to decompress before talking to Lloyd.

Eva dropped down into one of the soft seats, rubbed her neck and sighed. "After we speak with Ambrose, will you still need me?"

"Odds are that we will," Mason said.

"Oh." Eva Starling paused a beat while she searched for the right words. "It's just that I'm not exactly the type who goes around getting shot at and abseiling down buildings. I'm worried I might slow you down or get in the way."

"Are you kidding?" Milo said. "We couldn't have done any of this without you."

Eva was clearly flattered by the compliment, but waved it away. "Being chased around the world by crazies like the Hidden Hand and kidnapped by thugs like Linus isn't exactly my thing. Trust me when I say that this whole experience isn't exactly going to be my most treasured memory."

Caleb handed her a bottle of water. "What is?"

She gave him a surprised look. "I'm sorry?"

"What was your best and worst memory?" he said with a cautious smile.

She hesitated. "I guess my best would be the day I got married, and the worst when my husband died."

"I'm sorry," Caleb said. "I had no idea."

"Why would you? I've only known you for a few hours."

Caleb gave her another warm smile and turned to Ella. "What about you, El?"

"Best memory is easy – the day I graduated from Cambridge."

"Not when you met Ben?" Zara said.

Ella considered but shook her head. "No, Cambridge. I love Ben with all my heart because he came along at just the right time… pretty much saved me from myself, but that was a confusing time. The best memory was graduation day."

As Ella recalled the moment, her smile widened. "Mum and Dad were both there, and my brother James. It was sunny, and after the ceremony we all went for drinks and a meal at The Eagle on Benet Street. I was the first person in my family to go to university, and they were all so proud of me."

"Sounds great," Caleb said. "I graduated from the University of Brawling, Arizona."

"What did you study?" Ella asked.

The others cracked up with laughter. "Think about it, El," Milo said.

"Ah," she said. "Sorry."

"Hey, don't knock Brawling," Zara said. "I studied ass-kicking at Barfight College, Nevada."

"Nice," Milo said, nodding his head with approval. "That explains so much about you."

"Zip it up, Louise," Zara said, flicking his ear.

"Hey – that hurt!"

"*That* hurt?" she said. "Jeez, I only flicked your ear, you big cry-baby."

"Sooner be a cry-baby than have a negative IQ."

"Fifteen-Love," Virgil said.

"Fifteen-Love my ass," Zara said. "Tell us yours."

Virgil bit his lip as he thought it through. "Best was when Amy was born, and worst was when I lost a half a million at the poker finals. Damn that thing."

"What about you?" Ella asked Caleb. "What's your best and worst memory?"

"Best was when my son was born, and second best was when my daughter was born. Worst was when I took a bullet in Afghanistan and got medically evacuated back to the States."

"Zara?"

"Best, when we rescued Charlotte Nowak from that crap-hole in Budapest."

A strange silence fell in the cabin. Charlotte Nowak was the daughter of a New York billionaire who had been snatched by kidnappers while on holiday in Italy. They had demanded fifty million dollars within forty-eight hours or they would kill the girl. She was only eleven. The Raiders not only got her back, but took out all of the kidnappers into the bargain. Then, Zara broke the silence. "You all know the worst."

Another silence fell, this time a darker, sadder thing.

"And what about your worst, Ella?" Caleb said, breaking the silence. "You never said what it was."

"If we're going to talk about work then my worst was when we screwed up the Monaco job."

"Ah," Caleb said. "The Monaco job."

"That wasn't our fault," said Milo.

"It was our job, our team, our planning," Mason said. "Our fault."

"But we were double-crossed," Milo protested. "We couldn't have seen that coming."

"And that's why it was our fault. It was our responsibility to see it coming," Mason said. "My fault."

Caleb changed the subject. "Milo?"

"My best memory was when I pranced naked through the wildflower meadows of Old England, hand in hand with a supermodel – I forget her name now."

"You have to be serious, Toadstool," Zara said.

"In that case, my best memory is when I hacked into NASA and played havoc with their security systems. I don't give a metric fuck about fame, but that made international news, you realize."

"We realize," Caleb said with a smile.

"Worst was the day I left home to escape Dad."

Another silence. They all knew that story, too.

"All right, Mr Mason," Caleb said. "Your turn."

"Jesus, I hate these stupid games. I have to plan the mission."

"You're not getting out of it that easy, hun," Zara said. "Best and worst, right now."

Mason sighed deeply and ruffled his hand through his hair. It was a delaying tactic but it only bought him a few more seconds. "I suppose the best memory I have is when my brother and I got to the top of Everest, if I'm pushed to talk about it."

"And worst?"

"That's easy," he said bluntly. "Yesterday, when my girlfriend betrayed me and left me for dead."

That was the end of the game.

*

The Spiders had received their pay checks for snatching the American archaeologist and their business with the Hidden Hand was done. This was good. What was not good was that their plans to sell Eva Starling to Albanian people smugglers had been ended abruptly when their Frankfurt safehouse was raided by unknown specialists. They had taken her from right under their noses and their quarter of a million had gone up in smoke right there and then.

So when the English woman walked into the abandoned farm they were hiding in and told them she knew who had taken the American, Linus Finn saw a chance to right a few wrongs and get his money back.

"Sounds like this Mason is your hero," Finn said. "No man can serve two masters: for either he will hate the one, and love the other; or else he will hold to the one, and despise the other," he said slowly. "Matthew 6:24. Ye cannot serve God and mammon, Miss Addington, or in your case you cannot serve Jedediah Mason and SPIDER."

Led by Bjorn Brick, a low chuckle rumbled around the group of men and women sitting close to Linus. The only one who didn't laugh, or smile, was Kyle Cage. He was too busy sharpening his hunting knife to care what anyone was talking about.

"I understand that," Kat said icily. "And he is not my hero."

"I see."

"And it's Lady Addington to you, Colonel Finn."

A neutral grin spread across Linus's lean, unshaven face. He liked Kat Addington already, and something told him they were going to get along like a house on fire. "Lady Addington?"

"At least until we get to know each other a little better, anyway."

"And will we?"

"Will we what?"

The grin grew broader, and greasier. "Get to know each other better?"

"Many men have tried to get close to me, Colonel, but most of them end up very disappointed."

"I see you're a confident woman," he noted. "I like that, and you're beautiful, too."

"I'm not here to ask you out on a date, Colonel."

"Hear that, Linus," Brick called over. "She says keep your dick in your pocket."

The others laughed, but Kat Addington never flinched.

"So why did you reach out to me? Why are you here, exactly?"

"I'm giving you an opportunity to get the American back so you can fulfil your contract with the traffickers," she said.

"Not worth our time," Linus said in a flat, cold tone. "I've lost interest in it."

The aristocrat licked her lips and he could see she was thinking something over in her mind.

Linus drummed his fingertips on the arm of his chair. "Come on, *Your Ladyship* – out with it."

"They have something in their possession."

"What?"

"Something of enormous value and importance. Something I thought was mine, but Mason double-crossed me and now he has it. If we take it back from them we will each retire as multi-millionaires."

Linus sat up in his chair and paid closer attention to the woman. Her astonishing beauty had been obvious as soon as she entered the room, but now he saw something else – the same kind of cold, calculating cunning he saw when he looked in the mirror. It was there, behind her cornflower blue eyes, sparkling like a wicked kind of black magic. "Don't stop."

"We were hired by a very public institution to retrieve a stolen asset. They always approach the Raiders first because of their reputation. In this case, the asset had been stolen in a robbery of military precision and they were in trouble. Big trouble. If the theft ever went public there would be hell to pay with insurers and a million other problems. Mason's brief was simple: retrieve the asset and return it to its rightful owner."

"Only you cooked up another sort of plan?" he said, a smile creeping over his thin lips.

Kat looked almost offended. "I decided it was time Mason and I went our separate ways, and I knew I would need money to fund the lifestyle I wanted to live."

"So you made the decision to rip off your friends and steal the asset?"

"It wasn't like that."

"Don't be so concerned, Lady Addington – I like what I'm hearing. You sound like my sort of woman." A murmur of approval rippled over the small group. "You see here in SPIDER we all like to think of ourselves as a little like pirates. It sounds corny, I realize, but we're really all out for ourselves. There's not a lot of your 'all for one and one for all' bullshit here."

"But we have each other's backs," Iveta said. "Don't confuse the two things. We are a team, a solid unit, but we all know when we're done we fly away into different sunsets and never see each other again."

"I understand," Kat said.

"A different arrangement from what you're used to, no doubt," Kyle said, finally looking up from his knife. He slid it in the sheath hanging from his belt and walked over to her. "There's no marshmallows over the fire in this crew. We're business. In and out. No respect for the law of any land."

Linus smiled. He was enjoying this recruitment more than when he hooked Molly Cruise. "But you knew that already, right?"

"I guess so."

"And if you're here to betray us to these Raiders," Bjorn growled. "I'll kill you with my own hands, but not before you've seen me kill everyone you ever loved."

"There is *that*, yes," Linus said. "If you're here to infiltrate us and try and compromise any of our missions, you will die, certainly."

Linus could see Kat was confused; she was clearly struggling with many emotions. Switching crews was not an easy thing to do. Everyone had their own working culture and rules, their own dreams and nightmares. "So maybe we have a deal?" he said at last. "We work together to track down Mason and his crew, we get this mysterious asset and split it evenly, and we get to kill the Raiders for screwing up our Albanian contract."

The English woman nodded. "We have a deal, Colonel Finn."

"Call me Linus, *please*."

# CHAPTER TWENTY-FIVE

Kiya's cell phone rang. With Tekin at the wheel of the stolen BMW, she looked down and saw the Lion had responded to her request to identify the man she had fought with at the British Museum – the man who had snatched the codex from Dariush and driven him to take his own life. She would never forgive him for humiliating her in front of the Lion like this, and she would kill him for what he did to her loyal Raven.

In the soft, blue glow of the instrument panel, she stared down at the new message on her phone and a scowl etched itself on her face.

So, his name was Jedediah Mason.

Now that was an old name, a biblical name.

According to the Lion, he was a soldier once, and now ran a highly respected asset extraction company based in London. The others around him were the rest of his team. Between them they had a lot of experience, mostly in the military. Their skills included martial arts, urban climbing, mentalism, computer hacking, forgery – you name it. Quite the crew, and for some reason they were now looking for the Nectanebo codex. *What would a man like Mason want with that?*

"He's working for someone else," she muttered.

Tekin turned to face her. "What?"

She paused before replying. The only sound was the noise of the tires as the car cruised along the M40 on its way to Oxford. Tekin accelerated the car as they pushed through the chalk cutting known as the Stokenchurch Gap.

She sighed, and tapped a long, black fingernail on the screen of the smart phone. "I said his name's Mason, and he's working for someone else."

"Whoever he's working for, he's dead," Tekin said casually. "What difference does it make?"

Kiya tutted. "You will not make Bride with that attitude, Tekin. When you want to kill a snake you cut off the head. I want to know who he is working for, and the Lion is asking questions too – difficult questions. He wants to know why these people are pursuing the codex. He wants to know why we have not yet obtained the codex. He says the Persian is growing impatient with our lack of progress."

"The Persian?" Tekin said nervously.

Kiya nodded. "We are being watched carefully by those at the top."

"They are always watching," Tekin said. "Probably right now, through these very CCTV cameras."

Kiya glanced up at one of the cameras on the side of the motorway. Rumors like this could spread like wildfire in the Hidden Hand, but no one really knew if there was any substance to them or not and testing it would be taking that wildfire and playing recklessly with it. The Hidden Hand rewarded honesty and diligent obedience with lavish gratitude, but its punishments for failure and betrayal were too terrible to be contemplated.

"If they're watching, then that's all the more reason not to fail, Tekin."

"And you're sure about this professor?"

She managed an absent-minded nod. "He's the definitive authority on Napoleon and he has a professional relationship with Starling. That's where they're going."

"And they haven't gotten to him yet?"

"Not yet. Their plane was delayed at London City. They'll be landing in half an hour."

"I hope you're right, for both our sakes."

"I'm right," she said. "I feel it in my heart."

"What you feel, I feel," he said. "What you think, I think."

She gave him a sharp look. "What's your point?"

"I sense you are feeling doubt about the mission."

"You know only what my head knows, Tekin. You cannot know my heart." She closed her eyes, and saw the desert moonrise. "Just get us to Oxford Airport before they land."

# CHAPTER TWENTY-SIX

After the trip down memory lane, no one spoke for a while. The first to break the silence was Zara.

"Just what the hell is an ankh, anyway?"

"It's what we call an ideogram," Eva said.

Zara gave her a look. "That clears that up then."

"An ideogram is just a symbol representing an idea," Virgil said.

Ella said, "You mean like the time Zara drew a penis on Milo's head that time he passed out drunk on the Miami job?"

Zara and Ella laughed and shared a high-five.

"You did what?" Milo said, shocked.

"You heard."

"I never saw that."

"Of course not," Zara said. "I'm a professional. After I drew it, photographed it and put it on social media, I rubbed it off again."

Caleb shook his head and smiled. "Sweet."

"I'm not sure drawing *things* like that constitutes an ideogram," Eva said. "Ideograms are usually symbols that represent *important* ideas."

"I think the idea that Milo is a dickhead is very important," Zara said. "And that is why I did it."

"Perhaps we can get back to ankhs," Mason said from the seat in front, his eyes still shut. "And a good place to start might be the important idea that the ankh ideogram represents, don't you think?"

"Life," Eva said bluntly. "The design of the symbol perfectly represents the joining of the male and female. The ankh is one of the oldest ideograms on Earth, and we've found it on excavations all over the ancient world, in sites from eastern Persia, right through ancient Mesopotamia and stretching west into Egypt."

"So, pretty important in the ancient world then," Ella said.

"And in Christianity, too," Eva said. "Recently, the royal seal of King Hezekiah was uncovered in an archaeological dig at the base of the Temple Mount's southern wall in Jerusalem."

"King Who?" Zara said.

"You never read the Bible?" Eva said, astonished.

"Too busy getting shot at and beat up," Zara said, turning to the academic. "You got a problem with that?"

"I guess not," Eva said.

Mason gave her a sympathetic look. "You were saying?"

"King Hezekiah was mentioned in various books of the Bible, including Kings, Isaiah and Chronicles."

"So a big hitter in the Bible Belt, then?" Milo said.

"Ignore it," Mason said with a sigh. "And please continue to enlighten us."

"Yeah," Virgil said. "I thought we were talking about ankhs?"

"We are," said the Texan archaeologist with a frown. She was starting to sound more like an annoyed kindergarten teacher every second. "What makes this discovery so special is that in this case the bulla was…"

"The what?" Ella said. "Now even I'm confused."

"Bulla," Eva repeated. "Clay bullae are a kind of seal used by kings in ancient times. They've been dated back to at least the 8th millennium BC in parts of the Middle East."

Zara leaned back in her seat and closed her eyes. "That's it. Ankhs, Bulls… I'm bailing out. Someone wake me when we get to the interesting part."

"And you say that you failed school and dropped out of the system?" Eva said.

"Hey, the system failed *me*, sugarpop. That's a very different thing."

"We were on bullas," Caleb said, giving Eva a reassuring smile.

"The clay bulla found in Temple Mount recently – the seal of King Hezekiah – was special because it included a depiction of a two-winged sun disk which was flanked on either side by ankh symbols."

A loud sigh from Zara's seat. "So what?"

"So, you asked what the ankh was, and I'm telling you it's a symbol of life used not just by ancient mystery religions, but also by kings included in the Christian Bible. Their ideography is everywhere."

"Had to ask…" Zara muttered.

"How much of this did you tell Linus?" Mason asked. "Not too much, I hope."

Eva shook her head. "No, not at all; I only told him what I had to, nothing more. I pretended to have more so they wouldn't…" she paused.

"So they wouldn't what?" Milo asked.

"We know what you're trying to say," Virgil said, giving Milo a sharp look.

Eva lowered her eyes for a moment as she started to open up about the kidnap. She chose her words carefully, not wanting to look weak, but also conveying to everyone the ordeal that Kyle Cage and the rest of the Spider crew had subjected her to.

Mason listened carefully as she led them through everything that had happened to her in Germany. He was proud that his extraction team had yet again pulled off another great mission and rescued her from the Spiders, but he could see how badly shaken Eva still was by the kidnapping. He was especially moved when she told them all that just knowing the Spiders and OM were still out there, and knew she was alive, felt like their slithering fingers were running up the sides of her body and wrapping around her throat.

The pilot announced that they would be arriving in Oxford in a few minutes and that everyone should buckle themselves in for the landing. Mason took his seat and started to pray that the long, black arms of the Hidden Hand hadn't already grabbed Ambrose Lloyd by the neck.

# CHAPTER TWENTY-SEVEN

The Ashmolean was an impressive building that had dominated Oxford's Beaumont Street for nearly two hundred years. The collection inside its impressive walls was even older, housed before its move to the current location in another building on Broad Street. The construction of the original museum had commenced back in 1678 when the famous English antiquary Elias Ashmole had donated an impressive cabinet of curiosities to the University of Oxford.

Also known as Wonder Rooms, cabinets of curiosities were vast collections of items which the Renaissance era had not yet categorized. For this reason, geological artefacts like rocks were in the same collection as works of art or natural history specimens.

These encyclopaedic collections often comprised of various objects from the worlds of archaeology, geology and antiquities, but also relics and other religious artefacts. Ashmole's collection included the mantle which had belonged to the father of Pocahontas, the lantern used by Guy Fawkes and Europe's last ever dodo, stuffed and mounted for all to see.

The collection was moved to its present location in the 1840s. Mason and the others had learned this as Virgil briefed them on the museum on the drive down into the city from the airport just outside Kidlington. They had cruised south through Summertown along the Banbury Road and were now leaving Park Town and approaching their destination.

Virgil interrupted himself to give Caleb directions. "Turn right at the Martyrs Memorial, Cal."

"That's this statue thing up ahead, right?"

He indicated an impressive stone monument a hundred meters or so in front of them which marked where Magdalen Street, St Giles and Beaumont street came together. Completed in 1843, the monument commemorated the Oxford Martyrs – Bishop Hugh Latimer, Nicholas Ridley and the Archbishop of

Canterbury, Thomas Cranmer, all of whom were executed for their protestant beliefs during the reign of Queen Mary I.

"Executed huh?" Caleb said.

"Burned at the stake."

"Ouch," said Zara. "That's gotta hurt."

"And that happened here?" Milo asked.

Virgil shook his head. "No, just around the corner in Broad Street. There's a little cross in the street to mark the location of the execution. It was outside the city walls at the time."

"You're a quick study," Eva said.

"Not really," Virgil replied nonchalantly. "I did my PhD here. I wrote it in six months so I had to find something to do with my time. Local history filled that void."

Zara sighed and shook her head. "How many bars are there in this place, Virgil?"

"At least a hundred."

"And you filled the void with local history. Weirdo."

As they climbed out the car and walked up the stone steps at the front of the museum, Milo broke the banter. "You think Kiya and her thugs have already got to old Lloyd?"

"Not as of five minutes ago," Eva said. "He just emailed me to say he's in the lobby."

"No cops, right?" Caleb said. "We don't want any cops."

"Hey, I was a cop!" Zara said.

"You know what I mean, Z."

Eva stepped ahead and shook hands with the professor. Ambrose Lloyd turned out to be younger than they had pictured; no older than late forties, he obviously kept himself fit and had the easy-going smile and confidence of a man who was happy with his lot in life.

Mason was relieved to see that he had respected their request about the police, and the only other person was Nigel Sim, the Director of the museum, plus two security guards, neither of whom was armed, as was normal for the United Kingdom.

After a brief round of introductions, Ambrose and Nigel led the team into the museum and through a large room full of ancient Greek and Roman sculptures.

"Where are we going?" Ella asked.

"My office is just through here," Nigel said.

They passed through several smaller rooms dedicated to ancient Egypt and the Amarna Revolution before finally reaching the director's private office. "Here we are," Nigel said. He ushered everyone inside and closed the door. "Now, you say Ambrose's life is in danger, is that right?"

"We believe so," Mason said. "Not imminently, but there's a faction of people – more of a cult, really – and they want something we have very badly. If they get it, then the next thing they're going to want is Dr Lloyd here, because they'll need him to translate something."

Ambrose's eyes lit up like emeralds. "Ah yes," he said. "The note you say you found in Nectanebo's sarcophagus. You said you think it's going to lead you to the Nectanebo Codex."

"The *what?*" Nigel said, visibly shaken. "Is this some kind of joke?"

"Unlike Oxford's traffic management, this is no joke, Prof," Zara said.

Nigel was still too stunned to respond to Zara's barbed comment. "Archaeologists have been searching for the Nectanebo Codex since the dawn of the science of archaeology itself. What's this note you're talking about?"

Eva pulled the tiny copper tube from her pocket and held it up in the light. "Right here, inside this tube."

Nigel ran a hand over his bald head. "Good God!"

Eva unscrewed the tube and handed Ambrose the small handwritten note. "If anyone can interpret this code, then it's you."

The professor took the note with a trembling hand and stared down at the words scrawled by Napoleon so many years in the past. "Bugger me," he said quietly. "This is the find of the century!"

"What does it say?" Caleb asked.

"I need more time to translate everything," Ambrose said, his words hushed and uncertain. "But from what I've already looked at, I think you've struck gold."

# CHAPTER TWENTY-EIGHT

"Spill the beans, Prof," Zara said, checking her watch. "What's it say?"

"It's a note to the British," Lloyd said. "He's mocking them."

"Over what?"

"He says he has the codex, and writing it in one of his codes just adds insult to injury."

"The Nectanebo Codex?" Nigel said in awe. "I still don't believe it."

Mason moved closer to Ambrose. "What else does it say?"

"I'll translate it: *My British Friends, in here I found something more precious than all the treasures of Egypt that I will keep with me until my dying day, but I deny it to you with these parting words – you win the gold but you lose the gods. Napoleon.*"

"I don't understand," said Milo.

"It's easy," Lloyd said. "We know the Romans discovered the sarcophagus and moved it to Alexandria. We also know that Napoleon found it on his Egyptian expedition. We also know that he was forced to hand everything over during the capitulation at Alexandria when the British beat the French – including the sarcophagus you saw in London. But now we know Napoleon found the damned codex in the sarcophagus before the British got to him so he took it for himself. Leaving this note was just one of his famous flourishes. He had a very dry sense of humor."

"Yeah," Zara said. "Because this is truly hilarious right now."

"I don't know," Virgil said. "Seems pretty funny to me. The British were supposed to find this note hundreds of years ago. He was taunting them."

"I guess when he was talking about finding the gods he was referring to the Book of Thoth," Caleb said. "So he knew… Napoleon Goddam Bonaparte *knew*."

"But he never went back to Egypt," Eva said. "So he never found his gods."

133

"Quite right, my dear," Ambrose said.

Mason took a deep breath. "That's *our* job."

"So where do we go from here?" Caleb said.

Eva looked in silence at the note in Ambrose's hands for a few seconds and then turned to face him. "Any ideas?"

Ambrose smiled broadly. "Paris. You go to Paris."

"Paris?" Zara said. "That's a big place."

Eva said, "We all know how big Paris is. We need to go to Musée de l'Armée. The Army Museum, am I right, Ambrose?"

"Yes."

"And you're sure?" Mason said.

"She's right," Ambrose said. "The military museum also serves as Napoleon's museum and mausoleum. His tomb is there along with most of his personal possessions and even a recreation of his home on St. Helena where he was in exile. He says in the note that he would keep the codex with him until his dying day. He's buried in Paris, so that's the next logical place to go."

Mason reached out for the scrap of paper and studied it for a few seconds before handing it back to Ambrose. "And you're sure you made the right translation?"

Ambrose looked almost offended, but it was Nigel who replied.

"Dr Lloyd's the leading scholar on the subject, Mr Mason. You won't get a better translation anywhere in the world. If he says the codex is in Paris then it's in Paris."

Outside in Beaumont Street they heard sirens and then saw flashing blue lights bouncing off the Randolph Hotel. Milo darted past Nigel and looked out his office window. "Three vehicles – two police cars and one unmarked Jag. Judging by the guys clambering out the cop cars, I'd say they're all armed response."

"What?" Caleb said, marching over to the window. "Damn it!" He turned to Mason and sighed. "Looks like secret service as well, Jed. Two dudes in black suits looking pretty serious in the Jag."

Mason looked at Ambrose and the director with dismay. "I thought we said no police?"

Watching through the window, Mason watched as the men climbed out of the big, black car and walked with purpose up the museum steps a few steps ahead of a cluster of armed policemen.

They were too far away to see their faces, and now they slipped out of sight as they reached the main entrance.

"They'll be here in a few minutes," Nigel said. "And I never called them!"

He was right. A minute or two later they were striding through the Egyptian section, making a beeline straight for Nigel's office. Mason watched them as they approached the open door, his heart quickening as they drew closer. The way they moved reminded him of the men he'd seen on a documentary about the Men in Black, and now one of their jackets blew open in the wind to reveal the handle of some kind of service pistol in a shoulder holster.

Now they entered the office and flashed their ID cards at Nigel. The lead man was tall, with dark blonde hair and a strong jaw. His eyes glinted darkly in the low light of the office as he turned to the armed police officers. "We'll take it from here. Go back to the entrance and make sure no one comes in."

After scanning the faces of the small group, the senior agent walked up to Ella and took hold of her shoulders, kissing her hard on the mouth. Mason and the others watched in shock as Ella ran her hands up the man's back until they were wrapped around his neck. When he finally released her, Ella Makepeace sighed and said, "I always knew you were a hotshot, Ben, but I had no idea you were this good."

Mason and the others stared at Ella in disbelief for a few seconds as she stood on tiptoes and kissed her boyfriend for a second time. She turned back to them and smiled. "Everyone, meet Ben Speers, MI5 agent and world's greatest kisser, Ben, meet the Raiders."

"Wait just a goddam minute," Zara said. "This is Ben, as in *your* Ben?"

She nodded "Uh-huh."

"Good to meet you," Ben said, giving a shallow nod of acknowledgement. "Is that Raiders as in tomb raiders or something?"

"No," Mason said bluntly, and told him what RAIDERS stood for. "We're in asset recovery."

"Neat," said Ben. "I hope it's all above board and legal."

"Of course," Ella said. "You think I'd hang out with a bunch of crims?"

"Look," Mason said impatiently. "We're in a hurry. The last thing we need right now is the interference of the sodding SIS." He glared at Nigel and Ambrose.

Ella and Ben stopped to kiss again, and Zara pretended to vomit. "Can't you wait till you get a room, at least?"

"Sorry," Ella said, picking a piece of fluff of Ben's shoulder. "It's just been a while since we saw each other." She turned to her boyfriend and locked eyes on him. "I thought you were out of the country?"

"I was, but an hour after landing I got a call from Henderson in the Met. I'm surprised you never called me yourself, El."

"I can fight my own battles, Ben," she said defensively. "I don't have to call my boyfriend up every time I get in a scrape."

Ben looked momentarily offended, but then things changed fast. One of the security guards burst into Nigel's office without knocking, his chest heaving up and down with the speed of his breathing. "It's the armed police down at the entrance! They've been shot and the gunmen are heading this way!"

# CHAPTER TWENTY-NINE

Amadeus slowed his breath and worked hard to maintain his nerve. He had been initiated into the Occulta Manu rank of Persian too many years ago, and he was starting to think his career in the organization had reached its end. He idly speculated that someone, somewhere, didn't like him very much and was holding him back from the promotion to Sun-runner that he so richly deserved. Now, the Lion – Kranz – was on the line prattling about how his Bride was failing to complete her mission.

If the Bride failed Kranz, then Kranz would fail him, and that meant he would have to report the failure to Benedict, the Sun-runner who held his life in the precarious balance so familiar to those in the Order.

And Benedict's rank meant he had the ear of the Father.

None of this helped his nerves, and he quietly performed the ritual of unscrewing his little plastic bottle of Xanax and popping a couple of the tiny blue ovals. In a few short moments, the diazepam would work its magic and calm his frayed nerves.

Allow him to see more clearly.

When the benzodiazepine washed into his bloodstream, he took a deep breath and spoke into the phone. "His name?"

"Jedediah Mason," Kranz said.

"An old name. Details."

"Born in London. Troubled up-bringing and then the British Army made a man of him. The last few years he's been running an asset recovery service, apparently the best in the world and in great demand. His team are supposed to be at the top of their game, but they look like a bunch of rogues, renegades and dropouts to me."

"These dropouts are causing me a lot of trouble right now, Lion."

"I understand."

"I'm not sure you do. If they cause me a lot of trouble, then I will cause you a lot of trouble."

"I'm doing everything I can, Persian."

"Are you?"

"Kiya is the best, and Dariush gave his life for the cause."

"I'm not interested in the fate of a Raven who hands vital information like the Napoleon letter to the enemy. He is no hero. If he had not killed himself he would have been executed by the Order for his derisory failure."

He heard Kranz take a deep breath. "I won't fail you."

"That is what they all say, dear Kranz. That is what they all say, but it never pacifies Benedict. A man like that respects only results, not excuses."

Amadeus closed his eyes and felt the drug coursing through his body. It felt almost like someone was giving him a shoulder massage. The relaxation dispersed like evaporating water when the image of the Sun-runner appeared in his mind like a phantom.

Or more accurately the image of what he *thought* the man looked like. He had never seen Benedict in all his years in the Order. That wasn't the way things worked at this level. Benedict the Sun-runner was just a voice on the end of a phone, or a string of commands in a text or email. Like an apparition forming in front of him at any moment and then vanishing again, he had no idea when he would touch his life.

Just as poor little Kranz had no idea when Amadeus would pull his strings, either.

"If I want to progress from Perses to Heliodromus, then I must not fail in this mission, Kranz. Is that clear?"

*Heliodromus…Sun-runner…how he craved that rank.*

After a short pause, Kranz said, "Very clear, and there will be no failure. Kiya is hunting them now as we speak, in Oxford. She and Tekin are closing in on their prey and I think very soon I will have good news for you."

"For your sake, Kranz, I hope you do."

Amadeus cut the call and popped another Xanax. All their fates were hanging on a thread dangling from Kiya's hands, and if she failed, they all failed. He shuddered and closed his eyes. No one understood what failing the Sun-runner meant better than he did: he had heard the rumors of those close to Benedict and what he did to punish anyone who failed him. He decided to start making a few enquiries of his own about these *Raiders*, and see if he couldn't bring their adventure to an abrupt end.

These damn pills just weren't strong enough, he thought, and crossed the room to his drinks cabinet. Maybe if he washed them down with some Scotch he could calm himself once again.

# CHAPTER THIRTY

Nigel Sim looked like he was about to have a heart attack. "What did you just say?"

"Shot, sir! We was standing on the front door with those armed coppers, just like you told us to when these maniacs turned up out of nowhere and just started shootin'! When I saw them go down I legged it down here to tell…"

The guard's sentence was cut short when a bullet tore into his neck and exploded out the other side, smashing into the giant Turner reproduction on the wall behind Nigel's head. Before anyone could react or even scream, a second bullet hit him in the head and blew the front of his skull off.

The dead man slumped to the floor, and it was only then that Mason noticed that Nigel was also dead. The second bullet had continued on its trajectory after drilling through the guard's head and torn into the director's chest. Blasted out of his chair and back against the wall, his body had slid down to a heap beside his filing cabinet and left a long trail of blood painted on the wall behind him.

"Oh my God!" Ambrose managed to squeak out. "What the hell is going on?"

"How the hell did they know we were here?" Caleb said.

"They must have seen the Napoleon note after all," said Mason.

Milo frowned. "And trailed us from the airport, maybe?"

"Possible," Ella said. "The delay at the airport in London must have given them a head start."

"So they were waiting for us at Oxford airport," Virgil said. "Bastards."

"Dangerous bastards," Ben said.

Eva was in shock, staring at the body of the dead director, but Zara was already on the case. Pulling a Glock from her pocket, she had beaten even Caleb in the race to draw her weapon first.

"You're too slow old man," she said. "One of these days you're going to get shot."

"I can't believe they killed Nigel!" Ambrose said, his voice barely a whisper.

"And they'll kill you too if you don't get away from that door!" said Virgil.

Ben spoke rapidly, the tone of his voice deadly serious. "I don't know where the hell you got those weapons from but you're not licensed to use them in this country." He drew a Glock 19 and slid a round into the chamber. "No one fires except me, or we're all in a deep lake of hot shit for the next ten years, got it?"

Ben fired a short burst of shots, professional and controlled, and the enemy dived for cover in the darkened corridor outside the office. "We need to get out of here!"

"We have what we need," Mason said. "We have to get to Paris."

"What about me?" Ambrose said. "I can't go to Paris!"

"You're going to a safe house," Ben said. "Holloway – get on it."

The other MI5 man pulled his smart phone from a pocket and started to make a call.

Looking over his shoulder, Mason had a clear view of the path Kiya and the Raven were taking to approach the office. They had anticipated an armed response and were now taking cover behind a large glass case full of ancient Egyptian coffin lids arranged in a vertical display.

"They're behind that case," he said.

Zara nodded. "I see the bastards." She fired off a shot, then another. The sound of the Glock discharging in Nigel's office was crude and savage, and Ambrose clamped his hands over his ears and nearly jumped out of his skin.

"Dammit!" Ben said. "I said no one fires!"

"So sue me," Zara said coolly. "I'm not taking a bullet just because some James Bond wannabe tells me not to fight, even if you are Ella's boyfriend."

"Ballistics are going to love this crime scene…" Ben muttered.

Ambrose was now the color of putty. "I've never seen anything like this in all my life," he said. "Are they trying to rob the place?"

"Look," Mason said. "Ben's right. We have to get out of here. These guys are insane and it's obvious they'll kill anyone to get what they want."

Ambrose had an idea. "We have tunnels here, beneath the Ashmolean. They go all over Oxford."

Mason shook his head. "No way. I'm not leading my team, or you, down into some kind of labyrinth when I have no way of knowing how to get out. It's suicide. Think again."

"They're getting closer," Ella said. "Behind that giant thingy on the right."

Eva rolled her eyes. "That's the shrine of King Taharqa."

Caleb frowned. "Whatever you call it, it's great cover and gets them one step closer to this office."

"There are too many of us for one vehicle," Ben said. "Holloway, I want you to take Doctor Lloyd to the safehouse in Cumnor."

"The rest of us are going back to the airport," Mason said. "Don't even think about trying to stop us, Ben."

Ben fired another shot at the approaching enemy. "I'm only one, and there are seven of you. I can't stop you without shooting you and I'm not going to do that, am I now?"

"Come with us!" Ella said. "We need all the help we can get."

Ben glanced at Mason. "Well?"

Mason gave Ella a withering look, but relented. "Fine, but only to the airport, then we go our separate ways."

"So what now?" Virgil asked.

Mason blew out the window and holstered his gun.

"Dammit!" Ben said. "Did anyone hear what I said about guns?"

"We can get out this way," Mason said, ignoring him. "I'll stay here and hold them off and you get everyone to the cars."

Ben led the others to the safety of the cars parked outside in Beaumont Street while Mason and Zara let rip with their Glocks, emptying both magazines in an attempt to hold Kiya and Tekin back for as long as possible.

"I'm out, Jed," Zara said.

"Me too," said Mason. "Time to make tracks."

# CHAPTER THIRTY-ONE

Mason watched as Holloway and Ambrose jumped into the Jag. A second later it skidded away west along Beaumont Street and swerved left onto Worcester Street in a cloud of burned tire rubber and diesel fumes.

"Into the police cars," Ben said as they sprinted down the front steps. "I'll drive one and you take the other." He tossed Mason the keys and they all piled into the two marked police Volvos parked in the street; Ella, Milo and Caleb joined Ben, while Zara, Eva and Virgil climbed in with Mason.

The Londoner turned the key and the engine turned over.

Then the windshield exploded into a mess of shattered glass, but stayed wedged in the frame. "Looks like they've worked out where we are," Virgil said.

"You were top of your class, right?" said Zara, reloading her Glock.

"I don't think Agent Speers is going to like that," said Virgil, glancing down at the freshly loaded weapon in her lap. "He's going to be very disappointed in you."

"Your lives are like one, long rollercoaster ride," Eva said, rubbing her head. "I don't know how you do it."

"It's not always like this," said Zara. "Sometimes it gets really violent and dangerous."

Mason gave Eva an apologetic shrug of his shoulders and stamped on the accelerator. The front-wheel drive Volvo roared in response and the two wheels spun around like demons, producing a vast cloud of burned rubber. When he dumped the clutch the car surged forward into the night, leaving two long, black trails of burned rubber swerving all over the street outside the museum's entrance.

"Hey!" Virgil said, pointing at Ben's car up front. "He's got the lights on, and the sirens! Why can't we do that?"

Eva turned and gave Virgil a look of pity. "What are you, like five?"

"He's right," Zara said. "Trust me, I was a cop in LA for years. You slap those babies on and you're getting where you want ten times faster."

"Hit it, Z," Mason said, swerving the car into St. Giles and heading north.

Zara didn't need to be asked twice, and she quickly fired up what British police called the 'blues and twos', activating the flashing blue lights and sirens.

"Oh, man," Virgil said. "This is so cool, and now we get to go to Paris, too."

"I hate to dump on your lunch, Virgil," Zara said, tipping her head to glance in the rear view mirror, "but we have two douche nozzles on our six and they're gaining fast. Looks like they're in a BMW."

"She's right," Mason said, checking his mirror. "They're in an M6."

Eva looked concerned. "What does that mean?"

"It means the only way we're getting away from these punks is if Jed can out-drive them," Virgil said.

"And can you do that, Jed?" Eva asked.

Mason changed down and floored the throttle. Beneath the hood, the two litre turbo roared like a lion. His face lit a gentle mint green by the instrument panel, he smiled and said, "Only one way to find out."

"Is their car that much faster then?" Eva said.

Zara pushed her window down. "Not with their front tires shot out, it's not."

Virgil leaned closer to Eva. "Dr Starling, I suggest you put your fingers in your ears, because any min…"

The sound of Zara's Glock cracked hard in the night. Most of the sound was outside the car, but it was loud enough in the car to make Eva Starling jump in her seat and quickly follow Virgil's advice.

"No way are these assholes following me to Paris," Zara yelled as she squinted down the sights. "When I get there I want coffee, wine," she fired another shot. "Maybe a croissant, and some Me Time," another two shots. "I do *not* want to be wasting my time chasing a bunch of assholes who think they're in the next Matrix movie."

"She has a good point," Virgil said. "Paris is fantastic this time of year."

Eva held her head in her hands. "You guys are making my head spin. You really are."

Zara yelled from outside the car. "They're returning fire!"

Kiya leaned out the passenger window and fired a short volley from a pistol. The rounds sprayed up the back of the police car, shattering the rear window and exploding the lights on the roof.

They reached the north end of Banbury road and Mason plowed the battered and dented police Volvo over the roundabout and headed for the final stretch. Kidlington was fast approaching and that meant Oxford London Airport was just minutes away.

As Mason swerved off the roundabout and hit the Oxford Road he was doing more than seventy miles per hour, but the Raven was driving the BMW hard, and seconds later he had caught up with them.

As they raced through the center of Kidlington, the Raven smashed the powerful German car into the rear of the Volvo and they all braced against the impact. The police car was a heavy vehicle, and absorbed most of the energy, but Tekin had now placed the BMW right on their tail and given Kiya a clear shot at them.

Zara threw herself inside the cab. "MP5! Get down!"

Her words were still echoing in the car when Kiya fired the machine pistol and sprayed bullets all over the back of the Volvo. 10 mm auto jacketed flat point rounds drilled though the Volvo's bodywork, pinging off the side panels but puncturing the tailgate and shredding into the body armor and gun cases in the back.

Eva screamed, Mason looked ahead and saw Ben hanging a hard left on Langford Lane. "We're almost there!" he yelled.

Taking the same hard left, he stamped on the throttle one last time and pushed the Volvo as hard as he could. Slowly, they caught up with Ben and the rest of the Raiders who were now turning right and driving into the airport.

With Kiya and Tekin right on their tail, Mason turned right and drove into the airport. He was instantly relieved when he saw a bank of flashing blue lights up ahead, and saw half a dozen police cars parked in a line to block the entrance to the airport.

"Ben must have called for back-up," he said. "Thank God."

"They didn't have to come far," said Virgil, pointing to a series of new, two storey buildings to their right. "According to my smart phone, that's the HQ for the local police."

"They're forming a barricade!" Eva said.

Mason shook his head. "No, they've left a gap for us to get through. When we drive in they'll close the gap and open fire on our friends behind."

"I just hope Ezra wasn't right about so many people being under the control of the Hidden Hand," Zara said. "Because if they are, then those guns are for us, not Kiya and her insane boyfriend."

But they were safe, and seconds after screeching though the barricade, the police cars closed the gap and issued a warning to Tekin to stop the car.

The Bride and the Raven ignored the warning and increased speed, racing toward the police line with everything the M6's mighty engine could give them.

The police issued a second warning and when that was ignored they opened fire on the BMW.

Mason was now airside and bringing the Volvo to a halt on the apron beside Ben's police car. The team jumped out of the battered car and headed toward the Citation which was parked up where they had left it hours earlier.

Behind them, the sound of gunfire crackled in the night air.

"They're fighting back," Zara said.

Virgil nodded. "Sounds like they're using the MP5s against the police."

Mason was just pleased that someone else was watching their back, and as he approached the jet, he could hear the engines were already starting to spool up. When he climbed on board the jet he found the rest of his team, plus Ben, strapping themselves into their seats. "I thought we said you could stay with us until the airport?"

Ben shrugged and looked at Ella.

Mason looked at her too. "Well?"

"Come on, Jed! He saved our lives tonight."

"Plus he called the police to the airport," Milo said. "Even gave them a special codeword us civilian plebs aren't supposed to know about."

Caleb waded in. "Come on, Jed. He's MI5 and Ella's boyfriend."

Mason gave Caleb a look. "Can we talk for a second, *Cal?*"

The two men moved toward the cockpit, and Mason talked first. "Listen, we don't know the first thing about this guy."

Caleb sighed. "We know Ella's been seeing him for over a year and they're talking about getting engaged, and we also know he organized an armed road block that saved our asses and is at this very moment filling the Hidden Hand with hot lead."

Mason sighed and looked over Caleb's shoulder at his crew buckling themselves into their seats and preparing for the short flight to Paris.

"Fine," he said. "But you're telling Ezra about it."

Mason gave the order to take off, and seconds later they were bursting through the clouds and banking south to Paris.

# CHAPTER THIRTY-TWO

Jed Mason pulled the shutter on the Citation's window and banished the chaos in his mind. Lined the problems up and thought about them one by one. Heading up the Raiders was challenging enough, but Ezra Haven had introduced a new level of stress into his life. They had the ankh and Napoleon's note, and thanks to Ambrose Lloyd they had a translation. That translation was pointing to Napoleon's final resting place in Paris.

As the Citation soared above a thin layer of cirrus and hit its cruising altitude, Eva Starling wandered over to him and smiled. "Mind if I join you?"

Mason moved his bag off the leather seat. "Please."

"Ezra tells me your little group is called the Pirates, or something."

"Raiders," Mason corrected her. "Rapid and Incognito Deployment, Extraction and Rescue Service. Milo thought of it."

"And after your incognito deployment, what do you extract and rescue exactly?"

Mason gave a humble shrug. "This and that."

"Oh, come on, Jed," she said. "Don't be coy."

"We operate in a grubby world, Eva. It's a world full of thieves, smugglers, and kidnappers, but we try and throw some light on it and clean it up if we can."

"Sounds pretty nasty."

"It is, but there's satisfaction when we get a job right."

"What was your last job?"

"Retrieving some proprietary software. It was stolen by a team of Ukrainian thieves from the offices of a world-famous tech company based in California."

"Is that who I think it is?"

Mason gave her an apologetic smile. "We never talk about clients."

"Still, sounds very satisfying."

Mason was quiet.

"No?"

"Sometimes, sure. Other times we're hired to get people back, and when you succeed it's the best feeling in the world, but when you fail it's…" he stopped talking and closed his eyes for a second. "Like I said, we work in a grubby world."

"But you make a real difference," she said. "I can't say that."

"I thought being an archaeologist was roughly comparative to the Indiana Jones movies, no?"

She laughed. "Not at all, unless they made one about a woman sitting in an office reading lots of journals."

"They did not," he said. "But even if they had, that would still have been better than Crystal Skull."

"Hey!" Milo called out. "I loved that movie."

"I want to thank you again for saving my life back in Frankfurt."

"Like I said, think nothing of it," he said quietly. "We were hired to do the job we do and we did it."

"Seems to me like you're a force for good."

"We're not a bunch of holier than thou Robin Hoods, Eva," he said. "We all have things in our pasts we're not proud of, but we work together better than any family. We're stronger than a family. Closer, you know?"

"I'm starting to see that."

"And you're the Big Daddy, right, Jed?"

They both turned to see Zara standing beside them.

"Hey, how's it hangin', Dietrich?" Mason said with a smile. "Got 'em by the shirt tails?"

"Always, Jed. Always – you know that."

"Ezra's on line one."

Ezra looked less relaxed than the last time they'd seen him. He was sitting in an office with a bank of plasma screens behind him, and they could just about make out a window but the shades were drawn down.

"I just spent the last hour dealing with a long line of VIPs."

"Very Important People?" Eva asked. "Sounds interesting."

"No," Ezra said bluntly. "Very Incredibly Pissed People."

"Drunks?" Milo asked.

"He means angry," Zara said.

"Surely that would be VIPPs?"

Ezra gave a long, deep sigh. "The people in question include the Mayor of Frankfurt who wants to know why there was a terrorist incident in his city today, the British Home Secretary who is asking some seriously tough questions about the incident at the British Museum and just now the head of the Oxford Police who's talking about car chases and gun fights in his city."

"Did they get the Hidden Hand thugs?"

"No," Ezra said. "They did not. They escaped on a chopper that swooped them up and flew them away into the night."

"Great."

"I told you they have a long reach."

"In our defense," Milo said. "These OM guys are like a cross between ninjas and Spetsnaz on speed."

"Let me spell out very clearly that I do not want the Mayor of Paris on my phone under any circumstances."

"Got it, chief," Zara said.

"You are to get into the Musée de l'Armée, get what you need and get right back out again without incident, understand?"

Mason nodded. "No problem."

"Come on, Ez," Caleb said. "We go way back, man. We're good – the best – but these Hidden Hand psychos are like nothing we've ever seen before. It's like they're possessed by some ancient spirit or something and they don't care what it takes to get what they want. Throw in Linus Finn's crew and we're up against it here."

"Yeah, chief," Zara said. "Maybe a little back-up?"

"You know why I can't provide back-up," he said firmly. "I'm not in the agency any more. If I try and get more people on board, especially anyone with connections to any of the alphabet agencies it's going to raise concerns in the wrong places."

"It's raising some concerns right here," Caleb said. "And I have a nasty feeling this is going to end very badly."

\*

With her eyes shut, Zara skipped over her thoughts like stepping stones until she saw her father's face smiling at her warmly. He was sitting inside their old Airstream Cruiser and lighting a Marlboro while an old Howlin' Wolf song played on the stereo.

## THE RAIDERS

His famous 1959 Fender Strat was on the couch, the sun glinting on the frets, and the smell of fried bacon was still hanging in the air from breakfast over an hour ago.

It was a real memory – her twelfth birthday. Her dad had played in Phoenix the previous night and now they were parked up in the badlands south of the Painted Desert. They were headed to Denver. Another night, another gig. More noise, more smoke and probably more fights. It was her life.

Her childhood was a million motels, endless headlights on the highway and watching her father keeping one step ahead of the drug dealers and debt collectors... seeing him right in front of her now brought a sad smile to her lips.

She reached out to touch him, and he smiled again as he blew out some smoke.

"How you doin', Zara?"

"I'm fine, Dad..."

"I'm not your Dad, Zara," Caleb said.

She turned to see the former Ranger sitting beside her on the plane. He had two coffees in his hands. "I'm sorry, Caleb."

"Forget about it. We all know what happened to Jimmy and it was a shitty thing to happen to a kid of your age."

"Thanks."

"And you have a new life now," he said, giving her shoulder a fatherly squeeze. "And a new family."

True.

And she had no desire to go back to her old life. She hated most of it. Thanks to her dad's career she'd attended six high schools before she was fifteen. The friends she made were in and out of her life so fast she felt like a revolving door.

People pick on the new girl, and she'd been the new girl so many times she'd met every kind of asshole under the sun. They bullied her until she broke down and cried but she never told her dad. Instead, she enrolled in karate classes after school. Karate turned into Kung Fu, and then she found Silat. After that, it was a big mistake to give Zara Dietrich any trouble because she gave it straight back, with change.

Mason emerged from the cockpit. "Heads up, everyone. We're landing in Paris in fifteen minutes, and then it's straight to the Musée de l'Armée and Napoleon's mausoleum."

"Sounds great to me," Zara said. "Let's get this show in the road."

# CHAPTER THIRTY-THREE

The Raiders and Dr Eva Starling stepped off the airstair and set foot on French soil. More precisely, it was the asphalt of Orly Airport's private aviation apron. In the far eastern reaches of the sky, a fragile pink blush was the first sign of daybreak. Mason was last off the plane, hefting his canvas bag up over his shoulder. The steel tube containing the Istanbul asset poked out the top and caught the morning sun.

"What's in the tube?" Ben asked.

"Confidential," Mason said bluntly.

"Sounds mysterious."

"No mystery, just highly valuable. Until it's returned to its rightful owners, it goes where I go."

The air was already warm, and as they piled into the car, Ella Makepeace tied her hair back and tried to relax. "How far to the museum?" she asked.

"Not far," Caleb said. "We're less than fifteen Ks away, almost due south of the place. According to this app we'll be there in twenty minutes."

"Without traffic," Milo said. "I lived in Paris for three years and believe me when I say the roads won't be this forgiving when we get over the Périphérique."

Zara sighed and looked at Milo. "You're such a pessimist, baby."

"Not a pessimist, but a realist."

As he said this, Zara mouthed the same word, perfectly lip-synching him. "Heard it so many times before, Miley."

"Miley," Virgil said with a chuckle. "I like that."

"Any word from Gaston?" Mason asked Virgil.

The New Yorker nodded his head. "Just got a text right now."

"Who's Gaston?" Eva asked, looking at the entire crew one by one for an answer.

She was met by silence.

"Well? Come on, you guys!"

"Gaston Majerus," Mason said. "One of Virgil's former lecturers."

"I see," Eva said. "Helpful."

"He works at Les Invalides," Virgil said. "It's waste of his talent, really. He's a brilliant classicist but somehow he ended up curating. He also writes a mean verse in memoriam stanza."

"Huh?"

"It's a quatrain in iambic tetrameter."

"Huh?"

"He writes poetry," Ella said. "Virgil struggles with simple words."

"Poetry, huh?" Eva said. "He is French, I guess."

"He's not French," Virgil said. "He's a Luxembourger. Never call him French."

"I'll bear that in mind," Eva said.

Much to Caleb's annoyance, Milo was right, and just under thirty minutes after they had driven out of Orly they were pulling up outside Les Invalides. By now, the sun had broken the horizon but was still low and the city was shrouded in the last remnants of the dawn twilight.

Majerus was a sight to behold with his cream linen suit, flamboyant silk scarf flung casually around his neck and a trilby hat set at a coquettish angle on his head. "Virgil," he cried out, extending his arms. "So good to see you, mon ami."

They kissed on each cheek and Zara and Caleb exchanged a raised eyebrow.

"Thanks for being here, Gaston," Virgil said.

"I came the instant you called. I said to Bernard, that I must make haste."

Eva leaned into Milo. "Bernard?"

"My parrot."

"Are you *kidding*?"

"No kidding," said Virgil.

"And here I am. Now, we go to the archives. This museum holds some of the greatest collections of archives relating to Napoleon in the entire world."

"What's the book?" Virgil said, pointing to a small leather bound journal in Gaston's hand.

"It's the memoirs of Bon-Adrien Jeannot de Moncey," Gaston said. "He was the first Duke of Conegliano, Peer of France and Marshal of France."

"A little light bedtime reading?" Milo said.

Gaston raised an eyebrow. "De Moncey was the governor of Les Invalides when Napoleon's ashes were returned here. I thought it may be of some use to us."

They made their way up the museum's steps and entered a cavernous hallway.

Mason followed Gaston Majerus and Eva Starling as they made their way along the corridor and headed toward the archives. The Texan woman had already impressed him a great deal with her knowledge and calmness under fire, but now she went and did it all over again as she struck up an effortless conversation with Majerus in what sounded like fluent French to him.

"So what are you looking for exactly?" Gaston asked.

"Ultimately, we're searching for a codex," Eva said. "We think Napoleon found it in Egypt during his campaign there. We think the codex will contain a map leading us to Thoth's Book of Spells."

"So, nothing much then," Gaston said, aghast.

"Nothing so far, that's for sure," Ella called out.

"And you think this codex is in here?"

Eva shrugged. "We *hope* so. You said this is where most of Napoleon's personal belongings were stored after his death, right?"

Gaston gave a haughty nod.

"So it's got to be here, then."

The task ahead of them was daunting. The archives were of a scale that Mason hadn't previously dared to imagine, and even the section dedicated to Napoleon looked almost infinite. Long lines of metal shelving units stretched away into the gloomy, musty space; each one was stuffed with box files and a hundred other types of container – all of them filled to capacity with papers relating to the great emperor. More than that, the place was stacked with the emperor's personal belongings – chairs, tables, wardrobes, old clothes, chests, everything he had accumulated on his travels.

Mason silently admitted to himself that he had made an error in calculating how long the Paris leg of the mission would take. When Ambrose Lloyd had told him that Napoleon had hidden the map from the British and that they would find it in the museum he had reckoned on no more than an hour.

Now he realized this assumption was idiotic, and that even with all seven of them hunting through the paperwork they would be here for hours. No problem in itself, he considered, but the concern was the usual one: SPIDER and the Hidden Hand. Two forces of dangerous, highly trained killers who wanted him and his crew dead and the codex in their possession.

Two hours into their search, Gaston took Ella and Ben Speers upstairs to the restaurant bar and returned half an hour later with a tray of coffees and pastries. Like Mason, the others smelled the warm, buttery-chocolate delights before they saw them and when Ella and her ex stepped into their section of the archives they were all over them like vultures.

Milo disgusted everyone by cramming an entire croissant into his mouth in one go while simultaneously snatching up a hot cup of coffee just so he could pocket one of the pains au chocolat, but he'd worked harder than anyone else and was quickly forgiven.

Mason brought his coffee to a stack of boxes in the corner and sat on his own for a few moments, just watching his friends. They always blew him away by how fast they could mobilize and how versatile they were, but on this mission they had impressed him more than ever. Not that they were getting a raise.

As they reached the top of the fourth hour, Eva sighed and crashed down on top of a large chest. "We've been through everything and it's just not here, dammit."

"Let me see that inventory," Virgil said.

He walked over to Gaston and the Luxembourger handed it to him. As he ran his finger up and down the lists, a frown began to form on his face. Lifting his eyes from the papers he pushed his glasses up on his forehead and started to scan the archive room. "No, no…"

"What is it, Virgil?" Mason asked.

# THE RAIDERS

The young man looked over at the group and a broad smile formed on his scrawny face. "This inventory isn't right," he said. "Something's missing!"

"If something's missing then that must be where the codex is!" Ella said.

"Exactly! It says here there were two cassones but there's only one – the one Eva's sitting on."

Gaston flicked through the small journal once again. "And yet the entry in de Moncey's notes mentioned that it was definitely *two* Florentine cassones that Napoleon picked up when he was crowned King of Italy at the Duomo di Milano."

"What the hell was he picking up casseroles for?" said Milo.

Virgil sighed. "*Cassone*, not casserole. It's a marriage chest used to carry the personal belongings of a bride on her wedding day. It's going to be pretty spectacular if it caught the eye of Bonaparte – right, Gaston?"

The Luxembourger nodded. "I taught you well."

Caleb shook his head. "You mean we've just been wasting our time?"

"Bugger it!" Mason said. He turned to Gaston. "I thought you said this place stored everything Napoleon had?"

Gaston looked crestfallen for a few seconds and was unable to speak, then his face lit up with the realization of what had happened. "Wait a minute! I know where the missing chest is!"

Zara sighed. "We're waiting."

"In Rome!"

"In Rome?" Mason said "What the hell?"

"Damn, baby," Zara said. "What the hell's it doing in Rome?"

Gaston said, "Throughout history Rome was traditionally seen as the center of culture in Europe, for all the obvious historical reasons, but that all changed during the reign of Napoleon."

"If you ask me," Ben said wearily, "it doesn't sound like you know what you're talking about."

"How dare you!" Gaston said. "How was I to know what you were seeking wasn't to be found in this room, but was instead in the other cassone?"

"I guess so." Ben didn't sound convinced.

Milo faced Gaston. "You said everything changed during the reign of Napoleon – how?"

Gaston puffed his chest out. "The Emperor desired the consolidation of all the most important religious and historical records of Europe. For historical reasons these records and archives were collected and stored in Rome, *naturellement*, but Napoleon decided they should be brought here to France, to Paris, because he wanted to make this city the cultural center of Europe."

"Sure makes sense from an egomaniac point of view," Caleb said.

"He started seizing the Vatican's archives in 1799 during his initial Italian campaign, but he went much further, gradually taking the archives and records of the other lands he conquered."

"And that's why it's in Rome," Ben said. "Now I get it."

"Oui… c'est très simple," Gaston said nonchalantly. "When Napoleon died, the Pope demanded that the archives be restored to Rome, but not all of them made it. It proved to be too expensive for the Catholic Church to transport them all back, so many of them were left here in France, and there was much confusion. But you see, the codex you seek is inside the other cassone, and the other cassone was returned with the archives that went back to Rome. Today, it can only be in one place – the Vatican Secret Archives."

"Oh, that's okay then," Virgil said. "I'm guessing they'll just let us stroll in and take whatever we want. They're not the most secretive place on Earth *at all*."

"Listen," Mason said firmly. "We'll do what we have to do to secure the codex, and then…"

His words were cut short by an enormous explosion which lifted him from his feet and blasted him across the archive room.

"Grenade!" Caleb yelled. "Dive!"

And then all hell broke loose.

# CHAPTER THIRTY-FOUR

In the smoke and chaos, a dazed Jed Mason scrambled to his feet and made for the same cassone Eva was using for cover.

"Where's my bag?" he said, searching for the missing asset. A cloud of plaster dust drifted like snowflakes to the floor.

"Over there," Eva said, pointing to the blasted door.

"Dammit!" he yelled. "Cal! The bag!"

Caleb peered over the top of an upturned shelving unit and saw the bag.

Then they watched as a team of operatives in riot gear and gas masks burst into the room and fanned out in a defensive position. One of them headed straight for the bag.

"Spiders!" Zara cried out.

"And look whose company they're keeping," Milo said.

Mason stared with unbelieving eyes as he watched Kat Addington running alongside Linus Finn, Kyle Cage and the rest of the Spider crew. "I don't believe this... how *could* she?"

"What is it?" Gaston said.

Mason felt the rage rise in him. "It's time we made our excuses and left."

"Who are these people?" the Luxembourger asked.

"They're serious trouble," Zara said. "And now they've gotten the goddam Istanbul asset."

"Fuck it!" Milo said. "That's everything we worked for! That's my early retirement!"

"What's in the bag, El?" Ben asked.

She gave him an apologetic look. "Raiders Rule #1, Ben: never talk the job."

Before he could respond, she opened fire on the Spiders alongside the rest of her colleagues, but it was too late. It had been a lightning raid, and now they were disappearing into the grenade smoke.

"After them!" Mason said. "We need the asset secured before we go to Rome."

"I'll call the police from my office," Gaston said. "It's not far. Go on without me!"

Mason led the way, running back through the rubble-strewn floor of the archive room until he reached the blown-out entrance. The doors were hanging off their hinges, and several dead security guards were sprawled in the corridor outside. Arseholes, he thought. *How could Kat be part of something like this?*

"That way!" he said, pointing to another exploded door along the corridor to the right.

Bursting out into the day, it wasn't hard to locate the Spiders. Not too many people in Paris wore black riot gear and had machine pistols over their shoulders. They were sprinting toward the Place Vauban to the south of the military museum where they'd parked their getaway rides.

Climbing onto half a dozen black Vespas they quickly kick-started them and zoomed away west into the traffic.

"Fuck it!" Mason said. "What now?"

"There!" Milo yelled.

He pointed to a bright green street-cleaning truck parked up at the side of the road. Its driver was crouched down at the side of the truck and trying to free something that was jamming the circular gutter brush.

Zara glared at Milo. "Are you freaking kidding me?"

"It's all we have!"

They ran to the truck and Caleb climbed up into the driver's seat. Ella, Milo and Eva joined him in the tiny cab, and Zara clung onto the side mirror extender. Mason, Virgil and Ben climbed onto the back of the truck as Caleb hit the gas. The truck surged forward, leaving the driver on the side of the street with the brush in his hands, and a string of curses on his lips.

Caleb powered the truck west along the Avenue du Tourville in pursuit of the Spiders, who had jumped a red light and were weaving in and out of traffic on the Place Joffre. Swerving right like a fighter plane display team, they quickly disappeared into the expansive parklands of the Champs de Mars.

Caleb swung right and the Eiffel Tower loomed into view ahead of them. Tourists ambling around with ice creams waved fists at the reckless bikers, but leaped for their lives when Caleb left the road and plowed the street cleaning truck over the kerb and into the park.

With his hands squeezed hard around the wheel, Caleb Jackson swung the municipal vehicle hard to the right and hit the gas again, powering it forward as fast as its diesel engine would allow. Looking ahead, he saw the Spider crew weaving deftly in and out of panicked tourists on the gravel pathways which ran the length of the Champs de Mars and converged beneath the Eiffel Tower.

On his left, Zara tapped on his window with the grip of her Glock.

He pushed it down and looked at her. "What?"

"Can't you go any faster, Cal?"

He gave her a double take. "Sure I can, I just thought I'd take it easy for a while. You know, take in the sights. Enjoy the atmosphere."

"Damn it, Cal! We're losing them and you're making jokes."

"The pedal's on the metal, Z," he said, swallowing a string of abuse he felt like yelling at her. "We're going as fast as we can."

One of the Spiders riding pillion turned around and fired with a machine pistol peppering the front of the truck with bullets.

"My money's on Iveta," Zara said. 'With Cruise driving the thing."

Caleb swerved hard to dodge the attack and only just avoided plowing into one of the manicured plane trees marking the northern pathway.

"Holy crap, Cal!" Zara called out.

"We're trying to hang on up here!" Mason yelled, banging on the cab's roof.

The Spiders screeched across a wide boulevard which dissected the park in half and then mounted the opposite kerb to rejoin the gravel path leading to the world-famous tower.

Caleb was undeterred and ripped across the boulevard in pursuit while Zara opened fire once again. Her aim was low, and the rounds slammed into the gravel a few meters behind the rear Vespa, blasting clouds of dust and chips into the air.

"They're too damned fast!" she cried out.

"They have the asset, Zara," Ella said. "We are *not* letting them out of our sight."

"River's approaching," Caleb said.

Zara leaned into the cab. "They're not slowing down."

"Are they in Seine?" Virgil yelled.

"For *fuck's* sake, Virgil," Zara muttered.

The Vespas pulled together and raced under the Eiffel Tower, scattering crowds of tourists and forcing two armed gendarmes to draw their weapons and open fire. One of the policemen hit Iveta's arm and they all saw her crumple over in pain, releasing Mason's bag and crying out in agony.

Molly Cruise never stopped, and now she followed the others through the narrow path leading out to the Quai Branly. Seeing the bikers slow down to drive through the gridlock on the busy road, the gendarmes vaulted over the low fence which divided the road from the tower and fired more shots.

Zara said, "Can't believe they turned Paris into a warzone to try and snatch the asset," she said. "It's that sort of commitment that's so sadly lacking in today's youth."

"Did they get any of them?" Ella asked.

"No," Caleb said. "They drove right onto a boat and they're already half a click down the river. All planned. Total pros. If it hadn't been for those cops they'd have the asset."

"The bag!" Mason yelled out. "Iveta dropped it – get it before the cops!"

"Already on it," Caleb said, and slowed the cleaning truck as he steered it over to the bag Iveta had dropped when she was wounded. Pulling beside it, Zara hopped off the running board on the side of the truck and strolled to the bag.

A small crowd of bemused tourists had gathered, but they took a step back when they saw the American ex-cop stuffing a Glock in her belt before she stooped to snatch up the bag.

"What the hell's going on?" said an Australian tourist, staring up at the cleaning truck and then back to Zara. "You nearly killed those guys!"

Zara's face turned to a frown. "You got a problem with the city's cleaning policy, bigshot?"

"No," he said hastily, glancing down at the pistol. "Not at all."

"Good."

Zara waved the bag at Mason, and he nodded with relief when he saw the steel tube still safe inside it. "Thank God."

"You want to deliver right now?" Caleb said.

"No time," Mason said firmly. "We've got to get to Rome as fast as we can."

Virgil's upside down head appeared in Caleb's window. "So what are we waiting for?"

Caleb pushed his face away, closed the window and put the truck in first gear.

# CHAPTER THIRTY-FIVE

Gaston Majerus picked up the telephone in his office and moistened his lips as he dialled the number. Outside his window, police were swarming around the museum in response to the shootout, and yet more were driving in the direction of the Champs de Mars where the Raiders had last been seen chasing the Spider crew.

"Shelto?" he said in a solid, single tone, coldly spoken.

"Yes."

"Your life has been saved by serendipity."

"I don't understand."

"Guess who walked into my museum a few moments ago?"

"Mason?"

Gaston could almost hear his Lion thanking God. "Yes. Turns out I know one of them. When he called me I simply couldn't believe it, and they seem to have more enemies than just us. They were attacked in the museum by a team in riot gear."

"Who?"

"Could be anyone, but it wasn't us. No point in catching them until they have what we desire."

"Do you know where they're going?"

"Yes. They're heading to Rome."

"Leave it to me," he said. "This time, they're mine."

"No. They have run rings around you too many times. This time you are to order Kiya and the Raven to hang back and trail them. No more interventions. When they know precisely where the Book of the Dead is, I will give the order to kill them, and not before."

"Yes, Amadeus. As you wish."

"Good hunting, Lion – and don't let me down again."

"No, Persian."

Gaston cut the call and considered reporting to Benedict, but instead he lit a cigar and watched the police as they crawled over the museum in search of the Raiders and their attackers. He knew they would never find them – they were too good for the gendarmerie, and he didn't want them to find them either.

They were going to lead Kiya all the way to Thoth's Book of Spells.

*

Kiya felt her skin crawl as the man rubbed her shoulders and gave her what was supposed to be a reassuring smile. Schelto Kranz, or the Lion, as he was more properly known, was a weak but greedy man. These were two qualities that never mixed well and she always felt unnerved in his presence.

"Please, Kiya – take a seat."

Kranz released his sweaty grip and indicated a low, leather couch running beneath a window in his office. When she sat down on the soft, worn leather, she prayed he would not sit beside her. Her prayers were answered when he took one of the chairs opposite the couch, behind a small, glass coffee table.

"You're my third in command, Kiya. I trust you. I admire your skills, but you have let me down on this mission."

"I know."

"I'm covering for you as best I can, but Amadeus the Persian is starting to ask awkward questions about your performance. Tekin's failure to deliver for OM has also not gone unnoticed."

Kiya maintained her composure as she felt the sweat from Kranz's grip cooling on her shoulders under the ceiling fan. "I will not allow them to beat me. I have never failed a mission and I'm not about to start now."

He nodded but her words of reassurance had failed to lift the concerned frown on his face. "In Amadeus's eyes, Dariush is not seen as a hero, dying for the Order in a brave way, but a fool who lost us Napoleon's note. This is also how you and Tekin are being judged, and you have only one chance left before I will be forced to cut you loose. Without my protection, it will not take the Order long to hunt you down and have you neutralized."

"I understand, but I will not fail. What are my orders?"

"You are to go to the Vatican Secret Archives and wait for Mason there. The Persian believes the codex is somewhere in the archive, but we do not know its exact location. He forbids you from engaging with the enemy until they have found the tomb and the Book of Thoth. Only then are you to execute them and secure the Book. Is that clear?"

Kiya listened carefully to the Lion's words as he spelled out the Persian's orders. She felt a wave of disappointment that she was not trusted to take the codex from them in Rome.

But orders were orders.

# CHAPTER THIRTY-SIX

Thirty-eight thousand feet over the Swiss Alps, the Raiders, plus Eva Starling and Ben Speers were watching the worried face of Ezra Haven on a plasma screen on the partition wall. The American former NSA man dropped down into his seat and rubbed his neck. He looked troubled and tired. "It's great news that you know the Nectanebo Codex is in the Vatican, but I just got some bad news."

"What bad news?" Caleb asked his old friend.

Ezra passed a hand over his red eyes and sighed. "I was worried something like this might happen."

"What's the deal, Ez?"

"Titanfort is picking up some chatter about a terror attack somewhere in North Africa or the Middle East."

Caleb frowned. "ISIS?"

Ezra sighed and gave his head a weary shake. "No, OM."

"I thought they were focussed on finding the Book of Spells?" Mason asked.

"They are," Ezra replied. "But they're an enormous operation, Jed."

Milo said, "You mean they can rub their tummies and pat their heads at the same time, right?"

"Right," Ezra said. "They can easily run multiple missions all over the world at the same time, and often do so just to create extra confusion. Titanfort is suggesting the terror attack is a diversion designed to break our team and stretch our resources at this critical time in the mission."

"And they'd be right," Mason said, bringing his hand down on the table with a hefty smack. "We're already running on empty, Ezra. We can't afford to split the team and send half on some wild good chase all over bugger-knows-where while the rest of us secure some crazy Egyptian Book of the Dead."

Zara sidled up to Milo with a mischievous smile on her face. "Aww," she said.

"What?"

"You call them tummies."

"Just take it easy," Ezra said to Mason. "All we know at the moment is that there's increased chatter connected with the Hidden Hand with regards to some kind of terror attack. At this time, the location is unspecified and the time is unspecified. We're not splitting the team up based on that."

"But be ready all the same, right?" Caleb said.

"Be ready all the same," said Ezra. "The stuff we're picking up looks like they're working with the Spider crew again. After their success in snatching Eva it seems OM has found a solid crew of dogsbodies who will work for peanuts, doing the dirty work while the big boys focus on the grand prize."

"Linus is a busy boy," Ella said. "A few hours ago he was trying to hunt down one of our assets, and now this."

"Maybe the failure to secure that asset is what drove them back to OM," Ezra suggested.

"This is just insane," Mason said. "Tell me again why the US Government isn't going after these guys? Why isn't the CIA all over this, Ezra? Why us?"

Ezra rubbed his eyes then raised his head to face the Londoner. "I already told you, Jed. I already told all of you. The US Government, along with just about every other government is infiltrated at all levels by members of the OM secret order. There's no way to know who we can trust, and who we cannot trust. Titanfort was established by a private consortium, a select few – a small circle of good men and women who want to purge the Hidden Hand and bring daylight back to the world." He paused a beat while everyone soaked up the lecture. "That is why we can't call 911 and ask the nice people in the CIA to fight the bogeymen for us."

Caleb broke the silence. "You trust the source on this terror attack? This is our lives, Ezra."

"I wouldn't be passing the information to you if I didn't."

"Do I know him?" Caleb said.

"Yes, and it's a she. For now, we focus on getting the codex out of the Vatican and securing the Book of Thoth. In the meantime I'll have my people here at Titanfort try and get more details about the attack." Ezra leaned forward in his chair. "As soon as you land in Rome, you need to move faster than you ever went before, and I hope you realize that. These people are not your average internet conspiracy. These guys are serious business. Make no mistake," he said firmly. "This will be the biggest, hardest fight of your lives."

"You got that right," Zara said.

"Damn right," Ben said.

The team shared a mutual look of concern. Ezra was first to break the silence, his voice sounding thin in the cabin's speakers. "All right, Milo – what did you get on Napoleon's cassone?"

"I've got its rough location," Milo said. "So when we get there we should be able to move things along without too much delay. Hunting stuff down is where things start to slow down. I've been searching through some of the floor plans available on the Vatican tourists sites, but there's nothing for the Secret Archives, obviously."

"You are *kidding* me, right?" Zara said.

"Not at all, stuff like that doesn't really... ah – I see what you did there."

Zara winked at him and gave his hair a playful tussle. "When you grow up you'll be all right, kid."

"Thanks, wait – when I grow up? I'm the same age you are."

She fixed an eye on him and a smile crept across her lips. "What's age got to do with growing up, Milo?"

"Point taken."

Mason looked at the screen and fixed desperate eyes on Ezra. "Please tell me your Titanfort guys have got us into the Vatican?"

"No dice, I'm sorry. The authorities in the Vatican played hardball and we got nowhere," Ezra said. "They are not cooperating at all and we have no contacts there similar to Gaston in Paris. They rejected my requests to enter the archive outright, and when I spoke to some of my old bosses in the NSA and tried to get some strings pulled, they dug their heels in and started to get suspicious. There's nothing else for it – we're going to have to go in the hard way."

Mason sighed and shook his head. "Fine. No problem."

"I want a detailed plan before that aircraft touches down in Rome, and I mean infiltration, asset recovery and exit strategy planned to the second. When you hit a place like the Vatican you upset some very serious and powerful people. We're going to need to get in and out with the asset in double-quick time and without raising an alarm or we're not going to get as far as the airport on the way out, never mind the country."

"Fine."

"And no guns," Ezra said. "We're not getting into a situation where there's live rounds firing in the air in the Vatican and Swiss Guards getting killed on duty. You have to do this without firearms, is that clear?"

"We prefer to leave the shooting irons back at the ranch whenever we can, Ez," Zara said. "So that's fine with me."

Ezra gave a nod. "And the rest of you?"

"There are no problems with my team working without guns," Mason said. "Like Zara just said, we try and work without them whenever we can. They have a nasty habit of going off and killing people, and a lot of our jobs involve rescuing innocent and scared people, often children. Going in tooled up with automatic weapons can often make a job harder."

"Good. You proved you know how to handle weapons in Frankfurt, but this is not one of those jobs. Taking one of the Spiders out of the game is one thing, but killing a member of the Vatican Security forces is quite another, not to mention the chance of a senior member of the church getting killed in the crossfire if things get out of control."

"So that's settled," Mason said. "No guns."

He cut the call and Mason stood in front of the plasma screen. He looked at his watch. "We're running out of time."

"Wait just a minute," Eva said. "You're not seriously going to break into the Vatican Secret Archives?"

"Sure, why not?" Caleb asked.

"Because nothing like that has ever happened before! It would be the break-in of the century."

Zara looked unfazed. "Still not getting your point."

"All right – enough of this," Mason said. "Virgil and Milo: I want a plan to break into the Vatican Secret Archives and I want it before this aircraft touches down in Rome. We just entered Italian airspace, so you have forty-five minutes."

# CHAPTER THIRTY-SEVEN

Thirty minutes later, everyone was gathered around Milo's laptop staring at a jumble of terracotta roofs and winding cobblestone streets.

"You're looking at an aerial image of Vatican City," Milo began coolly.

Virgil spoke next. "And this is the Vatican Secret Archives. It's located to the north of the Apostolic Palace – that's the large building right here."

Mason quietly scanned the faces of his team and felt a surge of pride as he saw them studying the screen in front of them. This was why they were the best, the fastest and the safest pair of hands.

Virgil continued. "A significant amount of storage space was added to the Secret Archives in 1980 when a new underground facility was built beneath the original building, and this is where we believe Napoleon's chest is being stored, along with the codex. To say they're not very keen on visitors is an understatement. Postgraduate students and academics researching specific and relevant subjects to the archives may apply for a special entry permit, but undergraduate students aren't allowed anywhere near the place, and no one at all outside of the higher reaches of the church is allowed to see anything dated after 1939."

"No one?"

"Zero exceptions, and in some cases only the Pope himself."

"And the Raiders," Zara said.

Mason's smile widened. "Of course, the Raiders."

Eva rolled her eyes, but then gave Mason a reluctant, affectionate smile.

"Our first job is to get inside the Vatican itself," Milo said. "This isn't difficult as we can pose as tourists, but we'll look suspicious if we go in together mob-handed, so we're going to need to split up and stay in contact via earpieces."

"After this is gets harder," Virgil said, and nodded at Milo to change the image. "The main building that houses the archives is guarded twenty-four seven by the Pontifical Swiss Guard."

Zara raised her hand. "Question."

"Shoot."

"Are those the guys that look like clowns?"

Mason sighed and gave her a look. "Clowns, really?"

Virgil spoke up. "The Swiss Guard is basically a military unit within the Holy See and pretty much ceremonial. They guard the place ceremonially, but if you get any trouble when you're in there it will be from the Gendarmerie Corps – they're the main security force."

"I see," Zara said. "I never knew that. I'd hoped we'd be fighting the clowns."

"Sorry," Virgil said deadpan. "No clowns, but inside the archives themselves are over fifty miles of shelving packed with top secret papers going back well over a thousand years."

"In other words," Zara said. "It's hiding more dirty secrets than a politician's cell phone."

"Exactly, but we're only interested in one thing, and that's the codex."

"And that's on the lowest level of the archives inside old Boneparte's little treasure chest," Milo said, flicking the next image onto the screen. "And this is where it gets really hard, so I'll take over, thanks Virgil."

"Asshat."

"You're too kind."

"Step on it, Milo," Caleb said gruffly.

"Sorry. After we've got past the Swiss Guard," Milo continued, "we still have another major obstacle before we reach the asset. The section of the archives that we want to access is reached via a small elevator and then a set of bomb-proof doors. They can't be blown up or blasted open. The only way to open them is with a highly sophisticated vocal recognition function."

Zara sighed. "If we get caught, we're going down until Doomsday."

Ella shifted in her seat. "So, it's basically a bunker with steel doors that weigh tons and you need the Pope to ask the doors to open. More than that, if we get caught we cause a major diplomatic crisis and go to prison for the rest of our lives. Am I right?"

"You're not wrong," Milo said.

The team shared a few seconds of silence before a ripple of subdued laughter emanated around the cabin.

"It's the toughest job we've ever had," Mason said. "If we pull it off, we'll know we can do anything after this."

"That's a big *if* right there, Jed," Caleb said. "Sure, we've broken into some pretty tough places in the past."

Eva raised an eyebrow. "Care to elaborate?"

Caleb scratched his chin pensively. "I was thinking of the casino in Atlantic City."

"Then there was the monastery for the Misko job," Ella said. "That was hard work climbing up those cliffs."

Ella's reminiscence was broken by Mason. "This is nothing like any of those. This is more securely guarded and intensely political. There is absolutely zero margin of error on this job. When we light the touchpaper on this one we're on the ride to the very end, whatever that may bring. Are we all clear on that?"

Their faces said yes.

"Good. Anything else, guys?"

"Sure," Milo said. "Even the floors and walls are both dust-proof and fire-proof and every single item that's catalogued in there is fitted with a special computer chip that can be used to trace its location."

"This is a nightmare," Eva said. "I know you're good but no one's *that* good. Tyring to break into this place is suicide."

"The Raiders have never failed a job yet," Mason said. "We're not starting now. Give me some good news, Milo."

"The whole place was recently given a total security overhaul and now just about everywhere is covered by CCTV coverage as well. That will have to be cut when we make our move inside the archives."

"I said good news."

"I'm coming to that. A tower in the famous Belvedere Courtyard is used to transport documents they want moved from the bomb-proof bunker underground up to the various consultation rooms. I think this could be our way in."

"Break in via an elevator, huh?" Zara said, a smirk forming on her lips. "That's wrong on so many levels."

"Droll," said Ben. "Very droll."

"Just walk into the elevator leading down to the archives?" Ella said. "I think not."

"Of course not," Milo said. "According to the schematics I downloaded, we're dealing with a roped elevator, and that means the steel cables on both the elevator car and counterweight are connected to an electric motor at the top of the elevator shaft. This is where the shiv, or pulley, raises or lowers the car depending on which way you turn the motor."

Zara smiled approvingly. "Gotta hand it you, Miles – you sure do know how to get your nose in other people's business."

"The point is, the schematics show that there's a door behind the elevator housing which leads to the motor room, and from here there's a service panel where we can access the elevator shaft via a hatch in the top of the car."

"I thought that was an urban legend?" Ben said.

Milo shook his head. "The urban legend is right to an extent – you can't usually open the hatch from inside the car, but you *can* open it from the top of the car. If we can get into the motor room then we can get through the hatch and into the elevator car. After that we just have to get to the vault doors and break them open."

"Good work, Milo," Mason said. "That's a great start."

Caleb leaned back and stretched his arms. "You said there was a voice recognition system."

Milo nodded.

"Whose voice?"

"His name is Bishop Zurla," Virgil said. "He's the Prefect of the Vatican Archives, and don't worry about it," he added with a mischievous smirk. "I've got a great idea."

"I bloody hope so," Mason said, looking at his watch. "Because we touch down in Rome in less than ten minutes."

# CHAPTER THIRTY-EIGHT

"You're sure he bought it?" Mason asked Ella.

"Hook, line and sinker, Jed. You should have more faith in my skills."

"It's not your skills I have the problem with, it's Virgil's crazy plans."

They were walking across the center of St. Peter's Square in the heart of the Vatican City and approaching Bishop Francisco Zurla. He was surrounded by a small coterie of advisors.

"And you're sure Milo got the password right?"

"He worked at Flowdox until the US Government shut them down, Jed. He has Julian Assange's personal email address. If he hacks the Vatican and says he has the password, he has the password."

"Let's hope you're right."

"He hacked the BBC website and got my picture on there easily enough, didn't he?"

He *had* done that, it was true. Milo's dubious past at Flowdox, a long-time rival to Wikileaks was well documented in the world of hackers and government intel agencies, and the skills he had learned there had brought the Raiders' bacon home on many occasions.

Mason knew all about Flowdox. Milo had narrowly escaped arrest after the US Government had made a deal with Denmark and done a little raid of their own. They planned to shut down the servers and arrest as many hackers and journalists as they could get their hands on. Fortunately, a Washington insider had tipped off Absalon Mortensen, the enigmatic founder of Flowdox, about the raid and when they got there they found nothing but an empty building.

After that, Milo had gone to ground for months before resurfacing in Thailand where he used his hacking skills to make a living on some questionable day-trading. He'd racked up a good six figures before he ran into Ella Makepeace on a beach on

Phuket one day, and the rest was history. Mason knew there was much about the young man's past he had kept to himself, but that was part of the Raiders' code – no awkward questions and no awkward answers. "I guess," he said doubtfully.

"And fucking hell, this thing weighs a ton!" Virgil grimaced as he repositioned the TV camera on his right shoulder.

"It was your idea, so you get the donkey work," Mason said. "And where the sodding hell did you get a TV camera and sound boom from?"

"One never questions the genius and creativity of The Virgil, Jed," Virgil said. "One simple appreciates."

As they approached the Bishop, Mason felt a wave of uncertainty. The feeling was followed by a flashback of the day he'd led his brother to his death in Kenya. He'd felt the same thing then, too. The decisions he made on that mission cast a long, dark shadow over his life, and he worked hard to shake it away as he smiled and shook the bishop's hand.

After a round of pleasant introductions, and the presentation of Milo's hastily created fake news media ID cards, Ella said, "It's so good of you to speak with me today. Do you mind if my cameraman films some close-ups for the show?"

"Not at all," the Prefect said. "I'm only too happy to help."

Ella settled in opposite Zurla and gave him a broad smile, which he warmly returned. Behind her, Virgil was doing his best impression of a professional cameraman and filming non-existent footage of whatever he could to pass the time.

Mason stood beside Ella and pretended like he knew what he was doing with a sound boom, holding it vaguely over the top of the bishop as Ella started to interview him for the BBC.

Watching her at work like this always blew him away. The rest of team each brought tangible skills to the table – Caleb and his connections, Zara and her fighting prowess, Milo and his technical ability, Virgil and his polymath knowledge, but Ella was different. How did you put a price on the crazy mind games she employed to get what she wanted out of people?

He didn't know how to quantify her skills because he couldn't begin to understand them. He'd watched people like Derren Brown doing things like this to people but always dismissed it as TV fakery, but seeing Ella Makepeace playing people like violins in this way had converted him. He was a believer. Watching Signor Zurla open up like a flower and give Ella exactly what she wanted was like watching a witch work magic on a child. He reminded himself never to let her do it to him, but then, he thought with mild concern, how would he ever know if she had?

Ella flashed her famous smile. "Just one more thing – you mentioned that His Holiness is visiting the Shrine of Our Lady Fátima."

"Yes, that's right," Zurla said.

"When is that?"

"May."

"I see."

"And the repair work you're doing on the Basilica – do you think you can do it before the end of the year?"

"Yes, I think we can do it. That's the plan, anyway," he said with a forced smile.

"And did that cost you more than the previous work on the Sistine Chapel?"

"Yes, it cost us a great deal of money and aggravation. It's been a very long interview. Shall we end it here?"

"Of course. Thank you so much, Signor Zurla," Ella said. "You have no idea how helpful you've been today."

They walked slowly away from the Prefect and crossed the yard on their way back around to where the others were waiting for them. "All right, we got it."

"You got it?" Eva said.

Ella nodded and pretended to chalk a mark in the air. "Works every time."

"How did you do it?"

"Simple," Ella said. "The password was – what was it, Virgil?"

"The password was actually the first four words to Angele Dei, or the Guardian Angel prayer, spoken in Latin, and then only by Zurla," he said. "Qui custos es mei, me tibi commissum pietate superna, hodie, hac nocte, illumina, custodi, rege, et guberna, amen. It means, 'My Guardian Dear, to whom his love commits me here, ever to this day, this night, be at my side, to light and guard, to rule and guide, and obey'."

"And you got the Prefect to say that?"

"Just the first four words."

"I can't believe he would say the passwords out loud like that, when he knows they activate the archives."

"Oh, he doesn't *know* he said them," Ella said.

"I don't understand."

"We needed him to say the first four words in Latin," Virgil said. "Qui custos es mei. The voice recognition system is a computer, and they're remarkably unfussy when it comes to things like this. All the computer wants to hear is the phonemes, so Ella worked out a way to have the bishop express them and now Milo here will reconstruct them into the correct sentence."

"That's right," Milo said. "If anyone knows how to make a computer satisfied, it's me."

Zara raised a hand. "What happens in your bedroom, stays in your bedroom."

"Funny."

"So how did you have him say the right words?" Eva asked.

"Qui – I can build it from when the bishop said *I think we*; custos, I can get from *it cost us dearly*; es was easy – *less*; and *mei* was even more straight forward – I had the bishop confirm the Pope's trip overseas was in May."

"Now all we have to do is break in," Milo said as he shared a high five with Virgil.

"Yes," Mason said with less certainty. "Now all we have to do is break in."

# CHAPTER THIRTY-NINE

The Raiders pretended to be tourists as they meandered around the Belvedere Courtyard. Mason recalled a story he had read in a British newspaper about Joe Hawke and the ECHO team hunting notorious Mexican drug lord Silvio Mendoza across this very courtyard and creating a diplomatic storm after a shootout in the Sistine Chapel. Ezra Haven had been very clear about not providing an encore to that particular performance.

"This is where we split," Mason muttered. "Ella and Virgil, you go south to the Basilica. You know what to do. Just wait for the word."

"Can't I come with you?" Virgil said. "The library has a vast collection of incunabula I've been dying to see for ages."

"You're going with El," Mason said. "That's the way we rehearsed it."

"If you insist," Virgil said, and the two moved away with another group of tourists heading toward the world-famous Basilica dome.

Walking with Zara at his side, and Caleb and Ben a few paces behind, they crossed the courtyard and stepped into the shade of the Vatican Apostolic Library. The library had been in here for over five hundred years and contained vast bequests and collections from across the centuries.

"If Virgil were here he could tell us all about this place, I bet," Mason said.

Zara nodded. "Thank heaven for small mercies."

They reached the northern exit and emerged into another smaller courtyard. "There it is," Caleb said under his breath. He nudged his chin up at the Gregorian Tower, or Tower of the Winds, standing on the western perimeter of the palace. Taking two years to construct, the tower was finished in 1580, and its original purpose was to encourage the new science of astronomy.

Making their way into the tower, they checked their comms one more time. All of the crew were in radio contact with Milo and Eva back in their hired Fiat Talento via invisible Bluetooth wireless headset earpieces.

"Still with us, Miles?" Zara said quietly.

"Always, Z. Just think of me like your own personal God, always in your head."

"Piss off, Milo."

"That's no way to speak to the voice of your conscience, is it?" He lowered his voice to an eerie whisper. "You love Milo… you love Milo."

"Can it, Milo," Mason said. "We're on a job. You know the rules."

"Sorry, boss."

Inside the Tower of the Winds, it didn't take long to follow the route they had studied and reach where they needed to be. Occasionally, a priest walked past, but among so many tourists no one gave them a second look.

"I see the lift," Ben said.

"Got it," Zara confirmed. "Elevator at one o'clock."

Mason spoke into his mic. "You reading me, El?"

"Clear as day."

"Time for a smoke."

"Got it."

\*

Ella Makepeace and Virgil Lehman were walking arm in arm across the floor under the dome of St. Peter's when Mason's order came through their earpieces: *time for a smoke*. Rising over four hundred feet above their heads, the enormous, breathtaking structure dwarfed them like nothing either had ever seen before.

Mingling with the tourists, they broke apart and each reached into their bags. Pulling out what looked like two cans of Coke, they moved to separate parts of the dome before sitting down to take a drink. Placing the cans at their feet, they got up and wandered over to each other again before linking arms and strolling back out along the nave and emerging into the bright Italian sunshine.

Virgil pushed a button on his cell phone and looked at Ella. "Three, two, one…"

The first reaction was a woman screaming, and then several Swiss Guards left their posts and rushed inside to see what was going on.

"Smoke grenade diversions successfully deployed, Jed," Virgil said.

Mason spoke rapidly but calmly. "Good. Get out of there."

"That should keep them busy for a few minutes," Ella said. "Time to get back to Milo and the van."

\*

Ella and Virgil walked around to the Viale Vaticano and reached the safety of the Talento which was parked up adjacent to the Vatican Museum. They climbed inside through the side door and slid it shut behind them. Taking a seat behind Milo's mission control they nodded at Eva who was in the driver's seat up front and gave each other a silent high five for a job well done.

"All good?" Milo said without looking up.

"All good," said Virgil. "Even when they work out it's just harmless smoke grenades, they'll take ages to check the place for anything else. Protocol demands that they sweep the whole place."

They all heard Mason's voice over the speakers. "We're going toward the lift shaft, Milo. Check comms."

Milo silently adjusted the headphones on his head and checked the frequency of the radio signals to the team. "You guys inside yet?"

"Going in now."

"Still reading me?"

The replies came back clear and loud.

"This is Mason, check."

"Caleb here."

"I hear you, Milo," Ben said.

"I can hear everyone, but damn it…this thing isn't easy to wear," Eva said from the front seat, readjusting her headset. "Keeps falling out."

"Push it in harder," Mason said.

"Said the priest to the football coach," said Milo.

"Jesus, Milo," Mason said. "This is not professional."

"Sorry," the young man said. "What about you, Dietrich?"

"Yeah, I'm professional."

He sighed. "Are you reading me?"

"Kinda obvious, no? But yeah, clear as crystal, Schnookums."

"You sound weak," Milo said.

"Say that to my face and see what happens."

"No, I meant your signal. I'm increasing the gain. Gonna shrink the bandwidth but should boost the signal."

"Feels kinda good without a sidearm," Zara said. "Like I'm naked."

Mason gave a heavy sigh. "Keep it professional, Zara. We're almost there."

\*

Mason led the team through the door behind the elevator shaft and headed to the motor room, but a few meters in, a security guard appeared from a small room on their right and started to wave his hands. "Non… non! Back. Go back! No tourists here."

Zara apologized and stepped closer to him, pulling a map from her pocket and unfolding it. "Mi scusi…"

He looked at her and offered a smile, but then she struck, placing him in a lightning-fast chokehold, and squeezed until he gently passed out. "Thirty seconds until he wakes up," she said calmly. "Duct tape, please, Ben."

Ben Speers reached into his bag and pulled out the tape, and seconds later the guard was trussed up like a Christmas turkey under the desk in his office. He regained consciousness and started to squeal and writhe, but Zara gave him a loving pat on his head and then held her finger to her lips and gave him the hush sigh. "When we're done I'll call your boss and he'll come get you."

"All right, Milo," Mason said. "We're in the motor room." It was a small space, filled with equipment and smelling of oil, and in the center of it all was a large orange-painted electric motor. "What now?"

"There should be a trap door behind the motor," Milo said. "You see it?"

"I got it," Caleb said. "I'm opening it now."

"Well don't!" Milo said. "It's attached to an alarm!"

Caleb frowned. "What the fuck?"

The sound of Milo's chuckling drifted over the airwaves. "Just kidding, Cal. You can open it."

"You *asshole*, Milo." Caleb heaved the trap door open and they all peered inside.

"All right, that's the roof of the lift," Mason said. "And there's the hatch."

He pulled the hatch open and the empty elevator was revealed. One by one they lowered themselves into the car. When everyone was in the elevator, Mason hit the down button. "I want everyone on standby. When this shit goes down the whole Vatican's going to be on fire. If we don't make it, I want Milo and the van crew out of here, clear?"

The confirmations came in one by one.

Mason nodded once and slid on his gloves and mask. Caleb, Zara and Ben followed suit, and then attached their night vision goggles. "Good. Then here goes nothing."

# CHAPTER FORTY

The elevator doors opened to reveal a narrow concrete corridor stretching away from them, just as Milo had seen on the schematics. Mason scanned the area for a moment and then raised his palm-mic.

"Milo, cut the juice."

The reply was immediate, and this time there were no jokes. "Consider it done."

One second later the corridor was plunged into darkness. "Let's go," Mason said. "The vault's at the end of this corridor on the right."

Using their night vision goggles, they walked the length of the corridor, silently passing under a series of CCTV cameras, all reduced to meaningless plastic by the lack of electricity to power them.

"And Milo's sure the vault has its own power system?" Ben said.

"Dead sure," Zara said.

"It's a security feature," Mason said. "A failsafe in case anyone gets caught inside during a power cut."

"I bloody well hope so," Ben said nervously. "Because if I get caught down here the next thing I know MI5 will be giving me my P45."

"Huh?" Zara said.

"It's the reference code of the form you get when you lose your job," Mason said.

"Got it. Don't worry Benjamin – you're in safe hands with us, and just think how impressed Ella will be when you pull this off."

They continued along the corridor, but Ben still didn't look too convinced.

Mason pulled up at a set of enormous steel doors. "We're at the vault, Milo."

"Let's hope your voice voodoo worked, Miles," Zara said.

Caleb shrugged, and raised his iPhone to the mic. "Proof of the pudding, and all that – ready, Jed?"

Mason nodded and typed in the forty-seven digits that Milo had hacked. Immediately, a countdown began just as the young hacker had briefed them it would.

"All right, do or die, Cal," Mason said.

Caleb pushed his iPhone closer and played the Bishop's reconstructed voice: *Qui custos es mei...*

And the vault clicked open.

"Jesus, Miles," Zara said. "It actually worked."

"This is what I'm paid for, hun," he said smugly. "Tell me, what are you paid for again?"

"Take a long walk off a short dick, Milo."

Mason said, "Remember the Fubar Protocol, right, Milo?"

"I got it – if it goes pear-shaped then we make tracks and meet in Tahiti."

"Tahiti?"

"I added that bit to the plan. Always wanted to go there."

Zara sighed. "What the hell are we waiting for?"

They stepped inside and got their bearings. It was a vast space, bigger in reality than what they had imagined from Milo's hacked schematics, and mostly filled with documents packed into endless stretches of shelving. All of it was behind an enormous glass screen running from the ceiling to the floor, just as Milo had warned them. The purpose of the screen was to control the humidity and other aspects of the climate within the archives, but getting inside was simply a matter of punching another twelve digit keycode and popping open a door.

Inside the Secret Archives, Mason held one thought in his mind above all others, and that was how little time they had before the ruthless might of the Pontifical Swiss Guard came crashing down on their heads. A life spent in an Italian prison cell, serving time for one of the most notorious break-ins in history was not part of his plans for the future, so they had to work fast.

"How's the diversion going, Milo?"

"Like a dream, but it's not going to last forever." They heard the sound of tapping as he typed on his keyboard. "I'm just checking the monitors now and it won't be long before they work out they've been duped."

"We're going as fast as we can," Zara said. "And if anything goes wrong I'll find a way to blame you, Miles."

"I know you will, Z."

"It's in Aisle 17," Mason said. "Let's go."

They reached their destination and started to search for a cassone similar to what they had seen back in Paris. After a few minutes with no luck, Mason was starting to get nervous. He glanced at his watch as the team kept up their search. "Milo?"

"You don't have much time left," he said. "I can't keep blocking out the CCTV up top and our friends in the Swiss Guard have just sussed out our little diversion."

"Damn it!" Mason said. "We have to get out of here, codex or no codex."

"Wait." It was Zara. "What about this thing?"

Mason watched as she pulled an old dust sheet off a pile of furniture in the corner of the chamber. "Am I the best, or am I the best?"

Mason's eyes widened like saucers. "I think you found it!"

Stepping over to Zara, they beheld another magnificent fifteenth century cassone marriage chest with solid oak panels and gilded around the edges with fine gold leaf.

Zara ran her hand along the lid. "It's beautiful."

"It's priceless," Caleb said.

Mason grinned. "And with a bit of luck it's got Parennefer's codex inside it."

"So we got the fucker," Zara said. "Excuse my Castilian."

Mason stepped up and lifted the cassone's lid. Inside, his eyes feasted on a vast jumble of luxurious clothes, books and jewels. This was without a doubt part of Napoleon's private belongings accidentally brought back to Rome after his death.

He rummaged around for a few moments and then pulled a tattered and stained hardback book from the chest. It was covered in jewels, and an ankh-shaped groove was carved into the heavy, leather front. "We got it," he said, holding the codex in his hands. He spoke to Eva over the mic, a smile widening on his face. "I only hope you can make sense of the damned thing."

As he stared the ancient codex, the American archaeologist's voice drifted over the radio. "Sure, but I'll need time."

"Which is something you've just run out of." It was Milo's voice.

Caleb gave Mason a sharp look of concern. "Swiss Guard?"

"Yes," Milo said. "But they're calling back-up as well, the Gendarmerie Corps – just as we knew they would."

"All right, everyone," Mason said. "Back to the lift."

They exited the vault and jogged back to the elevator. "Power on, Milo."

"Got it, boss."

The lights came back on and they stepped inside the elevator. Mason hit the button to send it up out of the archives and they all said a silent prayer and as it jolted to life.

# CHAPTER FORTY-ONE

Commissario Nichetti kept his eyes focussed on the display above the elevator which showed the position of the car. "They'll be here in seconds," he said. "Guns ready."

Behind him, the uniformed men inside the Gregorian Tower stood without expression, their eyes shaded by the peaks of their caps. On Nichetti's belt was a Beretta 92, a semi-automatic pistol issued to police officers in Italy as their standard service weapon.

"No one's breaking into the Vatican archives on my watch," he said coolly, and then drew his weapon.

The Vatican Police Corps was formed two hundred years ago in 1816, and today there were only 130 members within its ranks. When the Pope wasn't present, the famous square was under the jurisdiction of the Italian State Police but when he was in the city the Gendarmerie took over once again. This had been the way of things for a long time. The rules were set out in the Lateran Treaty, a series of agreements made between the Holy See and the Kingdom of Italy back in 1929 when fascism ruled the country, but today things were much more peaceful.

Except for the criminals who had just broken into the archives.

The elevator arrived and the doors opened.

"Fire!"

Nichetti and his men opened fire.

*

Mason and the others heard the sound of Nichetti's gunfire as they sprinted up the stairs above the elevator motor room. Climbing up through the open hatch and riding on the roof of the elevator had bought the four of them a valuable few seconds, and as they hit the top floor and burst out onto the roof, Mason blinked in the bright sun and spoke to Milo.

"All right, we're out."

"The codex is still safe?" Eva said over the radio.

"Of course."

"Thank God."

"Don't sound so surprised," Zara said. "That's kind of what we do for a living."

"I can't wait to see it!" Eva said.

Mason's voice was calm, but he spoke quickly. "Are the bikes in place?"

"Exactly as planned," Milo said. "You're welcome."

"Get everyone in the van back to the plane," Mason said. "We'll meet you there when we're clear of the police."

"The raid's already on the internet," Milo said. "Pretty soon all of Rome's going to be on lockdown."

Mason, Caleb, Zara and Ben Speers sprinted along the apex of the tiled roof connecting the Vatican Library to the museum in the north. Reaching the edge of the roof, they opened their bags and started to pull out rappelling equipment. They quickly sorted the small collection of ropes and clips and then positioned their anchors to make the abseil safe.

"Man, that's a lot of police sirens," Ben said.

"You don't say?" said Zara. "Anyone would think someone just knocked off the Vatican."

"Point taken," he said.

"Less chat, more work," Mason said firmly. "We're not out of the woods yet."

With the screwgate carabiner attached to the anchor, Mason looped his rope into a clove hitch and clipped the doubled loop into it. Fixing the other end of the rope to a figure-8 descender, he then attached the descender to a second screwgate carabiner attached to his harness. Clipping the rope to another carabiner to a leg-loop, he lowered himself over the edge of the roof and started to rappel down toward the ground in between the Vatican library and the city wall. He was fast and efficient. He had done this countless times before.

Following his lead, Caleb, Zara and Ben went over the edge on their own rappel lines and ten seconds later all four of them were unclipping themselves from their harnesses and sprinting to where Virgil had parked the bikes.

Mason turned the corner and sighed with relief when he saw the two motorbikes – a Kawasaki and a Suzuki, parked up in the shade of an umbrella pine. *How the hell does he do it?* he asked himself. He and Zara climbed on one and Caleb and Ben took the second.

"Now we split up," Mason said. "Meet at the destination after we lose the cops."

Caleb kick-started his bike and Ben climbed on the back. Seconds later they were skidding away to the northeast.

Mason then fired up his bike, but nothing happened. "Shit!"

"What's up, Jed?"

"Flat battery!"

Zara kicked the bike's rear tire. "I'll fucking kill Virgil for this!"

"Steady as she goes," Mason said. "He's never let us down before."

"Over there!" Zara said. "I believe you were looking for a powerful superbike?"

She was pointing to a Ducati Panigale in a small car park outside the museum. It had two large panniers attached to it.

"Just one problem, Z – the driver's sitting on it."

"I don't see that as a problem at all."

They ran to the bike, and the man gave a cheery wave, but that all ended when Mason dragged him off the bike and jumped astride it, tossing the codex and his bag in one of the panniers.

Zara climbed on the back and rode pillion as he revved the 1.2 liter engine and skidded away into the traffic. In his rear view he saw Nichetti kick over a Vespa in rage and reach for his cell phone. The Italian police chief didn't exactly look thrilled with how his week was turning out – first the Director of the Vatican Library had been brutally murdered and now the culprits of the worst robbery in Vatican history had escaped and were on the run in Rome.

"Better hold on tight," Mason shouted. "Things could get nasty."

"You don't have to tell me that!" Zara said. "They've got guns and I'm the one sitting on the damned back!"

They took off into the backstreets of Rome, racing through the warm summer air as Mason negotiated the foreign city's maze-like roads. Zara slipped a Glock from inside her jacket and aimed it at the pursuing police.

"Bloody hell, Zara! Ezra said no guns."

"What can I say? I always come prepared for fubars like this."

"Just *please* don't kill anyone, Dietrich."

"Oh, ok then. I'll aim above their heads."

"That's what worries me."

Zara ignored the slur and fired a warning shot over the heads of the police. They ducked and scattered behind a line of parked cars for a few moments, but seconds later an irate Nichetti waved two men on police motorbikes rapidly forward to give chase.

\*

Kiya watched the Fiat Talento with passive eyes as Tekin followed Milo and the rest of the second team. They were still in Rome, and it looked like they were heading for a destination somewhere to the city's southeast.

"Keep on their tails," she said.

"I won't let them out of my sight," said the Raven.

She closed her eyes and sighed. "Looks like they're aiming for the military airport."

"Where they go, we go. I just hope Mason can escape from the police."

"He just broke into the Vatican Secret Archives with a few hours' notice," she said with respect. "He'll escape, all right. Keep up with the van."

He changed up into fifth, and pushed the stolen Alfa Romeo another hundred meters closer to the Raiders' Fiat van. "We've got them this time."

Kiya blew out a breath but her shoulder muscles were tight with stress. "Somehow Mason has somehow relieved the Vatican City of the Nectanebo Codex, and that will lead them to the Book of Spells, but if we lose them now… just one more error from us and we're dead."

"No more mistakes," Tekin said. "Soon we will have what is rightfully ours, and the gods will be revealed to us."

But Kiya wasn't listening to him. She was already dreaming of her elevation to a Hidden Hand Soldier. All she had to do now was hold her nerve and let Mason and his team lead her to the greatest prize of all.

# CHAPTER FORTY-TWO

With Zara's hands clamped firmly around his waist, Mason watched as Caleb and Ben skidded away to the northeast and then took off to the south. Rounding a sharp corner, he tracked the Vatican City walls until they hit some traffic on the Via di Porta Angelica. Checking the mirror, he saw police bikes and cars, as well as a van, on their tail and gaining fast.

Looking ahead into the traffic he saw a clear way through. He floored the throttle on the Ducati and it surged ahead, splitting the lane and scorching past the mostly stationary cars either side of them. They made a junction and he braked hard.

"Where did the police van go?" he asked.

Zara stood up and put her hands on his shoulders as she scanned the busy city in search of the police van.

"Got it," she said. "Three o'clock, turning into that side street."

"I see it. We'll go the other way."

Mason twisted on the accelerator again and steered the handlebars to the left. The Panigale reacted instantly as he cut across the other lane of cars and drew closer to their planned escape route. The powerful engine growled hard as he swerved into the side street and accelerated away from the police van.

"We lost him, Jed!"

"We're not free yet!"

The needle on the speedometer swept around the dial in a second, indicating in the clearest terms that the Ducati Panigale was not a machine to be messed with. Mason loved speed, but he had to admit he had never gone from nought to sixty miles per hour in 2.6 seconds before. It felt electric, and as the monstrous, liquid-cooled 1.2 litre l-twin engine roared beneath him, for one terrifying second he had visions of himself simply flying off the thing and coming to a bone-crunching end on the hot asphalt.

"You know how to control this thing, right?" Zara called out. "I don't think I ever saw you ride a bike before."

Mason acted cool. "Oh yeah," he lied. "No problem."

# THE RAIDERS

They raced away from the Apostolic Palace along the narrow, cobblestone road to the east, Mason furiously blowing the horn to clear the way of tourists gently ambling along with ice creams and cameras. They burst out on the Via de Mascherino, a broad two-lane road lined with shops and parked cars.

Mason had understeered the powerful bike and they mounted the kerb on the east side of the street and plowed their way along the sidewalk. He hit the brakes and slowed the Ducati from fifty miles per hour down to thirty, steering back onto the road and then increasing power. Soon they were speeding up to one hundred once again, and he felt a surge of adrenalin as he weaved the bike at high-speed through the Roman traffic.

The Vatican City was behind them now, but a Vatican Gendarmerie BMW i3 was sticking to their tail for all their life was worth. He watched them in the mirror as they powered up behind them. The bike was faster, but in the traffic there was a limit to how fast he could push things if he wanted to avoid spending the next three months in traction in a Rome hospital.

"Holy crap!" Zara screamed. "Tram! Tram!"

Mason looked up from the mirror to see one of the famous city trams rattling around the corner to his left and about to cross his path. He swerved the bike to the right and hit the brakes again to avoid smashing into the hood of a Nissan emerging from the traffic on Via Crescenzio.

Clear now, he hit the power and the bike surged forward out of the chaos behind them. "Holy shit, Jed!" Zara cried out. "You nearly killed us!"

Mason said nothing. He felt the same fear but time was running out and Nichetti was closing in. He could see in the mirror that the commissario was on the radio, no doubt calling back up six ways from Sunday and soon they would have nowhere left to run.

"So what do we do now?" Zara said.

"Just as we planned. We get back to the plane and get this codex the hell out of here!"

It was the only plan he had, even though the Citation was still miles way. They could get there if they were lucky and drove like the devil, but they would be cutting things fine, and there was nothing to say that the plane and the rest of the team hadn't already been shut down by the Italian carabinieri.

The road curved around to the right and he powered up again, racing up a long, straight road called the Via Cola di Rienzo. The road was clear and he decided to open the Ducati up and rag the hell out of it for a few seconds.

"Hold on, Z!"

It was a hair-raising experience.

With the throttle fully open, the superbike easily screeched past one hundred miles per hour, then one-twenty, one-fifty and was soon approaching its maximum speed of a little over one hundred and seventy miles per hour. It had taken a few short seconds and they were going faster than a jet plane at takeoff speed. As a result, they hit the end of the road before they knew it, and Mason saw a bridge fast approaching them.

It was the Ponte Regina Margherita, stretching over the River Tiber in the center of the ancient city. He hit the brakes and slowed to swerve around a line of cars and then revved up to roar across the bridge. Nichetti was still behind them in the BMW i3, but thanks to racing along the last road at nearly two hundred miles per hour, he was further back now and Mason had bought them some much-needed time.

East of the Tiber now, they were heading into the very oldest part of Rome, weaving the Ducati in and out of thousands of years of history. "Over there!" Mason said, looking ahead to a narrow side street. "He's not getting the Beamer down there."

He slowed down to walking speed and manoeuvred the bike around a tight corner and into a public walkway no wider than a meter and half. Checking the mirror, he saw Nichetti screech to a halt at the mouth of the walkway, curse, and then zoom away.

"He knows where this is going," Mason said.

"You think he's going to try and head us off?"

"He's not going for gelato, that's for damned sure."

"I was just asking a question!"

"Sorry..."

They reached the end of the walkway and burst out onto a small public square filled with tourists. Opposite them were the world-famous Spanish Steps near where Lord Byron had lived, but Mason's mind was firmly on the BMW i3 that Commissario Nichetti was racing furiously toward him on their left.

"Hold on!" he yelled. "He's found us already!"

"You're not going to… you have to be kidding!"

Mason didn't kid on missions, and now he revved the Ducati and aimed it toward the Spanish Steps. Tourists screamed and ran for cover as he hit the first step, and then increased power as he ziz-zagged his way up the famous landmark in a hail of tire squeals and burning rubber.

# CHAPTER FORTY-THREE

Reaching the top of the Spanish Steps, it was safe to say Jed Mason and Zara Dietrich had attracted the attention of the entire city's police force. The area was swarming with them, and everywhere they looked, a possible escape route was being blocked off by the authorities.

"We've fucking done it this time, Jed."

"Nonsense, we never screw up a job – ever! And this is just another job, right?"

"If you say so, but this asshole just doesn't know when to give up," she said with a glance over her shoulder.

The police bikes began to make progress, making use of shortcuts unknown to foreigners.

Up ahead Mason spied some red lights and a junction.

"Fantastic."

Zara fired at the police and they skidded out to opposite sides of the road to avoid her bullets before closing back into the center of the lane again. Pedestrians turned to watch the chase in amazement as the flashing blue lights and howling sirens of the police bikes drew the attention of half of Rome to the action.

Mason checked his mirror and shook his head. "Can't shake them off."

"Try back over the other side of the river."

The high walls of old Roman buildings towered either side of them, channelling them down toward a large crossroads and back to the river, but further south this time. They turned a corner and burst out onto a wide road on the east bank of the Tiber. A long hop-on-hop-off river cruiser was sailing slowly beneath the Ponto Vittorio Emanuele II.

They raced for the bridge, hoping to lose Nichetti in the old part of the city, but halfway across the bridge Mason saw the Italian commissario was a step ahead and had called for back-up. On the western bank were another two officers. They were going to catch them in a classic pincer movement.

Mason twisted the throttle and hammered the Ducati over the bridge, ripping over the Tiber like a demon.

"What the hell are you doing?" Zara cried out. "You're driving right into their trap."

"Oh, ye of little faith," he called back.

He powered along the bridge until they were about halfway across, and felt Zara's arms squeezing him tighter as they raced along the asphalt. Either side of him, angry drivers were honking their horns and winding down their windows to curse them as Mason weaved the Ducati in and out of the traffic on the busy bridge.

"I don't know what the hell you're planning, but it looks like we're running out of options, Jed," Zara said.

"We're running out of lives, more like."

He hit the brakes and brought the Panigale under control, dropping through the gears as he went. The massive engine growled beneath them as the revs shot up in response to the lower gears, but then fell to a low grumble. Mason steered the bike up on the sidewalk at the side of the bridge and they hopped off.

"Fancy a tour of the river?" he said, trying to slow his breathing.

Zara peered down at the murky brown water.

"It's now or never, Dietrich!"

"You can't be serious?" she said, shocked. "Swim in that?"

"Look behind," he said. "Speedboat heading this way."

He indicated behind them where a powerful speedboat was racing toward the bridge, its chrome rails and windshield sparkling in the Roman sun.

Zara shook her head in disbelief. "Oh, no, not that…"

He nodded and smiled. "When I say jump, we jump."

"You're shitting me, right? Please tell me that you're shitting me."

"I'm not shitting you, Z. If we time it right we'll drop right down into the boat and leave the rozzers far behind." He opened the pannier and snatched the codex and his bag.

"They'll call the water police, or a chopper."

"We'll cross that bridge when we come to it."

"Is that supposed to be funny?"

"In three, Dietrich. Three, two, one!"

They leaped off the bridge and dropped down through the air like stones, landing with a heavy crash on the rear deck of the luxury speedboat just as it emerged from beneath the bridge.

The captain turned, horrified, but Zara pointed the gun at him and told him to keep going, and to increase speed. "Just keep going, Capitano," she said. "And I'll cross your palm with silver. I'm no criminal."

The man shrugged and pushed the throttles forward. "I cannot lie," he said stoically. "This is not your typical day in Rome. Where are we going?"

"To the Aeroporto Militare south east of the city!"

The man gave an apologetic smile as Nichetti and his officers gathered on the bridge, cursing and shouting and making frantic radio calls. "This boat can only take you so far."

"Just get us away from the cops," Zara said. "That's half the battle won."

Mason sighed and rubbed his neck in the hot sun. "Something tells me the battle is only just beginning."

# CHAPTER FORTY-FOUR

The US presence in Egypt had a long and rich history, stretching back to the summer of 1830 when a merchant from Philadelphia named Charles Rhind signed a trade treaty with the Egyptian Government. Giving the US most-favored-nation status, the treaty allowed America to trade openly with the entire Ottoman Empire. The Consulate was opened five years later in Alexandria, and the use of the port exploded when demand for Egyptian cotton increased during the American Civil War. After a period of closure, the consulate reopened in 2016 in the Helnan Palestine Hotel in the city's Montazah area.

Now, Jed Mason and the other Raiders were sitting in a nondescript office in the rear of the consulate, working on their plan to retrieve the Book of Spells and patiently waiting for Ezra's "helping hand". This turned out to be three former Delta officers, all of whom were on first-name terms with Caleb Jackson thanks to their post-army careers in the CIA and NSA.

Caleb and the men exchanged a quick smile and after a round of meaty handshakes, he introduced them to the rest of the team. "Meet John Garrett, Chuck Ikard and Don French," he said. "Me and these guys go way back. Guys, meet my new crew. We call ourselves the Raiders."

"You're the guys who jumped off the bridge in Rome, right?" Garrett said, holding his iPhone up to show them the front page of the Italian newspaper, *La Republicca*. "Looks like you're famous."

Mason and Zara gave an apologetic shrug.

"Hey, we got the codex," Zara said at last.

"Ezra's not too happy about the publicity," Caleb said.

Zara sighed. "Ezra can kiss my…"

"Anyway," Garrett said. "Let's move on."

Following a few pleasantries and some jokes about life at Fort Bragg, the expanded team soon got down to the business at hand. Mason had full confidence that three NSA operatives and former

1st Special Forces Operational Detachment soldiers would have no trouble slotting into the team and he was grateful for the extra manpower. Maybe Ezra Haven had a use after all.

"Tell us, Dr Starling," Garrett said firmly. "You had time to study the codex on the flight from Rome. What does it tell us exactly?"

Eva looked at the map in the rear of the codex once again, her eyes widening as she made sure she had the translation right. She had opened the codex on the plane with the help of the ankh, which she slotted into the hole in its cover. Seeing it for the first time in centuries was already one of her career highlights. "The first thing it told me was to come here to Alexandria. As we had speculated, the codex is mostly written by an ancient Egyptian priest named Parennefer, and he was very clear about it being in Alexandria."

"Go on, please."

"Since we landed I've had more time to study it, and I think I understand it now. Parennefer writes here that he moved the Book of Thoth somewhere where the new Christian authorities would never find it, and I can hardly believe I'm saying this, but he says he hid it inside Cleopatra's tomb."

"Cleopatra's tomb?" Mason said. "Bugger me! That's one of the greatest missing historical relics of all time."

"Cleopatra wasn't a saint, Jed," Eva said.

"I'm sorry?"

"Relics are the personal belongings or even physical remains of saints. We're talking about a tomb containing the body of Cleopatra, who was a queen."

"This is the problem with having an archaeologist around," Zara said with a wink. "Sooner or later they're going to make you look like a total idiot."

"Hey," Milo said. "Jed doesn't need Eva to make him look like an idiot. He can do that perfectly well on his own."

"All right, all right," Mason said. "Dial it down. I'm still the only one here who can pull off aviator shades. Remember that."

"Aaaand, back to Cleopatra," Eva said.

"Oh yeah," Caleb said drily. "Let's do that. Just imagine I'm like my old friend Jed, here, and run me through Cleopatra for Dummies."

# THE RAIDERS

"First, she was Greek, and her full name was Cleopatra VII Philopator."

"She was Greek?" Milo said. "You learn something new every day."

"That's not hard starting from your baseline," said Virgil.

"Yes, she was Greek," Eva continued. "But she spoke Egyptian too. She learned it for her people, along with all their religious rituals. Essentially she became a kind of Isis, a sort of goddess. Back then it was important for rulers to be seen as divine, or at least appointed by the divine."

"Where's the popcorn?" Milo said cynically.

"Zip it, Miles," Zara said. "I'm interested in this stuff. Some of us never got a decent education, got it?"

"Sorry, Z."

Eva continued. "And she wasn't the only Cleopatra. Her mother was Cleopatra V of Egypt, for example, but history remembers her so much because of her relationships with Julius Caesar and Mark Antony, and the fact she was the last ruler of the Ptolemaic Kingdom of Egypt."

"What's the significance of that, sorry?" said Ella.

"The Ptolemaic Kingdom was a period of Hellenistic rule in Egypt."

"Helen who?" Zara said.

"Hellenistic," said Eva. "It means Greek."

"So say Greek if you mean Greek."

"Thanks for your input Zara," Eva said. "I'll be sure to publish an article in the American Journal of Archaeology about how we all have that wrong and be sure to change it."

"You're welcome."

"So what was so special about Helen's Greece?" Caleb said, winking.

Eva returned his smile. "This is when Egypt starts to change from the one we all think of, pyramids and mummies and pharaohs, and slowly starts to shift, first to Greek culture and then into Roman and Byzantine. It's a critical time in the history of Egypt and Cleopatra was right there front and center during the pivotal point."

"When did she die?" Mason asked.

"30 BC," Eva said. "She was only thirty-nine. She died just a few days after Mark Antony killed himself by falling on his sword. He did it because he thought Cleopatra had already died. Her death is one of the great mysteries of our entire history. Orthodox opinion has always recorded that she killed herself with an asp bite, but some revisionist theories suggest she was murdered by Octavian. It was a bloody and electric few days in history."

"And her tomb has never been found, huh?" Don French said.

"Their tomb," Eva corrected him. "Cleopatra and Mark Antony were buried together."

"I thought it had been found?" Ella said.

Eva shook her head. "No, but plenty of people claim they've found it. The most famous of which is the site at Taposiris Magna, a ruined, ancient city just to the south of Alexandria. The name refers to both the city and a temple there, and there is some evidence pointing to Cleopatra but the jury's still out."

"Nothing concrete, huh?" Caleb said.

"Not yet – not unless you count this." She lifted Parennefer's map and a smile widened on her face. "Our priest friend is very clear that the tomb is in the Catacombs of Kom El Shoqafa."

"The what?"

"The Catacombs of Kom El Shoqafa, Eva repeated, slower. "It's an ancient necropolis and a very famous archaeological site."

A tense silence filled the space at the end of Eva's sentence. She wondered if any of them truly realized the gravity of the situation. If the map could really lead them to Cleopatra and Mark Antony's tomb, that alone would shatter the world of archaeology. The contents of a tomb of this significance might even change world history, and that was before you started thinking about something as ancient and dangerous as the Book of Thoth.

They had rescued her in Frankfurt, and watching them at work in London, Oxford and Paris has been an eye-opener in terms of how the evils of kidnap and theft were fought, but none of them had any real experience with the ancient world and priceless archaeological or historical treasures. It looked like they really were a team who needed each other. They needed her and she needed them, and for the first time since this nightmare had

## THE RAIDERS

begun back in Boston she could really understand why Linus Finn and the Hidden Hand were so desperate to win this fight.

"Looks like we've got our hands full then," Zara said. "Book of Thoth, Cleopatra's tomb and an unspecified terror threat somewhere in Africa that could kill millions... if saving the world is our new mission statement, Jedediah Mason, I'm going to need a big raise."

A low rumble of laughter went around the small team but Eva could feel something approaching anxiety among them, not least in herself. Things were moving up a gear and she started to get the impression they were setting out on a one-way road. The sort of people who lurked in the ranks of Occulta Manu were unlikely to forget an enemy, least of all one who had killed their own.

Ezra Haven had been very clear about the extent of their reach, and how high their influence went in government and international agencies. Was she really ready to have her life trashed like this? Up until Kyle Cage had kidnapped her she had been happy in her life as an archaeologist researching quietly for Ezra on the side, but now she could see that was rapidly turning into her *former* life.

"So when do we get started?" Virgil said.

"It's not that simple," Eva explained.

"Problem?" said Garrett.

"The main issue is that Cairo will never give permission to drill out a section of the catacomb walls without a lengthy application process. The Supreme Council of Antiquities is a strict regulator of all archaeological works in the country, and anyone with a professional need to excavate in Egypt needs to contact the council and secure its permission first."

"I'm not liking the sound of this," Mason said. "First, we have to break into the Vatican Secret Archives and now you seem to be telling us we have to blow our way into the catacombs, too."

"I'm sorry, Jed," Eva continued. "Even in normal circumstances this is a long and arduous process, but right now the Ministry of Culture is cracking down and has even banned all new excavations in Upper Egypt. Luckily, Alexandria isn't in this region, but the chances of securing a permit at all are low, and in the next twenty-four hours the chance is zero."

"So there's definitely no way we can get a permit?" Ella asked.

Eva shook her head. "Applications have to be submitted at least three months ahead of the dig. They'll want to see what the mission objectives of the excavation are, the names of everyone involved, exactly where and when we'll be digging, you name it – they want it, in triplicate, signed in our blood."

"This is a nightmare," Mason said with a heavy sigh.

"It gets worse. When they get the application it then goes to the Permanent Committee of the Supreme Council for review, and it can move glacially slow – believe me, I've been through it many times. If we want to get into the catacombs in a hurry then we're going in without permission."

"And that's against the law in a big way, I'm guessing?" Milo said.

"Oh yeah," Eva replied. "The Egyptian Law on the Protection of Antiquities goes back to the early eighties. Excavating without government sanction can get you sent to jail for two years, and thieves smuggling antiquities out of the country get jail time with hard labor and a fifty thousand dollar fine. It's not recommended."

"Which is why we're here," Ella said. "Breaking into places is our bread and butter."

"But getting in is usually the easy part," said Caleb. "Looks like if we do the catacombs none of us is coming back to Egypt."

"We don't get caught," Mason said. "We never have and we never will. We go in and out and we're on the plane."

"Damn right," said Zara. "If we can get inside the Vatican's Secret Archives we can do anything, remember what we said?"

# CHAPTER FORTY-FIVE

Chuck Ikard was one of the NSA's top hackers, and he and Milo worked for several hours together, breaking into the Ministry of Culture's online operating systems and searching for anything that might make their lives easier during the mission. Plans of the catacombs were easy to find, as were schematics of the city's underground sewer systems. The recent discovery of a number of Ptolemaic buildings and tunnels in the city's Shallalat Gardens had given Milo the idea that maybe one of those underground passageways might lead to the catacombs, but there was no evidence that any existed.

A sense of frustration increased in the room until one of the consulate staff members knocked on the door and pushed a trolley laden with sandwiches and coffee into the room. Milo cracked a window and a sea breeze blew in from Tea Island in the east.

Mason rubbed his eyes and sighed. "We're going to need to speed this up, people," he said wearily. "The clock is ticking and we have no idea what the Spiders, or the Hidden Hand know about the Book of Thoth, or Cleopatra's tomb being in Alexandria. If either of them gets to it first then everything we did is for nothing."

"Wait – there's something here on the Ministry's system," Milo said. "According to this there's an underground system between the catacombs and Pompey's Pillar."

"What's Pompey's Pillar?" Ella asked.

"It's a triumphal column erected by the Romans not far from the catacombs, and the biggest of its kind outside the main centers of Constantinople and Rome. Made of red granite. Weighs nearly three hundred tonnes."

Zara allowed a low laugh. "Please tell me we don't need to move the damned thing."

"Not at all," Ikard said. "The information here says that the tunnel system beneath it was found just a few years ago during government restoration work. They kept it secret to stop people using it to get into the catacombs."

"The pillar was put up by the Romans in 297 AD, so it's way after Pompey," Eva continued. "It was to commemorate Diocletian's victory of an insurrection in the city." She turned to Milo and Ikard. "How far exactly is it from the catacombs?"

"Five hundred and fifty meters by foot, but the tunnel is direct so around four hundred and eighty meters. We can walk that in no time at all, right guys?"

Agreement. Four hundred and eighty meters was just over the length of four American football fields. They were all fit enough to make the trip in around fifteen minutes, even loaded up with the kit they would need once at the catacombs.

"One more thing – according to these plans, there's a small aquifer in the area. Just something to bear in mind when we're blowing things up down there."

"Got it," said Mason.

"Wait," Caleb said, spinning his laptop around. "It's Ezra, and it looks like it's urgent."

"I bet even when he takes a crap it's urgent," Zara mumbled.

They stared at the screen as the now familiar face of Ezra Haven flickered into view once again. He looked pretty shaken up.

"What's the problem, old friend?" Caleb asked.

"We got confirmation on the terror attack," he began.

"Target?" Mason asked.

Ezra's reply shocked the room. "It's SPIDER, as we thought, and the target is the Aswan Dam."

"Jesus, Ezra," Caleb said. "That's a big deal."

"You bet it is," said Ezra. "It's one of the biggest dams in the world."

"I don't know the first thing about it," Ella said. "Mini-briefing?"

Ezra went first. "The Aswan Dam spans the Nile, and is what's called an embankment dam. This means it's built artificially to ensure there's zero seepage erosion, but what we're interested in is the fact that this particular dam is holding a hell of a lot of water back in Lake Nasser. If the dam bursts millions of people living along the Nile to the north will be drowned."

"Oh my God."

"It gets even worse," Ezra continued. "Not only will the water kill millions of people, but when it's gone, it's gone. The Nasser reservoir is one of the biggest man-made lakes on Earth, and the water within it is essential to Egyptian agriculture, plus it's also used to provide critical power via several hydroelectric pumping stations. These generate billions of kilowatt-hours of power to the people of Egypt every year. If that dam breaks we're talking about the total destruction of Egypt. First, a devastating flood of Biblical proportions, then long-term blackouts for the survivors, and in the long-run, the total destruction of their agriculture sector, and, ultimately, their entire economy,"

"Could have done without this today, Ezra," Caleb said.

"Why the hell would the Hidden Hand do such a thing?"

"It could be a distraction," Ezra said. "Or maybe the Egyptian Government has upset them in some way and it's revenge, coercion… you name it."

"If it's a distraction, it's not going to work," Mason said. "We'll split the team so we can secure the Book of the Dead and stop the attack on the dam. We get some help from the Egyptian authorities for the dam, right?"

Ezra nodded. "I've already spoken with a Colonel Shafik of the Egyptian Army. He's putting together a small team of Special Ops guys from Unit 777, the Egyptian counter-terror force. You're meeting them on site."

"Who's doing what Jed?" Caleb said.

"I suggest Chuck Ikard stays at the consulate. We'll need a centralized HQ with someone we trust. Cal, you, Zara and Virgil go against the Spiders on the Aswan Dam. They'll need someone with bomb disposal skills when they get through Linus and his team and you have those skills, Cal."

"Got it," Caleb said.

"What about me?" Ben said.

"Go with Cal to the dam. We want as much firepower as possible if we're going to take out the Spiders."

Ben nodded. "No problem."

Mason said, "I'll lead Garrett, Milo and Ella into the Catacombs, and I'm going to need you too, Eva."

"I can do it, I think."

"Great, then that leaves you, Don. Up for a fight?"

French cracked his knuckles and grinned to expose two missing teeth. "What do *you* think?"

"Then let's get on with it," Mason said. "We'll meet up here when the missions are over. No failures. I want the Book secured for Ezra and Titanfort, and I want the Spiders taken out and the dam made safe. No one dies, clear?"

They all nodded, but a strange silence had fallen over the small hotel room. Things were moving too fast, and they all knew they had a long way to go before the mission was over.

Mason sensed their nerves. "Darkest hour's always just before dawn, everyone, and the same goes for this mission. Stay safe, make sure you've got each others' backs and we'll all make it to sunrise."

It was time to bring the fight to the enemy.

# CHAPTER FORTY-SIX

Schelto Kranz knew his star was rising in the Hidden Hand's glittering firmament. He had done well. He had served the Order faithfully, but Jed Mason and his Raiders still posed a mortal threat to his ambitions. If he let them take the Book of Thoth from his masters, his punishment would be of the capital variety. Those who failed the Order were usually offered the chance to end their own lives first, but if they couldn't do it, the end was swiftly provided by another servant desperate to show the Sun-runners and Persians their loyalty.

Watching the sun set over Alexandria was peaceful enough, but it had done nothing to settle his nerves over Mason. And no matter how hard he tried, he could never shake off the feeling that he was being watched, monitored, studied for weakness and tested for loyalty. He felt the Hidden Hand's eyes crawling all over him, as if he were under a hundred hidden cameras. It made him shiver. But... to be the man behind those cameras! To be higher in the Order and leading a contingent of Sun-runners! It was all worth it, he reminded himself. All he had to do was please Amadeus.

Kiya had served him well, reporting a few hours ago that the Raiders were in Alexandria on the Egyptian coast. He had flown to join her at once, keen to be part of the glory when the ancient Book of Spells was finally secured for the secret order.

Now, as he waited for her report, he noticed his hands were trembling with the anticipation of pleasing his lord Amadeus, the Persian.

Matthias entered the hotel room and closed the door.

"Speak."

Matthias licked his lips. "Kiya says they are in the American Embassy, Lion."

Kranz's voice purred like a sated beast's. "I see. Where is the Bride now?"

"She and the surviving Raven are waiting outside the embassy as instructed."

"Good. Kiya is a loyal acolyte, but if she fails me again she will be terminated."

Matthias gave a shallow nod. "She desires her promotion a great deal. I'm certain she will not fail us."

"Fail me, not us, Matthias. If she fails then it is I who must answer for it to the Persian."

"I understand, Lion."

Kranz doubted that the young Austrian Soldier understood at all. Members of the Order down at Matthias's level were not privy to the sort of ruthless business conducted higher up the ladder. They would never recruit anyone if the sort of darkness he had witnessed ever became common knowledge among the lower levels. It was the sort of thing that might keep most people up at night, but Kranz had long learned to deal with it.

"I want to know the second they leave the embassy. There is no way this mission can be allowed to fail, Matthias. If she secures the Book of Thoth then our initiations into the higher ranks of the Order are guaranteed. If she fails, we are all dead."

"Yes, Lion."

Both men were silent for a long time. Outside, the sun was now gone. It had slipped beneath the sandy, western horizon while Kranz was dreaming of his promotion. Now, a new night had fallen over the land, and the darkness it brought with it was reflected in the cold, bitter heart beating in his chest.

It was unfortunate that Mason and his team had stumbled into such a terrible conflict, but such was the way of things. If he had turned Haven down and minded his own business, he and his team would live a long life in their asset recovery business, but instead they had made the suicidal decision to challenge the might of the world's oldest and most powerful Order. They had decided to wade into a war older than they could understand, and they would be punished for it, savagely.

Alexandria, he thought once again with a smile. *Of course.*

Back when this place had become the Patriarchate of Alexandria in 42 AD, the ancient religions had been driven out by the Christians. The priest must have hidden the Book of Spells to protect it, he thought, and then secreted the codex in Nectanebo's sarcophagus as a final, mocking twist.

But then Parennefer was in the Hidden Hand, after all.

The Raiders had done well, but now was the time to fight back and finish them.

"You are dismissed, Matthias. Inform me when they leave the embassy."

"Yes, sir."

The Lion closed his eyes and took a deep breath. He was so close to the ancient Book of Spells he could almost reach out and touch it, and yet... Kiya would track Mason and the Raiders to the book's location, and then he would take it from them personally before ordering their execution.

Nothing would please Amadeus more.

# CHAPTER FORTY-SEVEN

"I thought we would at least have to solve an ancient riddle about the gods or something," Ella said. "But a storm drain?"

"Milo says this is the place," Mason said with an apologetic look at the others. "And Milo's….well, *Milo*. He's never wrong, right?"

"That's about the size of it," Milo said. "Sorry."

"So how do we get the grate off?" Eva said.

Mason looked at the CIA man. "Got anything to tow with in the Escalade, Garrett?"

The American nodded. "Sure. Length of tow chain." He took a closer look at the storm drain, wobbling the loose grate with his hand. "Ought to pop that open as easy as pie."

It popped open easy as pie the second Garrett hit the throttle and drove the Escalade forward a couple of meters. Even though it was after nightfall, Mason and the others had formed a ring around the offending article to stop any rubberneckers seeing what was going on, and seconds later their handiwork had successfully revealed the entrance beneath the famous pillar.

They kept lookout while members of the team lowered themselves into the storm drain one by one, and when they were all inside, they saw a large metal door built into the interior of the drain.

"Looks like the entrance to the catacombs all right," Eva said. "I'd say fifth dynasty."

"Very funny," Mason said, running his hands over the lock. Without uttering another word, he pulled his Glock and blasted the lock to pieces, releasing the old door.

Ikard's voice crackled over the radio. "I hate to break up the party, guys, but you've got company."

"Who?" Mason said.

"Your starter for ten," Ikard said. "Even in the Egyptian heat, they're wearing black trench coats."

"Huh?" Mason was dumbfounded. "How they hell are they tracking us?"

"And that's the good news, the bad news is there are now three of them."

"Three?" Eva said. "This just gets better."

Mason shook his head and cursed himself for sending so many of the team south to the dam. He was sure no one else knew about the tomb's location, but now he saw he had made a terrible error.

"Who's the third, Chuck?" Garrett said.

"No idea. Average height, receding hairline, definitely not the type to kick back with a couple of blunts and the best of Miles Davis."

"That's not helping me picture him, Chuck." Garrett said.

Mason faced the team. "The presence of the Hidden Hand means that things are now time critical. We have to find the tomb and the book and get out of here before they do."

They cautiously made their way inside the new entrance, and began to descend down a dusty spiral staircase cut into the stone. Garret closed the door behind them and plunged them all into darkness. He rolled a boulder behind it and dusted his hands off. "That should keep them busy for a while."

Mason switched on his flashlight and the narrow tunnel was instantly illuminated in a ghostly white light. "Well, here goes nothing, I guess," he said, and started to lead the others down the steep tunnel.

A little under five hundred meters later, they reached a narrow archway which led into the part of the catacombs, but not before they had to blast another door open to give them access. "The authorities really don't want anyone coming in this way," Milo said. "Must be trying to hide the location of the tomb from the world."

"Their main concerns are vandals and thieves," Eva said. "Not archaeologists searching for the tomb of Cleopatra."

Way after closing time, the catacombs were empty and silent, and the Raiders had them entirely to themselves. Located in Alexandria's Karmouz district, the Catacombs of Kom El Shoqafa are considered to be one of the Seven Wonders of the Middle Ages. The words meant Mound of Shards in English in reference to the vast quantities of smashed pottery fragments to be found in the vicinity.

"This is amazing," Ella said in hushed tones.

Eva agreed. "The whole place is cut directly out of the rock and is pretty much a cave really."

"How many levels are there?" Milo asked.

"Three. They're accessed via a central spiral staircase in the rotunda. They lead to a banquet hall, an antechamber and various burial chambers."

"Sounds like my kind of place," Milo said with a casual laugh. "Reminds me a bit of the Christian catacombs in Rome."

"Except this place was basically a private Roman cemetery," Eva said, her voice echoing weirdly off the damp walls towering above them. "It goes down into the earth to a depth the equivalent of a five story building and contains around three hundred corpses."

"Delicious," Milo said. "How did they get the corpses down here? These goddam stairs are a nightmare."

"They lowered them on ropes down the center of this spiral staircase."

"It looks sort of strange," Garrett said.

"That's because of the time it was created," said Eva. "It was at a very critical time for Egypt when there were many foreign influences, not just Egyptian, but also Roman and Greek."

"When was it discovered?" Mason asked.

"When a donkey fell into a pit on the surface. The catacombs themselves date way back to the first century AD."

They reached the bottom level. "Water," Mason said, waving his flashlight at the floor.

"We must be on the lower levels," Eva said. "They're well-known to flood from time to time."

Holding their flashlights up they saw beautiful carvings all over the rock walls, and enormous, complex statues rendered from white marble, and thick marble pillars holding up a carved ceiling.

"There," Eva said, pointing to a mural of a priest on the wall. "That's our way to the necropolis. Parennefer has an identical drawing in the codex. He says it's the gateway."

After shooting a vulnerable glance at Eva, Mason stepped forward and started to tap the wall with his flashlight. Precisely where Eva had said, over the painting of the priest, the tapping produced a more hollow sound.

Without saying a word, Mason pounded the flashlight on the painting and knocked a hole through the priest's face. "Looks like we found it."

"All right," Eva said, stepping forward. "It's time to bring this nightmare to an end." She took a deep breath, and slowly edged inside the narrow slit in the chamber's smooth, marble wall.

She moved carefully into the dark, damp tunnel which stretched away from the chamber at her back. Behind her, she heard Jed Mason and the others shuffling through the new entrance, but she knew this was now her territory.

Cautiously now, she stepped into the cold tunnel and tried to prepare herself for whatever nightmares lay ahead.

# CHAPTER FORTY-EIGHT

With the whole team now assembled in the void behind the chamber, Eva Starling knew this was her chance to shine – or humiliate herself. In the lead, she shone her flashlight into the gloom and confirmed what her legs were already telling her – the tunnel's shallow incline was now getting much steeper. They were getting deeper into the ground beneath the catacombs, and at a faster rate with each footstep.

The tunnel was barely wider than her shoulders, and so they marched down the slope in single file, and Mason, the tallest among them, was forced to lower his head to stop it scraping on the hard rocky roof of the passage. "Now I know what a god-damned sewer rat feels like," he said. "Please tell me, Eva, that we are almost wherever the hell we're going."

"You're in luck," she called back over her shoulder. "Up ahead the passage seems to widen a little and I think I can see the bottom."

They made it to the wider section and spread out until they were all able to shine their flashlights down into the final area. Making their way toward the archway they reached a narrow ledge covered in dust and broken pieces of rock. Peering over the edge, Eva's head started to spin as she stared down into a pitch black abyss.

For a moment, she felt a wave of nausea and thought she was going to fall inside it, get swallowed up by its gaping mouth, but then she felt a strong hand grip her upper arm and turned to see Jed Mason standing right beside her. "I'd take a step back if I were you."

She gasped and then realized what had almost happened. "It just *disappears*," she half-whispered. "I never saw anything like that in my entire life."

"Looks like we have a long way to go," Milo said, peering over Eva's shoulder. "This place is like the god-damned Grand Canyon or something."

"He's right," Ella said with an impatient sigh. "How on Earth are we going to find a tomb in all this? It's like an underground city."

"You're exaggerating, surely," Garrett said pushing his way forward to the front. "Oh, Jesus," he gasped. "I guess not. This place is massive."

"No one's been down here for centuries, or maybe longer," Eva said. "Just look at the dust and cobwebs over everything."

"So let's get on with it," Mason said. "We're wasting time."

He and Eva took the lead, shining their flashlights along the ledge and making their way around a curve in the path until they reached a series of steps stretching down into more gloom. "Here," Mason said. "Looks like we can follow the path to the bottom, this way."

Once again, they set off into the darkness until they finally reached the bottom of the steps and found themselves in another stone chamber. On the opposite wall, three archways stood like gaping mouths.

"So, which is the right one?" Milo asked.

Eva stared up at the inscription and started to chew her lower lip as she tried to translate the crumbling hieroglyphics. It says that to know the gods, you must know yourself. It's an ancient Egyptian proverb."

"So what's it trying to tell us?" Ella said.

"We go through the central one," said Eva. "The glyphs above the other archways are warnings."

Eva spun around and shone her flashlight back up the tunnel behind them. "What was that?" she whispered.

"What was what?" Milo said.

They stared down the beam of her flashlight until it dwindled away to nothing down the long, dark passage.

"I thought I heard something," Eva said.

"Heard what?" said Mason, moving beside her and adding his beam to the search.

"I don't know," she said quietly. "Maybe it was nothing."

"Great," Ella said. "Now she's imagining scary noises."

"I did *not* imagine it," Eva said. "I just mean maybe it was nothing *significant*, like a loose rock tumbling down or something."

Mason looked sceptical. "I think any loose rocks around here did their tumbling a long time ago."

"Maybe we dislodged something," Milo said.

"Or maybe those freaking maniacs with the leather coats are right behind us," said Garrett, sliding a round into the chamber of his SIG. "In which case, they'd better start praying they're pretty damned fast."

"We can't start jumping at our own shadows," Mason said. "This place is giving us the creeps, that's all. Let's keep our wits about us and get on with the mission. We're nearly at the necropolis. We're not going to start losing it now, all right?"

They reached a crevasse which was too wide to cross. A brief consultation resulted in Mason suggesting the grappling hook gun. He pulled it from his bag and fired it at a ledge on the other side, providing a taut rope they were able to traverse by monkey crawl. They crossed one by one and when they were all safely on the other side they followed a narrow passageway until they emerged into a large underground chamber. It was mostly natural, with stalactites descending from high above, but a pathway of smooth stone slabs divided the cave floor. They continued along the path, lighting their way with the gentle, buzzing light of the flashlights.

Walking in silence now, stunned by the scale of the chamber beyond the catacombs, they started to see more evidence of Parennefer's handiwork – hollowed out sections in the walls for torches, and ornately carved statues of a host of ancient Egyptian deities staring down at them.

"Well, these things aren't freaky at all," Ella said.

"Looks like they're hiding something from us."

Emerging from the narrow tunnel, they entered a manmade chamber. Compared to what had come before, it was an anticlimax. Small, plain and damp, it was almost empty apart from a low balustrade which ran along the far end.

Nearing it, the flashlights illuminated something beyond the balustrade. A series of stone steps descended away from the chamber and led down to a narrow river. Beside the gently running water was a neat, rectangular sarcophagus. At each corner was a statue of a warrior, each armed with a khopesh.

Eva raised her hands to her mouth for a moment, speechless with surprise. "This is it," she said at last. "Cleopatra's tomb."

Milo walked to one of the statues and raised his flashlight to illuminate the strange, jagged blade in its stony hands. "What the hell's this?"

"It's a khopesh," Eva said. "A kind of Egyptian sickle sword. They inherited them from the Canaanites. They were greatly feared and with good reason. The khopesh was a savage weapon."

They all stepped forward and Mason shone his flashlight over the sarcophagus for a few seconds, before sweeping it over the ceiling and down to the river. "This place looks like a death trap to me. Are you sure this is Cleopatra's tomb?"

Eva leaned in closer and examined the carvings on the stone lid. "It's written in ancient Greek for a start, which was her mother tongue, plus there's another reason you can tell."

"What's that?"

She ran her finger along some of the letters. "This says Here Lies Cleopatra Philopator."

"In that case, let's see what's inside this bad boy," Milo said, rubbing his hands together.

Mason ordered the team to remove the sarcophagus's heavy stone lid, and when they had gently placed it on the sandy river bank, he shone his light inside the sarcophagus and saw a stone carving of Cleopatra.

"That's her, all right," Eva said. "From the little we know about what she looked like, this is a pretty close likeness."

"See anything?" Ella asked.

Eva looked inside. "There!"

She reached inside and pulled out an object wrapped in leather. Carefully opening the small package, she gasped. "The Book of Thoth!"

"I can't believe we found it," Milo said.

"Hold it right there!"

Mason spun around to see three figures approaching them. Two were wearing leather trench coats, just as Ikard had described, but the third was an older man he had never seen before. He was wearing a black suit with a white shirt, unbuttoned and no tie. He looked like an accountant.

"Who the hell are you?" Garrett said, raising his gun.

"I am Schelto Kranz. Surrender, or I will order these soldiers to kill you where you stand." As he spoke, several armed men in combat fatigues rushed into the chamber.

Mason could see they had no chance. After Ikard's warning that there were three of them, he had figured he could take them on and win, but seeing so many heavily armed soldiers standing behind Kranz, he knew he had little choice but to submit to his demands.

Ordering the surrender with a heavy heart, he watched sullenly as the Raiders lowered their weapons. Even Garrett dropped his gun on the sand.

"Raise your hands!" Kranz yelled.

Again, they obeyed. Seconds later the soldiers were swarming around them, removing their weapons and shoving them roughly away from the sarcophagus.

"It was brave of you to challenge Occulta Manu, Mason," Kranz said with something approaching respect in the tone of his voice. "But also foolish. The punishment for meddling in our affairs is death."

"Your affairs!" Eva said. "You make it sound like you're an international charity, when you're no better than Hitler."

"Hitler?" Kranz scoffed. "Hitler was OM. I'm surprised you never knew that."

"Hitler was Occulta Manu?"

"Naturally. Now there was a burgeoning talent."

Eva shook her head in disgust. "Adolf Hitler was a genocidal tyrant."

Kranz raised his eyes to the prisoners and gave them a triumphant smile.

"I'm sure he'd appreciate the compliment."

"You disgust me."

He grinned. "Why not join us, Dr Starling? We could use your talents?"

"I'd sooner die!"

Kranz laughed and dabbed the sweat from his forehead. "As you wish. It's a shame you reject the offer of joining the Hidden Hand, Dr Starling. Locating Cleopatra's tomb and the Book of Thoth is an admirable achievement, but sadly you have instead chosen another path. For me, the initiation into the rank of the Persians, for you and your friends, a painful and lonely death."

"We'll see about that, Lion man," Ella said.

Kranz ignored her, and kept his eyes locked on Eva's. "Now, Dr Starling, if you would be so kind, please hand over the Book of Thoth, and the ankh key. Now."

Eva Starling hesitated for a few seconds, but just like the rest of the Raiders she knew her time was up. Kranz, Kiya and Tekin, plus the Egyptian soldiers they were now controlling, outnumbered and outgunned them by too great a margin. Any attempt to fight back would be suicide, and they all knew it.

She held the ankh and the book out at arm's length, and Kranz lifted them from her hands. His eyes sparkled in the white light of the flashlights as they crawled all over his precious prize.

"Kiya," he snapped. "Kill them all."

# CHAPTER FORTY-NINE

The Egyptian Army helicopter had flown through the night, low and fast over the silent sands of the Eastern Desert, lit blue by the powerful full moon hanging like a lantern on the horizon. On board, Caleb turned from the window and scanned the faces of his sub-unit – Zara, his 2IC, Virgil, Ben Speers and Don French. Sitting behind them was Major Shafik, Sergeant Sharaf and some hand-picked men from Unit 777. Between them, he had zero doubt that he could take out Linus Finn and the other Spiders.

A few months ago, when his ex-wife dropped the kids over to stay in his place in Arizona, Caleb Jackson had taken them out to the Hoover Dam. That had been a great day, and the dam was an impressive sight, but what he was looking at right now was another kind of monster altogether.

At ten times longer than the Hoover Dam, the Aswan Dam seemed to go on forever, and seeing it in the moonlight only increased the sense of awe he felt. It stretched over three kilometers toward the horizon, and as the Sea King Commando swooped down to land it felt like he was about to be swallowed up by the thing.

Now, they finished their attack plans and prepped for the worst. Dam security had contacted Shafik's superior officer and told them the terrorists had broken into two teams, with one heading to the powerhouse to plant the bomb while the others were defending their escape chopper on the dam's crest.

Recalling the briefing, Caleb shook his head. "I still don't understand why Linus is locating the bomb in the powerhouse. If he wants to blow a hole in the retaining wall and flood the valley, then he's on the wrong side of the dam. Either we're not getting something or he's a total idiot."

Zara shrugged. "Judge not, lest ye be judged yourself, Cal."

Without warning, the pilot pulled back on the collective and the chopper violently jerked upwards, almost throwing everyone out of their seats. They all heard him cursing in the cockpit as he increased power to the engine and turned sharply to the right.

"Incoming!"

They braced for impact, and then Caleb felt a substantial explosion somewhere off the port side of the chopper.

Zara spoke first, her voice loud in everyone's headsets. "What have we got?"

Caleb looked out the window and scanned the area below them. To the north, on the dam's crest not far from the spillway, was a heavy-set man in combat fatigues. He was crouching on the concrete and reloading a weapon.

"Shoulder-launched missile," he said. "Looks like Kyle Cage down there, having some fun with us. He's firing again!"

The pilot took more evasive action, this time thundering to the left and pushing down on the collective. The chopper descended fast, and everyone clung to anything they could find to stay in their seats. The second RPG screeched past them with only meters to spare before detonating, this time even closer than before.

The pilot fought hard to keep the chopper in level flight as the shockwave blasted them through the air. When he had regained control, Caleb and Shafik shared a knowing glance and the decision was made to get the chopper out of here as fast as possible – and that meant getting the unit on the dam right now.

Caleb fixed his eyes on the team. "Everyone, get ready for a go."

They were already wearing most of their kit, and helmets, but now they slid their visors down and put on double-leather palm rappelling gloves. Zara took the extra precaution of sliding a snub nose revolver in an ankle holster.

"You leave nothing to chance," Caleb said.

"I worked plain clothes vice in LA, Cal," she said.

"Enough said," he replied with a smile.

The pilot had taken the chopper out of range of the RPGs as the team finalized their preparations for exiting the aircraft, but now he was turning the machine back into the line of fire to allow them to rappel into the battleground.

The helicopter swooped low and raced toward the dam. The colossal retaining wall approached them fast, looming out of the moonlight.

Kyle Cage shouldered the RPG launcher and pointed it at them, preparing to fire once again. Iveta Jansons and Molly Cruise ran to his side and watched the event like it was a reality TV show.

The pilot barked orders at his 2IC who then opened his window and started furiously firing on the Spiders with a submachine gun. Cage slipped the launcher off his shoulder and both he, Iveta and Molly made a break for the cover of the crane which regulated the dam's mighty intake gates.

With the enemy temporarily subdued, the team checked their hookups and rappel seats and finally the rappel rings before testing the ropes. With the chopper swaying hard from side to side in another evasive manoeuvre, they finalized the prep by checking the anchor point connection to the inside of the helicopter.

Caleb swung open the door and the hot Egyptian night air blasted inside the cabin. He tossed his rope outside the chopper, ensuring it dropped over the outside of the portside skid, and with the wind buffeting him from every direction he swung his legs outside the chopper, flexed his knees and pushed himself outside.

The hot air washed over him as the father of two descended from the chopper. He was an old-hand at rappelling from buildings and helicopters, and as the rope slipped through both his brake hand and his guide hand, his main concern wasn't the descent but the maniacs on the crest of the dam with the RPG launcher.

Going over ten feet per second now, he looked up and saw the rest of his team piling out the chopper and making their way down toward the top of the dam's retaining wall. Glancing down, he saw the ground approaching fast as he lowered himself, but the chopper couldn't hover there forever.

Just above the ground now, Caleb braked and released some of the tension on the rope, carefully controlling his rate of descent with his brake hand. Hitting the ground, he cleared the rope through the rappel ring and freed himself. The others hit the ground and did the same.

"We're off rappel!" Caleb yelled, and the soldier in the chopper cut the ropes, allowing the pilot to turn and fly away into the night.

"All right," Caleb said. "As we planned, Zara and Shafik plus two soldiers come with me to the hydropower generator plant and deactivate the bomb. Virgil, Ben and Don take Sharaf to the crest and take out Kyle, Iveta and Molly."

The team split up, not knowing that one of them would be dead within minutes.

# CHAPTER FIFTY

Kiya raised her gun but before she could fire, Eva threw a fistful of sand in her eyes, temporarily blinding her. The Bride cried out and took a step back, instinctively dropping her weapon in order to raise her hands to her eyes and rub the sand out.

Kranz also took a step back, his eyes swivelling down to Kiya's gun on the sandy floor of the tomb.

Mason saw it too, and snatched it up, firing at the cultists seconds before launching himself into a forward roll and tumbling behind Cleopatra's tomb. The other Raiders took cover as Mason fired again, this time on the fleeing figure of Schelto Kranz.

Striking him in the arm, Kranz released the Book of Thoth and clutched his wound as he staggered to the safety of the chamber at the top of the steps. Kiya was a step behind him, still struggling to see through her sand-streaked, red eyes.

"Tekin! Finish them! And retrieve the Book of Spells!"

Tekin ordered the soldiers to open fire, and they did so with a vengeance as they gradually advanced toward the book.

Returning fire on the soldiers, the Raiders cut down several and drove the rest to seek cover before any others were slaughtered.

"Fuck! They've got grenades!" Ella cried out.

"Things are getting desperate, Jed!" Milo said.

Eva shook her head in disbelief. "Whose frigging idea was this?"

Kiya and Tekin threw their grenades through the chamber and they rolled to a stop at the base of the pillars either side of the river.

"I'm not liking this one bit," Ella said.

"Time to throw them back?" Milo called over.

Mason looked grim. "No chance."

The detonations were ear-piercing, and achieved precisely what Kranz desired – the explosions had blasted enormous chunks of marble out of the supporting pillars and fatally weakened them.

Mason watched in horror as the damaged pillars began to buckle under the strain of supporting the chamber's ceiling with so much of their strength now destroyed by the grenade blast.

"The chamber ceiling's starting to crumble!" said Milo.

"It's the weight of the aquifer," Mason said. "And it's coming down on top of us in about ten seconds!"

Eva pointed across the chamber. "The book!"

Mason looked up and saw Kiya sprinting for the Book of Spells.

"No way," he said to himself, and broke cover. He scrambled across the tomb under a hail of bullets and falling ceiling plaster, determined to reach the book before Kiya.

Reaching it a few seconds before him, she snatched it up with a good fistful of sand on the side and ran back to cover under a barrage of cover fire.

Ella fired on her, forcing her back once again, but it was too late. They were out of rounds, and the Hidden Hand had pinned them down with their superior firepower.

"Damn it all!" Mason yelled.

"What the hell are we going to do now?" said Milo.

"He asks a good question," Ella said. With the terror rising inside her, she tried to reload her weapon.

Eva watched Kranz as he ordered Kiya to bring him the ankh – the strange, jewel-encrusted artefact that had started everything back when they murdered Scala in the Vatican.

Ella saw it too. "What's he doing now?"

"Not flash tuning his Aventador, that's for sure," Milo said.

Kranz held the book in his hands. "You failed, Mason! I have it! The Gods have given it to me at last!" He placed the ankh in the hole in the cover and they all heard a click. The front cover popped open, and Kranz's eyes started to widen as he gently lifted the heavy cover and looked inside the Book of Spells.

The Dutch aristocrat began to read, quietly at first. As his confidence grew, he repeated the words louder and faster until his trembling voice reached fever pitch and the strange mantras tumbled from his mouth like birds escaping a cage.

"That is one weird-sounding language," Milo said.

"It's Coptic," said Eva. "Kranz is better educated than I thought."

"What happens if he finishes the spells?" Ella said. "Does he get to speak with the gods or what?"

"No one's speaking with any gods today!" Milo yelled. "The ceiling's collapsing!"

"Please tell me this is happening because of the grenades and not that freaky book!" Ella said.

Eva gave her a strange look, and Mason looked up and saw the ceiling finally give way under the tremendous weight of the water. Kept in place for millennia by the support pillars, it now tumbled through the hole in the ceiling in an awesome jet and immediately started to fill the chamber.

"Jed Mason," Eva said. "You'd better have a damn good idea about saving our lives, you son of a bitch!"

Yes, Mason thought with an inward sigh.

*If only I did.*

# CHAPTER FIFTY-ONE

Virgil felt his heart pumping hard in his chest as he sprinted along the top of the dam in pursuit of Kyle Cage, Iveta Jansons and Molly Cruise. It was one of those insane Raiders moments he could hardly believe was happening. Just a few days ago he was cuddling his newborn daughter in their New York home and preparing for his second PhD viva, and now he was on another job, working for Jed Mason. All the madness and excitement that usually entailed were here tonight in spades.

Ben Speers was ahead of him a short distance and Don French on his other side as they drew closer to the crane. It loomed into the starry sky, flashing dully in the Egyptian moonlight. Were it not for the terrorists taking refuge within its walls, it would have been almost beautiful.

"This way!" Ben said. "They're up ahead."

Don French raised his SIG 552 Commando and buried the stock in his shoulder as he paced forward, raising the muzzle and sweeping it from side to side. "We have to knock that Caracal out of action!" he said, referring to the Spiders' chopper.

They heard the chatter of submachine gunfire.

"Up there!" Ben said.

"They're using flash hiders!" French said.

It was too late. French took a hit direct to the chest, and then a second. He dropped like a rock onto the concrete, crashing into the side of the crest wall and gasping for air. When he spoke, his voice was thin and hoarse. "Dammit... take... cover!"

Virgil, Ben and Sharaf scattered to avoid the incoming fire.

They pulled up behind one of the support struts of the crane's base tower section and took a second to reload and scan the area for the enemy's location.

"There!" Sharaf said. "I see them over there behind one of the transformers."

"One of them's climbing," Ben said.

Virgil saw it too. Iveta Jansons was scaling the side of one of the lightning arresters. Not only that, she was doing it with a wounded arm from the bullet she took in Paris. He could hardly believe what he was seeing. The arrester's function was to protect the system's conductors and insulation from the harmful impact of a lightning strike, but it stretched up into the sky hundreds of feet. One slip, and she was dead.

"Is she crazy? She must be silly as a sack of shit."

"She wants a better angle to try and take us out," Ben said. "She's got a rifle over her shoulder."

"She won't get the chance," Sharaf said, and started to climb up the side of the support strut.

Virgil stared up as he watched the Egyptian Special Forces sergeant ascend into the darkness above him. He reached the gantry crane at the top moments later, and was now even more elevated than Iveta over on the lightning arrester. Far below, the moonlight sparkled on the distant Nile silently collecting in the reservoir.

"Where the hell's Cage and Cruise?" Ben said. "You see them?"

Virgil nodded. "They're making a break for the Caracal! Are they abandoning Iveta?"

"Not a chance," Ben said. "They'll pick her up from the arrester."

His words were drowned out by the crackle of gunfire. Sharaf and Iveta were exchanging fire high above them now. Virgil watched Sharaf's muzzle flash high above him, but then he heard an agonized cry and watched in horror as the sergeant clutched his throat and tumbled off the gantry crane.

The man fell silently in the darkness before crashing down on top of a bank of circuit breakers, dead.

Virgil's heart quickened. He had seen men die before on previous missions, but watching Sharaf's dead body convulsing like a marionette as the electricity coursed through it was something else. Driven by rage, he raised his weapon and fired on Iveta, striking her several times with the automatic fire until his gun was out of ammo.

She cried out, released her rifle and fell backwards off the lightning arrester. Tumbling into the darkness, she fell out of sight behind the machine hall and landed with a cannon-crack smack on the concrete platform behind the access gallery.

Virgil ejected the empty magazine and looked up at Ben Speers, expecting a nod of support but instead he saw something which turned his blood cold.

\*

Across the other side of the dam, Caleb Jackson led his team toward the enormous generator. There were twelve of them in total, each powered by the gigantic dam, and had during their time provided up to half of the entire country's electrical output. "Keep going, everyone!" he said through the headsets. "We're almost there."

Passing the service gallery and a line of transformers, they finally reached the turbine generation room and made their way inside the colossal structure in search of Linus Finn and his bomb. "I see Linus and Kat," Caleb said. "But where the hell is Brick?"

The Spiders saw them and opened fire with a savage volley of automatic rounds.

"Cover!" Caleb yelled.

They hid from the onslaught wherever they could: Caleb tucked down behind the generator's rotor housing and Zara and Shafik slid deftly under the platform of an observation deck.

"Just give yourselves up!" Linus shouted from across the other side of the generator room. "Resistance is futile."

"Why would I give up?" Zara called back. "Explain it like I'm five!"

"You'll find out."

"Fuck off, Linus," Zara called back over.

"I hope you don't kiss with that mouth, darling," said a cool English voice.

Caleb peered over the concrete housing and saw Kat Addington beside Linus. She was holding a pump-action shotgun in her hands, and Linus was making the final adjustments to a suitcase nuclear device.

"My God!" Caleb's eyes filled with terror. "It's a pocket nuke!"

"That answers your question about how he's going to blow a hole in the retaining wall from the powerhouse, I guess," Zara said drily, but then she gasped.

Caleb looked up to see Bjorn Brick holding a gun to the back of her head.

"And I guess that answers your question about where Bjorn Brick was," Caleb said.

Zara dropped her weapon. "It certainly does," she said, deflated.

"You too," Brick growled.

Caleb lowered his gun to the floor, but Shafik spun around and fired on Brick.

"No!" Caleb yelled. "You'll hit Zara!"

Shafik was a crack shot, but this time his aim was off and the bullet plowed into the concrete wall behind Brick's head. Brick fired back, hitting the Egyptian colonel in the stomach and chest and blasting him over the edge of the wall into the generator. He fell out of sight and they all heard the screams as he disappeared inside one of the turbines.

Linus ordered Brick to bring them forward, and moments later they were face to face with their old teammate and her new boyfriend.

"How the hell could you do this, Kat?" Zara said. "This guy's a real cock holster, you know that?"

Kat slapped her face and the sound echoed off the smooth, concrete walls of the vast generator room. "You always were a coarse bitch."

Zara wiped the blood from her mouth. "And you're a fucking traitor. Jed's totally destroyed. You ripped his heart out."

"He can give as good as he gets, I'm sure."

"You can believe it, Kat," Caleb said, his voice low but firm. "He won't stop until he settles his account with you. You must know that."

"He'd be a fool even to try," Linus crowed. He slipped his arms around Kat and they kissed on the mouth for several seconds.

"You make me sick," Zara said. "If Jed doesn't get you for what you did, you can count on me doing it."

"Sadly, you will not be able to indulge your depraved revenge fantasies, my dear," Linus said. "Because you will be dead in less than five minutes when that suitcase nuke detonates and triggers the greatest natural disaster in human history."

"Why the hell are you doing this?" Caleb said.

"Money," Linus said with a wink. "Greenbacks. My employers are very generous."

"Your employers are an insane death cult," Zara said. "You can't be stupid enough to think they'll actually pay a couple of lowlife bottom feeders like you two?"

"That's our problem," Linus said. After telling Brick to collect their weapons, he ordered everyone out the hall. "We're locking you in here – for your own safety, of course," he said with a chuckle.

Caleb watched as Linus, Brick and Kat started to ascend one of the stainless steel staircases beside the nearest turbine. "Dammit! They're getting away!" he said.

"Not so fast, Tonto," said Zara, and reached down for the snub nose pistol she had secured in her ankle holster. She shuffled behind Caleb's broad body for cover as she raised it into the aim and then fired over his shoulder, striking Bjorn Brick in a direct hit and sending him tumbling over the staircase.

He smacked into the cold concrete floor with a wet crunch. A spray of blood exploded outwards from his body and flicked up the side of the turbine. His pump-action shotgun and shells skidded across the polished concrete floor toward Caleb and Zara.

Linus saw the disaster unfolding and screamed at Kat to leave.

"What about the bomb?" she cried out.

He glanced at his watch. "Ninety seconds! They have no chance, but we have to get airborne right now!"

Caleb skidded across the floor, stuffed the shells into his pockets and snatched the pump-action off the deck with a greedy swipe.

"Time to make it rain fire, baby." Zara fired pot shots from her revolver but with only five remaining bullets it was empty in seconds.

Caleb took up the slack. Folding out the stock of the Mossberg 500 and clicking it into place, he loosed a savage volley of fire from the PA shotgun, blasting chunks of concrete out of the wall above Linus and Kat as they fled for the exit.

"Give me the gun, Cal!" Zara yelled. "I'll go after them while you shut the timer off!"

As Caleb threw her the shotgun and ammo belt and ran over to the suitcase nuke, Zara pushed more shells into the bottom of the Mossberg and then racked the weapon, sliding a live round into the chamber. Supporting the fore grip with her left hand and gently tucking the stock into her shoulder she aimed down the length of the matte black barrel and fired the gun at Linus and Kat. She peppered the door in front of them but it was too late. Her aim was wide and they were through, slamming the steel door behind them and locking it.

She ran to Caleb who was now crouching beside the nuke.

"We're locked in, Cal!"

Caleb barely heard her words. He was too focussed on the nuclear bomb in front of him. Linus had not been bluffing – the timer was now at sixty seconds and rapidly moving toward zero hour.

"Please tell me you know how to do this?" she asked.

"Sure, it's a piece of cake," he said, and started to remove a panel on the side of the weapon.

"Aren't these things fail-safe?"

He shook his head. "A device like this is made to fail-fatally, not fail-safe."

"You mean…"

They shared a glance. "I sure do. Like air brakes on a truck. In your car, if your brake fluid leaks then your brakes fail, so they fail fatally. With air brakes on a truck, they're kept open by compressed air. If there's a leak then the brakes close and the truck stops, so it fails safe."

*Forty seconds.*

"Same with this. The timer's a fail-fatally, and it's connected to the conventional explosives that are required to trigger the core. If I cut it, then it goes off, so the only option is to cut the connection between the trigger and the core."

*Thirty seconds.*

Zara watched as Caleb started his search inside the weapon. "I see what he's done here, the bastard."

"You can stop it?"
*Twenty seconds.*
"Pretty sure," he grunted, and started to unscrew an internal panel. "The connection between the trigger and the core should be in here."
"Pretty sure? Should be? Jesus."
*Ten seconds.*
"Think I got the bastard," Caleb said, and pulled his hand back out. "All we have to do is see what happens when the timer gets to..."
Zero.
*Click.*
Zara gasped.
Caleb smiled. "That was the trigger firing against nothing."
"Christ, Cal. You're an asshole sometimes."
"I stopped it though. Don't I even get a kiss?"
She leaned up and kissed him on the cheek. "I could kick your balls in for that little stunt."
He pointed at the shotgun, which was now dangerously close to his head. "Is that thing still loaded?" he asked with a wink.
"I'm sorry," she said. "Got a little fazed right there." Pushing the pump button, she pumped the gun back and cast an expert eye down the barrel to ensure the weapon was empty and then slung it over her shoulder. "We're done here," she said. "Let's back to Virgil."

*

Virgil watched as Ben Speers gently pulled the hammer back on his weapon and raised it until it was pointing at him. The young polymath looked at the barrel of the gun, glinting in the moonlight.
"I can't let you destroy that helicopter, Virgil," Ben said quietly.
"What's going on, Ben?" Virgil said
"It's time to die, said the Spider to the fly."
"I don't understand."
Ben gave a fiendish smirk, and his next act was the brutal firing of his weapon at Virgil.

Virgil heard the sound of the discharge echo over the dam as he clutched his stomach and fell forward onto his knees. He was dimly aware of Cage and Molly running over from the chopper to Ben. They pounded up the concrete steps and made it to the base section of the crane.

He felt his life slipping away now.

Stared up at the moonlight glinting on the gantry crane.

Heard the distant sound of the turbines in the generator room.

He prayed Caleb and Zara had stopped Linus in time, and as he clenched his teeth in agony he knew he had to tell them about Ben, but knew there would be no chance because he was already losing consciousness.

Cage and Molly approached Ben, and they gave each other a hearty slap on the back. Comrades in arms.

"Those RPGs got a bit close for comfort, Kyle," Ben said.

"It worked though, right? Delayed the landing and gave Linus time to set the bomb. If you hadn't been on board I could have blown them right out the sky."

"Am I coming with you?" Ben said.

Molly shook her head. "Nuh-uh. Linus says you stay with these guys and get cosy with them. He wants an inside man."

"No problem."

Virgil heard them laughing, and then he saw Linus Finn and Kat Addington arrive on the scene. They were out of breath and there was no sign of Bjorn Brick. Cage and Molly explained about Iveta, and Linus exploded with rage, pacified only when Kat kissed him and ran her fingers through his hair. All of them climbed up into the Caracal and then it powered up and lifted them all out of sight.

Ben turned back to Virgil.

"Sorry, old sport, but I have to get back to the Raiders and tell them all about how Kyle Cage took you out, after a brave attempt by me to stop him, naturally."

Virgil tried to speak, but he was too weak.

Ben raised his gun and fired one final time.

And then everything went black.

# CHAPTER FIFTY-TWO

Mason clung to the pillar as the water smashed over him and rapidly started to flood the chamber. The power of the bursting aquifer was forcing his hands away from the smooth marble pillar and it took everything he had to stop himself getting sucked away into the underground river.

Hearing a blood-curdling scream to his right, he turned to see one of the Hidden Hand soldiers lose his grip on the base of a statue. The aquifer's mighty power swept him away as if he were made of straw, and then he was gone, dragged by the churning water, kicking and squealing into the darkness of the subterranean tunnel.

Instinct commanded Tekin to throw out a hand to save his friend, even though it was already too late. He screamed an impassioned cry. "Kaaper!"

"Leave him!" Kranz yelled.

Tekin look shocked at the ruthless order, but Kiya's face was passive and inscrutable.

Mason was struggling to stay afloat and hold onto the pillar at the same time. His clothes were completely waterlogged now, and his weapons long gone. Fighting against the force of the water, he raised his head to check on the others, but saw only Ella who had crawled to safety on top of one of the sarcophagi, and Milo was now sprawled in a wet heap at Kiya's boots, with the muzzle of her gun jammed into his neck.

Straining with all his might, he pulled himself free of the water's fatal tug and clawed up onto the relative safety of Cleopatra's tomb. Seeing Tekin's Steyr TMP, he snatched up the weapon and fired, sweeping it back and forth in a wide arc, covering the entire breadth of the chamber. The muzzle flashed as the weapon spat fire all over the enclosed space, blasting chunks off the marble statues and tombs and forcing Kranz and the rest of the Order to scramble away up the spiral steps for cover.

Mason gave chase, but when he turned the corner he was met by a hefty palm strike that came close to knocking him out. He fell back, releasing the Steyr and nearly cracking the back of his skull on the flagstone floor. Dizzy and with blurred vision, he was just able to see the imposing figure of Tekin pad over to him and then pile drive a fist toward his face.

Mason dodged to the left and followed his evasive manoeuvre with a sideways roll to avoid a second punch. Scrambling to his feet, he slipped over on the wet tiles and went down again, only just stopping himself by throwing his arm out and grabbing hold of the side of a boulder.

Tekin marched over, a macabre grin cracking on his face. He said nothing, but beckoned the Londoner forward with his hands.

"If you want me, come and get me," Mason said, stalling for time.

The Raven marched forward, but slipped on a wet tile and went over. Before Tekin could get to his feet, Mason spun around and planted the sole of his boot squarely in the other man's face, grinding his skull down into the marble floor.

Ella winced. "Ouch."

"It'll stop him Tekin the piss though," Milo said.

Ella groaned. "Did you have to say that?"

"I thought it was funny!" Milo said.

Mason ignored it. The blow had done nothing more than give Tekin a few seconds of blurred vision, and now the enormous Raven was rising to his feet like some kind of avenging vampire. He raised his hands and pulled back his fists for another round, and his black leather trench coat billowed out behind him as the wind rushed down the tunnel.

Mason saw it first: a mini-tsunami was racing up behind Tekin. He felt a vague undertone of hope and his heart quickened. He took a step back, all the time trying not to alert the Raven to his fate.

Tekin grew suspicious, turned and screamed with terror but it was too late. The water smashed into him and carried him screaming into the under ground tunnel.

Mason dived back onto the top of Cleopatra's tomb and narrowly avoided the same fate of being swept away by the torrent like Tekin and the other Hidden Hand acolytes. Tekin was dead, but Kiya and Kranz were alive and kicking, and still desperately trying to get away with the Book of Spells. Pausing to find a way out, Milo screamed out at them.

"You can run but you can't hide, Kranz! The hell you gave other people is going to come back around again and kick you in your arse."

Kranz sneered at him and waved the Book of Spells in the air. "The gods are giving me what I deserve, you pathetic sewer rat!"

Before Milo could reply a chunk of plaster fell from the ceiling and smashed on Kranz's head, instantly killing him. He collapsed in a heap on the floor and the book fell from his hand and came to a rest in the wet sand.

"They certainly did give you what you deserved," Milo said, scrambling over and picking up the book. He tossed it over to Mason who caught it in one hand as he watched Kiya fleeing through the exit, but seconds later she returned with her hands in the air.

"What the hell?"

Then he saw. When she stepped inside the chamber, she was followed by a unit of Egyptian soldiers. "Looks like Ezra finally got in touch with someone of influence," Mason said, eyeing the Egyptian army as they poured into the chamber.

He walked over toward the commanding officer, pausing on his way to look at the dead body of Schelto Kranz with a mix of disgust and pity. The Dutch politician had dreamed of being the puppet master, but in reality he had been nothing more than one of their many marionettes.

"I am Colonel Nazif," the officer said.

Mason handed the book over to Nazif with a heavy heart. "I suppose you want this."

Nazif shook his head. "I'm under orders to let you take it. Apparently your boss Ezra Haven knows how to pull strings with the Egyptian Government." He stopped and looked at Kiya with contempt as his men cuffed her and led her out of the tomb. "And *she* will go to prison for rest of her life," he said.

"I don't think so," Kiya snarled. "Not with the sort of people I know."

"All right, that's enough," Nazif said coldly. "Take her away."

The Raiders watched as the soldiers dragged Kiya from the tomb. Just before they rounded the corner, she looked over her shoulder and cried out to them. "Each one of you will die for this, and everyone you love. Occulta Manu!"

Mason and his team shared an uncertain glance in the chaos of the tomb.

"You think she means it?" Eva said.

"Fuck what she means," Milo said. "We beat them once, we can beat them again."

"Threatening us is one thing," Ella said, "but threatening our families is something else."

"Come on, chucklefucks," Milo said. "The beers are on me."

Mason kept his counsel, and led the team from the tomb. Where they had rushed earlier, they now walked back in their own time, leaving Nazif and his men to catalogue the destruction behind them. When they hit the surface, they walked back to the Escalade, broken with the exhaustion of the securing the book.

Milo's cell phone rang. He answered it and had a brief conversation.

"It's Caleb," he said grimly. "Virgil didn't make it."

Mason felt his stomach turn over. "What? Virgil?"

Milo nodded, and handed Mason the phone. The leader of the Raiders spoke to his old friend for a few moments and then cut the call. "It's true. I can't believe it. Ben said he died trying to stop the Spiders escaping in a helicopter. Cage killed him."

"Christ," Milo said quietly. "Not Virgil. What about Jen and Amy?"

Ella's eyes filled with tears. She shook her head gently in denial. "There must be some kind of mistake."

"No mistake," Mason said firmly. "He's dead. Chuck Ikard's liaising with the US authorities about flying his body back to the States."

Eva searched for something to say. "I'm so sorry."

"I want to go home, Jed," Ella said.

"Me too," Milo added, his voice low, hollow.

Mason nodded once.

Ezra Haven had his ancient Book of Spells, but they had lost a dear friend and valued member of the team. Jen had lost a husband, and Amy had lost a father she never even had a chance to know. "All right," he said at last. "We go home."

Mason started walking again, feeling as if someone had just hollowed him out with a giant knife. He led the team toward the Escalade, the Book of Thoth in his hands, unopened.

# CHAPTER FIFTY-THREE

Jed Mason walked along Fifth Avenue with one hand in his pocket. In his other hand he held a sturdy steel tube.

The Istanbul Asset.

He glanced to his left where a blackbird flew over the street and cruised over the trees into Central Park; it was a perfect day, but any sense of achievement or pride he would normally feel after completing a mission was destroyed by the terrible murder of Virgil Lehman. Killed in cold blood by the Spiders when he was defending the dam from their terror attack, his old friend was a hero, but not one the world would ever know about. He'd had to break the news to Jen and that was not a moment he would ever forget.

He looked at his watch. Ezra Haven had summoned them all to the mysterious Titanfort for a meeting just before sunset. He still had time to draw a line under the Istanbul job and get to Hell's Kitchen long before the sun went down.

Stepping into the shade of the French Consulate's awning, he was met by a tall woman with shoulder-length brown hair. She wore dark red lipstick and a smart black suit.

"Mr Mason, I'm so glad you made it in one piece."

"So I am, Madame Bernard," he said. "Believe me, so am I."

Her eyes danced over the steel tube. "I see you have it."

"I do," he said coolly. "And I presume you're ready to wire the money?"

"When its authenticity has been appraised by us."

Inside the lobby, they took the elevator up to Pascale Bernard's office where a small, wiry man was waiting for them with a compact briefcase. His name was Sapin, and Pascale Bernard introduced him as an art appraiser from the Louvre.

Made sense.

Mason carefully unscrewed the tube and gently pulled out the painting, handing it to Sapin.

The Frenchman unrolled the work of art amid a chorus of tuts, sighs and headshakes. "And this has been taken care of, you say?"

Mason nodded. "I took every realistic care of it, Monsieur Sapin."

Sapin gave him a doubtful look and then turned his eye to the Mona Lisa which was now flattened out on Pascale Bernard's desk. A few moments of careful study ensued as Sapin made his tests. "A painting can be forged to absolute perfection," he said absent-mindedly.

Mason got the impression only Madame Bernard was being addressed.

"Mais... the craquelure – the maze of miniscule cracks in the varnish – cannot. These can never be reproduced with any degree of realism." He took the jeweller's loupe from his eye and looked at the Consul General. "Il n'y a pas de doute, Madame. C'est authentique."

Pascale Bernard faced Mason and offered a polite smile. "Monsieur Sapin is satisfied this is the original Mona Lisa by Da Vinci. I will have the five million dollars wired to your Swiss account immediately."

Sapin raised an eyebrow. "Five million dollars is a lot of money for retrieving stolen art."

"I was paid only one million for retrieving the art, Monsieur Sapin," Mason said coolly. "The other four is for keeping my mouth shut about your museum letting it get stolen in the first place."

The chastised Sapin said nothing.

"The reputation of not only the Louvre, but all of France was at stake, Mr Mason," Pascale Bernard said gratefully. "You certainly lived up to your reputation. Extend my gratitude to your team, please. I hope they enjoy their reward."

"I will," Mason said, thinking only of Virgil. "Goodbye."

# CHAPTER FIFTY-FOUR

Mason looked out over the Manhattan skyline and watched the city turn from gold to red in the sunset. Out here on the balcony the summer night was hot and humid and fifty storeys below the streets buzzed with life. He shook his head as he thought about where he was standing. This entire skyscraper was off-limits to the rest of the world and it was all his.

If he wanted it.

He turned and went back inside the strange but comforting cocoon that was Titanfort and smiled at his friends, old and new. Gathered in Ezra Haven's office they were waiting for the great man to return from what everyone around here simply called Olympus. The seat of the gods. The men and women upstairs.

They didn't have to wait long.

Ezra opened the heavy door and stepped over to his desk. He sat in the soft leather chair and stared at them for a few moments. The last of the day's light shone on his face and he looked proud.

After several long moments, he leaned forward in his chair, rested his arms on his desk and steepled his fingers. "Not bad."

Mason and the others shared a look, and then Zara said, "Is that it?"

"That's it," he said flatly. "What did you expect? Milk and cookies?"

"No," she said. "Maybe a thanks. We risked our lives for that goddam book. Our friend died."

Ezra locked his eyes on her. He looked like a father trying to explain to a child why not to touch the fire. "Listen, you're sitting in Titanfort. This is the most secret spy hub in the entire world, even more so than Titanpointe just across town. Here, you a part of a team that has the most extensive intelligence contacts and surveillance the world has ever seen. People spend thirty years working for the CIA and they're still not getting into this place. There's your thanks right there, so you're welcome."

Zara tried to look nonchalant, but everyone could see Ezra had delivered a fatal blow. "Right."

"And the book?" Caleb asked.

Ezra managed a neutral smile. "The book is currently in a secure location."

"How reassuring," Ella said. "But tell me, did Kranz reading from the text have anything to do with the necropolis falling apart, or was it just the grenades?"

"You're not in Titanfort yet, Miss Makepeace," Ezra said with a knowing smile. "So there are some things I can't answer."

Milo broke the tension. "I must say, the place is impressive."

"And all fifty floors are ours," Ezra said. "We need them. We're engaged in a covert battle here, guys. This isn't child's play or some stupid action novel. This is real. This is a vicious war with a shadow power that is very clear about wanting our destruction and the whole thing is fought under the radar. The people of the world have no idea this war is being waged. They can never know, and if you join this office you leave your old lives behind forever."

He got up from his desk and looked out over the city. The stars were coming out over Central Park. "When you join Titanfort you move into another world and it's a one-way journey. Do I make myself clear?"

Mason answered at once. "Yes."

"There's no going back, guys." Ezra's voice suddenly grew cold and deadly. "Let me make this totally clear: no one ever leaves Titanfort. You get me?"

Mason got him, and so did the others. A mission like the war against Occulta Manu was the highest level of classification. While they were on the team they would have access to the most highly classified information in the world. The only way to leave Titanfort was death. If you joined, you joined for life.

"So how does this work?" Zara said.

Ezra smiled. "Like I said, the entire building is ours. Three entrances. Palm print, eye scan and voice recognition to get in. You tell no one about what goes on in this place. We have residential quarters on several floors and a gym and a pool. We take personal fitness very seriously at Titanfort and we have annual medicals."

"What if you fail?" Milo said. "I thought you said no one ever leaves?"

"You don't fail your medical."

"Got it."

"Looks like you need to get yourself some treadmill time, Piglet," Zara said, and squeezed Milo's stomach.

"Hey! Get off."

"She's right," Ezra said. "Lose twenty pounds."

Zara burst into laughter. "Man, I *love* this place! Please, please, please can I be his personal trainer?"

"You cannot," Ezra said. "We have people for that." He turned to Milo. "Start in the morning. Floor 25."

"Got it."

"Say goodbye to those pastries, Chunk," Zara said.

Milo sighed. "I'm really not that bad," he said. He turned to Ezra, his face getting very serious. "Is there a drugs policy at Titanfort?"

"Of course. Drug tests every month."

Milo turned to Zara and smirked. "Oh *dear*, a drugs test every month, you say Ezra?"

"Yes."

"And is that another one of those tests that you can't fail?"

"It is."

Milo intensified his gaze at Zara and widened his smirk. "Thanks for clearing that up, Ezra."

"You bastard," she said.

A ripple of laughter went around the room, then Ezra raised his voice to regain their focus. "We have another more extensive training facility in Wyoming. It's about ten times more secret than Area 51."

Milo laughed.

"Why are you laughing?" Ezra said.

"The Area 51 thing, I was… *nothing*."

"I'm not joking," Ezra said flatly. "Our facility in Wyoming is called The Ranch. Less than five hundred people know about it and they're all top level former military or intel. Now you know. If you want to work with me or not is up to you."

# THE RAIDERS

Zara said, "If it means having a chance to get revenge on the people who killed Virgil, then I think we should do it. We owe it to him."

Mason cleared his throat. "So what's the next mission?"

Ezra turned on the laptop and a large picture filled the white screen at the end of the office.

They all stared at it for several seconds in awed silence. "That's the next mission?" Mason said.

"Yes."

Zara whistled loudly. "I do *not* believe what I'm seeing."

Each of them was unable to move their eyes away from the image on the screen.

After a minute or so, Ezra spoke. "So," he said, his voice cutting the stunned silence. "Are you in?"

# CHAPTER FIFTY-FIVE

"I can't believe this is happening," Ella said. She was holding a small bouquet of white lilies. Behind her the skyline of New York City rose like an old friend as she approached the coffin. Just a week after landing in New York and meeting with Ezra at Titanfort, and already it seemed like a dream.

"None of us can," Mason said. "Virgil saved my life more times than I can remember."

"I knew him for years," Caleb said. "We played poker together whenever we had the chance. Attended tournaments together."

Milo was silent. His hands were stuffed in his pockets and he turned his head down to the ground. His face was obscured by his floppy fringe, just the way he liked it. No one would see his grief today.

Mason watched now as Virgil Lehman's family and friends filed out of the church and walked sullenly across the cemetery to say their final goodbyes. As the coffin was lowered into the earth, Zara spoke through gritted teeth. "He didn't deserve this."

No, he didn't, Mason thought. "We risk our lives every day doing what we do. Virgil was the same. He cared more about other people than himself."

Ella began to cry, and Mason squeezed her shoulders. "Are you all right, El?"

"I'm fine… at least I will be."

"At least you've got Ben," he said.

She nodded. "He's on a mission in Russia at the moment. I miss him."

A heavy man in a black suit walked over, beside him was a frail woman behind a black veil. She was clutching a handkerchief in her trembling hands.

"Jed," Virgil's father shook the Londoner's hand firmly. "Thanks for coming."

Mason gave a polite nod.

"I miss my son so much, Jed," Virgil's mother said, the mascara-stained tears tumbling down her cheeks. "And he's only been gone a few days."

Mason said nothing; there were no words.

John Lehman fixed a firm, dry eye on Mason. He was an ex-CIA man who had been around the block more than most. He knew the score and now he wanted it settled. "You know who did this to my boy, right?"

"We do," Mason said at last.

Lehman worked hard to keep the rage in check. "You know what I'm going to say then."

"You don't need to say it, sir."

Virgil's father turned silently and waved at an old friend as he filed away into the crowd. When he turned to look at Mason his eyes were starting to fill with tears. "I didn't think so."

There was no talk of wasted life here. Everyone paying their respects today knew how much Virgil had packed into his young life. He'd written two doctorates, stopped terror attacks all over the US homeland, climbed mountains, explored shipwrecks, and skydived over tropical islands. Now, he had died bravely, thwarting the plans of a shadow network of villains who wanted only to destroy and harm anything in their way.

More than any of that, he'd married his high school sweetheart and had a beautiful daughter. It was the thought of that little girl growing up without a father than had pushed most here to inconsolable tears. Mason watched now as Virgil's widow drifted out of the church, dressed in black and holding her baby in her arms. He clenched his teeth to maintain some degree of control until she had faded back into the crowd.

The Raiders joined the other mourners as they slowly filed away from the church.

"That was as tough as it gets," Zara said.

Caleb had said nothing since they left the church. Now he was breaking open a fresh pack of robusto cigars and searching for a lighter. With the cigar clamped in his mouth he fired it up, blew a cloud of smoke into the air and said, "I'll never forget you, Virgil."

"None of us will," Ella said quietly.

Mason's reply was cut short by the sight of a long, black limousine pulling up outside the cemetery. Getting out of the car, Ezra Haven closed the door softly so not to draw any attention to himself, and then he casually leaned against the hood with his arms folded across his chest.

"He keeps his word," Zara said. "I'll give him that."

Caleb allowed a gentle laugh. "I told you he would."

Mason had never doubted it. He trusted Caleb with his life, and if his old friend told him Ezra was on the level, then he trusted him too. The only problem was that trusting someone was different for working for them. Ezra's proposal would draw them into a very different world, a dangerous world. Mason glanced back at the mourners saying their final farewell to his old friend and fellow Raider for confirmation of just how dangerous.

Milo looked at Ezra and then followed the path of an Eastern Bluebird as it flew up into the sky above the Cadillac. "So are we joining his outfit or not?"

Caleb, Zara and Ella all joined Milo and turned their eyes toward Jed Mason. This is one of those moments, he thought, when your whole life pivots on a single decision, only this time he was making that decision for four other people as well as himself. Joining Ezra Haven at Titanfort meant a massive upheaval in all their lives. It meant more danger, it meant losing some of their independence. It also meant giving the Raiders the chance to do much more than they could under his sole guidance.

And it meant the chance to avenge Virgil's murder.

Mason looked up at the sky and took a deep breath.

The answer was obvious.

THE END

# ABOUT THE AUTHOR

Rob Jones has published fifteen Kindle international bestsellers, and is the author of the Joe Hawke series, the Cairo Sloane series, and the Avalon Adventure series. *The Raiders* is the first novel in a fast-paced archaeological thriller series featuring a brand-new team of adventurers. Part two of the series, *The Apocalypse Code* will be published in 2018.

Please visit his website, www.robjonesnovels.com for more information about his latest releases and other information, or join him on Facebook at www.facebook.com/robjonesnovels for audiobook and paperback giveaways, or Twitter at @AuthorRobJones.

Printed in Great Britain
by Amazon